I Am Tony Blanco

Written by:
Durell Eubanks

Cadmus Publishing
www.cadmuspublishing.com

Acknowledgements

The cities in I Am Tony Blanco are all real, but are used fictitiously in this novel. The same is true of actual places of business that Tony Blanco, Quincy, and his associates frequented. The events that take place are all fictitious and came straight from the authors imagination.

I would like to thank God, and everyone who is down with Team Banks. All my family and friends, to my two daughters, Areeon and Zynah, who inspired me to take my writing seriously. To my mother, who passed her writing talent down to me and helped me push this project along. To my wife, who's been there for me since day one. Special thanks to my brother, Ricardo Banks, who's been holding the fort down since I have been away. I salute you, Bruh. Dad would be proud at how you're handling things. Thanks to Seven Montana, Mattie Rich, 6/9, and Latif. Shout out to my dawgs: Smoke, Tru, T. Mack, Debo, A.D, Pinn, Sisco, Ali, Tiny Wrench, Big Boi, Kali, Q, and to everyone that's locked behind the wall knee deep in the struggle. Hold your head up, it gets better before it gets worse. And, last but not least, shout out to all of my haters; please keep hating. Your energy is the fuel to my fire.

Dedications

I Am Tony Blanco is lovingly dedicated to my father, Henry Eubanks, who passed away October 17, 2020. His dream was to see my books published. I will always love you Dad; your teachings are forever instilled in me. This is for you.

CONTENTS

CHAPTER 1

My name is Tony Blanco, but everybody calls me Tony. Presently, I am in the county jail facing the death penalty for a double homicide. Here's my story.

On the morning of July 4th, 2011, Tony woke up to the smell of fried chicken. He got out of bed, took a shower, and got dressed. He tied up his Jordans and walked to the kitchen. Tony's wife was hovering over the stove cooking food for the Blanco family reunion.

"The food smells good baby." Tony said, as he walked over to her and gave her a sweet morning kiss.

"Thank you baby, I've been up all night cooking." Replied Tony's wife.

Tony Blanco's wife was the best thing that ever happened to him. She was his dream woman. Long hair, hazel eyes, brown skin, slim waist, body like a coke bottle, and to go with her gorgeous looks, the woman knew how to handle business and take care of her man. Her name was Jessica Blanco. Jessica and Tony have been together for twenty years and married for eleven. They had two daughters together, Trina and Tracy. Trina was five and Tracy was seven. Tony Blanco had a perfect life, a few businesses, a great woman, and two beautiful kids whom he loved more than life itself. Tony Blanco was happy, living the American Dream with his family.

As Tony began to help his wife Jessica with the food, he realized that he needed to go over to the office and grab some paperwork, so he could finalize a deal on the sale of one of their houses.

"Jessica?"

"Yes, baby."

"I have to run over to the office and get some papers so that I can finalize the sale of one of our houses. I will be back in about thirty minutes."

"Ok baby, that's fine. But can you stop by Food Lion, and pick up some cornbread mix?"

"Yeah baby, I can do that. Anything for you." Tony said as he walked over and kissed her. Tony walked up stairs to his daughters' room and gave them both kisses as he watched them play with their Barbie dolls. "God, I love them." Tony thought to himself.

When he left the house, it felt good outside as it was 70 degrees. He felt good about himself today, to be able to enjoy his family without any undesirable distractions was a blessing. He thought to himself, "I think I'ma drive my Maybach."

Tony walked out to his driveway, and got inside his Maybach. Proud of his success, he took a long look at his eight-bedroom home. Nice cars, nice houses, and a lovely family. Life couldn't be better for Tony. He then crunk his car up and pulled off; headed up the highway listening to R-Kelly. He took the Green Street exit, the light turned red ahead in the distance. When he got to the intersection, it took too long to change, so he ran it. Tony didn't see any police cars, so he figured he was good. Just as the thought began to clear his head, Tony spotted a black SUV run the light also. Once Tony got a few blocks up, he busted a quick right, just to see if he was being followed. "Shit, they are still behind me."

Tony pulled into a gas station and began to panic, as he realized he was being followed. "Damn, out of all the days." Tony thought to himself as he sped out of the gas station parking lot. He shot up the boulevard and ran another light. This time, they were stuck in traffic. Whoever it was, or how many, Tony couldn't see because of the tinted windows on the black SUV. He took his Glock 40 out of his glove compartment, and placed it on his lap, just in case. Minutes later, Tony pulled up to his office. He saw a patrol car about 300 yards up, but that was normal because his office sits across the street from a bank. Tony got out of his car and walked into his office. Once inside, he made sure everything was straight, and then grabbed the papers that he had come for. Then, he headed out the door.

As he walked towards his Maybach, he looked up and saw the same black SUV that was following him pulled up. Tony eased his Glock out, which was tucked in his waistband, and was now hanging it at his side. He reached for the door handle of his Maybach. Just as he began to open the door, the black SUV came to a stop. Two Black guys jumped out pointing guns in his direction. Without thinking and as if on instinct, Tony raised his Glock and squeezed off three shots in rapid succession before taking cover behind his Maybach.

"Are these guys trying to rob me or kill me?" Tony thought to himself as he hung his Glock over the hood of his Maybach and fired off two more shots.

"Bloc, bloc."

One of the guys fell grabbing his neck. Dead, Tony hoped.

"Bloc, bloc, bloc."

Tony was forced to seek cover behind his Maybach once again, as his attackers began to fire back. He could hear windows being shattered as round after round hit his Maybach. "Lord, please don't let me die." Tony raised and fired his Glock once again.

"Bloc, bloc, bloc."

Slinging rounds like never before, until he felt the pressure; as he was hit in his chest and stomach. He was knocked back to the ground. Tony felt his body. His hands were covered in blood. He reached to his side and picked his Glock back up, which was knocked to the ground when he was shot. Tony could hear sirens coming from everywhere. He was in so much pain that he felt like he was going to die.

"Not like this, Lord, please not like this." Just as Tony finished his short prayer, one of his attackers came around the hood of his Maybach with his gun raised.

"Bloc, bloc, bloc, bloc, bloc, bloc, bloc, bloc." Tony fired all eight rounds into his attacker, killing him, but not before his attacker squeezed off a round that hit him in the side of his head.

"Jessica." Tony whispered as he lost consciousness, and everything went black.

"Breaking news, Good Morning. I'm Tamara Lane reporting live in front of SunTrust Bank on 22nd and Brooke. I'm here with first on the scene FBI agent Jeff Hurns. He has informed us, that while serving tax papers on Mr. Tony Blanco, they were fired upon, even after identifying themselves as FBI agents. Two federal agents have died on the scene from multiple gunshot wounds. Mr. Blanco is in critical condition at this very moment. Agent Hurns, can you explain to the public what took place here today?"

"We were in route to serve Mr. Blanco a warrant for his past taxes. As we were pulling up, two agents were getting out of a black SUV identifying themselves. Mr. Blanco just started shooting. I don't understand why he would do this. I guess he didn't want to face his responsibilities, or maybe he was high on drugs. I am at a loss for words. Today, two agents lost their lives. My heart goes out to them, and their families." Agent Hurns replied.

*   *   *

Across town, Tony and Jessica Blanco's phone began to ring. "Ring, ring, ring."

"Hello?" Jessica said as she answered the phone.

"Baby, turn on the news." Jessica's mother replied.

"Mama, I don't have time. I'm trying to prepare this food for the family reunion." Jessica said.

"It's Tony, he's on the news." Her mother said.

"There's no way, he only went to the office to pick up some important papers."

"Something must've happened on the way there, Jessica. Just turn on the news, Tony's been shot."

"What?"

"Baby, it's on the news and they are saying that he killed two agents."

"Mama, don't be playing like this."

"I'm not. Turn on the television and see for yourself."

Jessica stopped what she was doing and turned on her TV to the news.

"Oh my God, Mama, I see it. I'm on the way to the hospital right now." Jessica said and then hung the phone up. She rushed upstairs, got Trina and Tracy ready, grabbed her pocketbook, and headed for the door.

It took Jessica thirty minutes to get to Duke Medical Center. She parked her Benz, gathered her children, and rushed inside of the emergency room.

"Welcome to Duke Medical Center, my name is Tammy. How may I help you?"

"Yes, I'm Jessica Blanco. I'm looking for my husband, Tony Blanco. Can you tell me where he is?" Jessica asked.

"Excuse me, Mrs. Blanco, my name is Agent Pennell." the FBI agent said introducing himself.

"Sir, can you please tell me what's going on?" Jessica replied.

"Ma'am, we went to serve tax papers on your husband, and he started firing on us. Can you tell me why he would do something like this? Is he on drugs or anything?" Agent Pennell asked.

"No, of course not. He doesn't do drugs. Where is he? I would like to see my husband, right now." Jessica said, becoming frustrated. Just as she was about to spaz out on the agent, a nurse walked up to her.

"Mrs. Blanco, your husband is in surgery right now." The nurse said.

"Will he make it?" Jessica asked.

"Yes, but he's hurt really bad. Ma'am, just have a seat and the doctor will be with you in a few." The nurse replied.

After a brief moment, Agent Pennell walked back up.

"Mrs. Blanco, I know this is not a good time. I have to inform you though, that your husband, Tony Blanco, will be charged with two counts of murder in the first degree." The agent said.

After hearing the words from Agent Pennell, Jessica felt like she was in a nightmare or having an out-of-body experience. She broke down crying while holding her children, not fully grasping the moment she was living in. "This can't be happening." She thought to herself.

Hours went by with no words of Tony's health. Jessica walked over to the receptionist desk. "Excuse me, could I please see the doctor concerning my husband, Tony Blanco?" Jessica asked.

"Ma'am, someone will be with you shortly, I'll try to call him out."

"Thank you." Jessica replied turning and going back to sit with her children.

Another hour went by and still no word on Tony. Just when Jessica was about to breakdown, the doctor came out.

"Mrs. Blanco." The doctor called out to her.

"Yes!"

"I'm Dr. Petterson. Your husband's surgery went well. He was shot three times in his chest, stomach, and face. He will survive. That's the good news. The bad news is, he's in a coma."

"Huh…"

"Let me finish. Don't stress yourself. He will pull through in due time. You just have to be patient." The doctor replied.

"Dr. Petterson, can I go see him?" Jessica asked.

"Yes, but only immediate family since he is under arrest. Mr. Blanco visits will be for five hours a day, but one person will be able to stay until he comes out of his coma." The doctor stated.

"Thank you, Doctor. What number is his room?"

"334. Do you have any more questions?"

"No."

"Okay, I'll be seeing you then. Don't worry, he'll be fine." Dr. Petterson said just before he walked off. Jessica went and gathered her children, then walked to her husband's room. When she walked in the room, Tony was lying on the hospital bed with his eyes closed. If you didn't know the situation, you would've thought that he was sleeping. He had IV's running from his arms with a tube coming from his mouth that was hooked to a breathing machine helping him breathe. He looked like he had lost 50 lbs. since she had last seen him. Jessica went and sat her kids down, then walked over and sat next to her husband. She reached for his hand and began to speak to him.

"I'm here baby; the kids are here also. I don't know what happened, but whatever it is, we'll get through it together. Everybody is praying for you. Nobody understands, and what the agents told me just doesn't add up. God, please let my husband pull through this. He's a good father, and husband, and I love him."

CHAPTER 2

Four days have gone by. I am struggling emotionally, trying to hang on to my husband. Tony still hasn't come out of his coma yet. I'm beginning to worry about my husband's wellbeing. I can't believe they have him handcuffed while he has all these tubes running through him. Our kids are at my mother's house; they're asking me every day how their daddy is doing and if he woke up yet. I don't know what to tell them, so I just say soon, just to make them feel better. But truly, I don't know when, and the uncertainty is bothering me more with each passing day. The FEDs have kept three agents here with us, like my husband is some type of terrorist from Iraq, planning a great escape. They just sit looking stone faced, lacking emotion, as my husband fights for his life. I really hate these muthafuckas, so much they have me over here talking to myself."

Five days later, Tony Blanco woke up from his coma confused, not knowing where he was at. He tried to lift his arm, but soon realized he was handcuffed to the bed. He was on the verge of panic until he looked around and saw that he was surrounded by his wife and kids.

"Baby, you're awake! I'm so happy you're okay." Jessica said as she squeezed his hand.

"Daddy, you're awake." Trina and Tracy hollered as they ran up and hugged their father.

"Yes, Daddy's awake. I missed you girls." Tony replied in a weak voice.

"We missed you too, Daddy. I thought you would never wake up." Trina said.

"Let your father rest, y'all go over there, sit down, and play with your toys." Jessica said.

"Okay Mommy." Tracy replied as she pulled her sister to the corner of the hospital room.

"Baby, what happened to me?" Tony asked.

"You've been in a coma for nine days, baby." Before Jessica was able to finish talking, three federal agents walked in.

"Doctor, Mr. Blanco is awake." One of the federal agents hollered. The Doctor rushed in.

"Glad to see you with your eyes open, Mr. Blanco, my name is Dr. Petterson. Your surgery went well." The doctor said.

"Surgery? What happened?" Tony asked.

"Why yes, uh, Mr. Blanco, you took gunshot wounds to your chest, stomach, and face. I seriously thought that you weren't going to make it. It's a blessing they got you here when they did."

"Here? Where am I?" Tony asked.

"You're at Duke Medical Center. Now, let me check your vital signs, so that these good men here can do their jobs." Dr. Petterson replied while pointing at the three agents standing behind him. When the doctor finished checking his vitals, he exited the room. The three agents approached his bed and informed him that he was under arrest for the murders of two federal agents. When the agents finished reading him his rights, Tony looked over to his wife and watched tears flow down her cheek. He couldn't believe what he was hearing. He was in so much pain and felt even worse after seeing his wife Jessica shed tears. He just laid back on his bed as his wife came and sat next to him rubbing his arm.

"Everything's going to be okay, baby. We will get through this." Jessica said while trying to comfort her husband.

Tony closed his eyes. It was true the federal government had been on his back for over 15 years now. When Tony was 33, he was in a bad car wreck. His Honda Accord was totaled after a transfer truck ran a stop sign as the driver was drunk and speeding. The driver couldn't stop. They had to use the jaws of life to cut open his Honda in order to get him out. It was as if an angel was protecting him. He only suffered a broken arm, collarbone, and a few broken ribs. It was the equivalent to a scratch as to what looked like certain death. Tony ended up suing the truck company, and received a settlement of $200,000 after lawyer fees were paid. Tony took his settlement and invested it in real estate and made himself a future and a fortune off flipping property. But the FEDs thought that he was a drug dealer, because a few of his family members have gotten themselves busted for selling cocaine. They tried to tie Tony to them, but as always, it didn't work. He was a successful Black man, and they hated to see that. If it isn't taxes, it's something every year; it never fails. His paperwork is always right, so nothing they ever throw his way sticks.

One week later, he was fully recovered. Or at least fully enough to be sent to jail. That day was July 21, 2011.

"Mr. Blanco, will you please stand. You are here today for a bond hearing. My name is Judge Timmons. I will be hearing this matter today. Mr. Holt, you may speak on your client's behalf."

"Your Honor, my client, Mr. Blanco, is married with two kids and has a lot of ties to this community. Mr. Blanco is a successful businessman, who does not have a record. Not even a ticket violation. Your Honor, on July 4th, 2011, my client thought that he was being robbed, so he discharged his firearm, which is registered and he has a license to carry. My client states that the agents never identified themselves. They just jumped out with their weapons drawn."

"Your Honor, I strongly object to Mr. Blanco being released on bond. Mr. Blanco is here on double murder of two federal agents, not a speeding ticket. Since I've been the prosecutor here in Wake County, I have never seen a crime like this against the government. Mr. Blanco has access to millions, and he could easily leave the country. With this type of money in hand, it's a fact that we will never see him again if he is released today. I request that his bond be denied."

"Was there anyone on the scene at the time of this incident?" Judge Timmons asked.

"Yes sir, your Honor." The prosecutor replied.

"Please stand and state your name for the court." Said Judge Timmons.

"My name is Agent Jeff Hurns. I am a local FBI agent. On the morning of July 4th, we were going to serve a tax fraud warrant on Mr. Tony Blanco. Agents were fired upon after identifying themselves, and two were killed. Mr. Blanco was hit several times. That's my account of what happened your Honor." Agent Jeff Hurns replied and then sat down.

"Agent Hurns, I'm Mr. Holt. I have a few questions. When my client, Mr. Blanco, was in route to his office, why did the agents not blue light him and pull him over to serve his warrant? Or better yet, once you knew he was in his office, why not pull up with your blue light then? Why jump out of a tinted black SUV with guns drawn? I have no further questions your Honor." Mr. Holt finished then returned to his seat.

"Mr. Blanco, please stand. Due to the severity of this case, I must deny your bond. There are two federal agents dead, and it would be a great injustice to our system to let you out on bond. Bond denied."

"Your Honor, on behalf of the government, we would like to seek the death penalty in this case." The prosecutor said.

"I suspect you would, prosecutor. Let the record show this will be a capital case. Court is adjourned." Judge Timmons replied.

"Mr. Blanco, we will figure out a way to get you out of here. You just have to be patient." Mr. Holt said.

"It looks like I'ma be here for a while. But whatever it takes to get me out, I want you to do it." Tony replied as he turned and was then taken into custody by the Wake County Jailers.

Once Tony got back into the county jail, he was still dressed in his Armani suit with his arm in a sling. Two guards stepped in the room and handed him a jail uniform so he could switch clothes. When he finally switched into his jail uniform, the craziest thing happened. A third guard walked into the room; he looked like he could have been a heavyweight boxer. Tony could tell that this man had rank because he had captain bars pinned to his shirt. His name tag displayed the guards name as Johnson. The door slowly shut. "Must have been closed by one of the other two guards" Tony thought to himself. Johnson stepped closer, so close Tony could smell the big man's breath.

"So, Mr. Blanco, you like to kill cops, huh?" Johnson asked.

"I don't want any trouble. I would just like to go to my cell." Tony replied.

"You brought trouble on yourself when you killed two cops."

Tony's instincts kicked in, as he had a foresight of what was about to occur. Unable to use his hands, Tony kicked the heavyweight guard in the stomach, knocking his breath out. The other two guards in the room closed in. Tony spun and kicked the smaller guard in the knee cap. He instantly fell to the ground screaming, gripping his knee. Tony Blanco was a black belt in Taekwando; which made defending himself easy; and at the same time nearly impossible because of the pain that was shooting through his body with every quick movement he made. The heavyweight Captain recovered from the blow he had taken in the stomach. He rushed Tony, slamming him against the wall. The third guard ran up and hit him with a riot stick. They continued to beat him; blow on top of blow rained upon his body, until he fell unconscious.

When he woke up, he was in the infirmary, body aching. For the next six months, these beatings would continue every week. The same Captain and two guards came to pay him a visit. He was denied phone calls, they took his mail and never sent it out. Until one day, the beatings stopped. Tony had guessed maybe Captain Johnson figured he had had enough, which was probably a fact he would never admit to himself or anybody other than himself. Tony was determined that he would stay strong and never break. He had to be strong for Jessica, and his two girls, Trina and Tracy. He could not show weakness, because showing weakness would break his wife Jessica, and he couldn't have that. She was his everything, his ride or die, his Bonnie to his Clyde.

"Blanco, pack it up. you're going to population." An unknown guard came in and screamed.

Tony packed his things, what little he had. The door popped, and he followed the unknown guard to population.

CHAPTER 3

It's been a year now, and after settling in six months ago into general population, everything has been going smoothly. Tony had plenty of canteen, he got to talk to his wife and daughters every day, and he had a strong workout routine going on with a few guys in the block. Tony's attorney, Mr. Holt, said this will be the toughest case that he has ever taken to trial. Tony didn't want to hear that, but he was still being optimistic about winning his freedom. After being locked up for a year, he was beginning to feel what his cousins were going through. He could remember how he used to send them money, and he figured that they were good. He was beginning to realize that money doesn't mean anything when you don't have your loved ones around. Tony's two cousins, Dee and Dre, were both currently serving a 27-year sentence for selling cocaine. They had both lost their women during their lengthy prison sentences. Even though Tony hadn't been convicted of the double homicide of the federal agents, he couldn't help laying on his steel bunk wondering if his wife Jessica would leave him. Only time would tell.

"Today is Thursday and a new group of guys will arrive today. I hope they don't give me no cell mate; these young guys just don't know how to act these days." He thought to himself as he got up and used the bathroom.

"Tony Blanco, you have a visit." The guard on duty came in the block and announced.

"A'ight, I am getting ready now." Tony replied as he reached for his toothbrush and toothpaste and began to brush his teeth.

When he was finished, he washed his face, put on his shoes, and headed out of his cell. As he walked out of the block, he could see nothing but young guys coming in. A couple of guys dapped him up and some nodded out of respect. When he entered the visitation room, it was all smiles. Trina and Tracy rushed him and gave him a hug.

"Daddy, we miss you." Tracy said.

"When are you coming home?" Trina asked.

"I miss you too, and Daddy will be home soon." As soon as Tony said those words, he looked up at Jessica and could see the lack of faith in her eyes.

"Hey baby, how are you doing? You look beautiful. I miss you." Tony said as he hugged his wife.

"Hello baby, I miss you too. I see you've been taking care of yourself. Looks like you've been working out." Jessica replied.

"Yeah, I've been doing a little something; pushups, dips, pull ups."

"Well, you look good."

"Thanks, love."

"Have you spoken to your lawyers?" Jessica asked.

"Yeah, I talked to him, but he isn't talking about nothing. He keeps saying be patient, let him work."

"Baby, I'm just so frustrated." Jessica replied through tears.

"Jessica baby don't cry. We are going to get through this. I promise you baby, we just have to stick together as a family."

"I know Tony, but it's hard. It's just so hard, I miss you so much; the kids miss you too. I'm scared, Tony."

"It's okay to be afraid. I am too, Jess." Tony replied.

"Yesterday I was at home, cooking your favorite, steak and fries. After I finished fixing the girl's plates, I started fixing yours. Until I realized you wasn't home. All I could do was cry."

"Baby, please don't stress, because it only hurts me more. I am always thinking about you, and the girls, and how this bullshit is affecting y'all. I'm so sorry about this Jess."

"I know you are, baby, I know." Jessica replied.

"So how is everyone doing?" Tony asked.

"They're doing okay. Momma told me to tell you hello, and that she is praying for you. Your sister stopped by the house and watched a movie with me Sunday night. I thought that was so sweet of her."

"Yeah, that's what's up. I got a letter that Cindy wrote me laying on my bed. I gotta write her back."

"I wrote you and sent some pics. Did you get them yet?" Jessica asked.

"Nah, not yet. When did you send them off?"

"Thursday."

"I'll probably get them sometime this week."

"I hope so."

"Jessica, have you gone over to the office lately?"

"Yes, I went and cleaned up some and then returned most of the business calls."

"So how did that go?"

"Well of course I paid all of the bills. Most of the calls were about renting one of our houses. Oh yeah baby, I almost forgot. This woman asked if you would like to sell the building?"

"Did this woman make an offer?"

"No baby, but I told her 3.5 million was the selling price."

"And what did she say to that?"

"She said that she wanted to buy it."

"Okay, that's good. Sell it to her, as soon as you can."

"Are you sure?"

"Yeah, we will need that money. Clean the basement, and run the business from there." Tony said as he squeezed his wife's hand.

"Time is up, visitation is over." the C.O. stepped in and hollered.

Tony, Jessica, and the girls stood up, gathering their things and said their goodbyes.

"Okay, times up. I'll call you later. I love you Jess, please don't stress, okay?" Tony said as he hugged and kissed his wife.

"We love you too, Daddy." Trina said as she and her sister Tracy walked over and gave him a hug.

"I love you both so much, make sure you are good and take care of mommy for me, okay?"

"Okay Daddy, we will."

Tony waved at his family as he watched them walk out the door. Feeling the same pain in his heart as he did at the end of every visit

After watching his family leave, the guard called him to the back room for a strip search. Tony hated this part the most after every visit. Every inmate had to be checked for contraband.

"Squat and cough." The guard said, and then he handed Tony back his clothes. "Next!"

Tony grabbed his clothes and put them back on. "Damn, I hope I didn't get a cellmate." He thought to himself. Tony walked straight back to his block and back to his cell. When he got up the steps, he saw a young, light skinned, slim guy in his cell unpacking his property. "Man, this shit is crazy. Hope this dude ain't no rat." He said to himself shaking his head.

"What's up, man?" Tony said as he walked inside his cell.

"What's good?" Quincy replied softly while still unpacking his clothes.

"What's your name man?" Tony asked.

"Quincy."

"Quincy, huh."

"Yeah, that's right. You got a problem with that?" Quincy asked.

"Nah, young buck. I'm just making sure I got your name right." Tony replied.

"Oh, my bad fam. I ain't mean to come off on you like that."

"It's alright, don't worry about it. By the way, my name is Tony Blanco." Tony said while shaking Quincy's hand.

"You're the one that killed the two FBI agents."

"Yeah, that's me."

"Damn, I can't believe that I am sharing a cell with you. Don't you own like half the city? Why don't you just bond out?"

"I have a lot of property, but I don't own that much. I would've made bond, but I don't have one. Enough about me, what are you locked up for?"

"I got a shooting charge."

"How much is your bond?"

"$250,000."

"Do you think you're going to get out?"

"Nah Tony. I'm in for the long haul. My bond is too high, and my money is too low. I have some bros out there but ain't no telling about them."

"Listen Quincy, I want to be straight up with you because that's the only way I know how to be."

"A'ight, what's up? Spit it out."

"I don't allow no homos or no snitches in my cell."

"Hold up, bruh, before you say another word. I ain't no snitch and I am certainly not no homo. So, you don't have to worry about that, homie."

"Good, good. That's good to know. Now that we got that out of the way, where are you from Quincy?"

"I am originally from LA, South side of Compton, but my mom moved us to North Carolina when I was 15. I've been living in Raleigh for a while now. I have a son and a daughter, and I have been married four years now.”

"Yeah, I am married too, young buck. I have two kids myself; two girls. This jail shit is driving my wife crazy.”

"I already know. Mines going to have a fit when she finds out I am in jail.”

"Yeah, we both gotta get out of here.”

"So Tony, do you think that you will beat your charges? They were saying a lot of crazy shit on the news about you.”

"I don't know, youngster. I just take it one day at a time, and try not to think about it. Are you hungry?”

"Yeah, I could use a snack.”

"Well, look in that bag that's hanging on the wall. Get you enough to last you for a couple days. We won't get canteen again till Monday.”

"Thanks Tony.”

"No problem youngster, you good.”

Two weeks later at the prosecutor's office

"Mr. Lockline, I fully understand the nature of my client's case, but the agents are at fault here, not Mr. Blanco.” Mr. Holt said.

"Mr. Holt, your client, Mr. Blanco, killed not one, but two federal agents, who were doing their job, I might add. How dare you walk up in my office and have the nerve to ask for a manslaughter charge. Life without parole will be the only plea I will offer Tony Blanco. You can take it or leave it; it matters not to me.” Mr. Lockline replied.

"Well, Mr. Lockline, you leave me no choice but to go all the way with this case.”

"If you do Mr. Holt, your client will die.”

"And if I don't, he will die. Mr. Lockline, you have a nice day!” Mr. Holt exclaimed as he stormed out of the D. A's office. "Damn, he's playing hard, but I believe my client. I know he didn't shoot unless he felt threatened first. I'll just have to prove it. While I am out, I'll go see Tony and let him know our plans.”

He thought to himself.

Mr. Holt gathered his thoughts as he opened the door to his Ford F-350. He looked at his phone and then crunk his truck up. He thought about calling Tony's wife, Jessica Blanco, but decided that he would go visit Tony and tell him first. Mr. Holt snatched his gear shift into drive and headed to Wake County Jail.

Once at Wake County Jail, Mr. Holt went and checked in at the front office.

"How are you doing Mr. Holt?" The guard asked.

"I am doing fine, thank you for asking." Mr. Holt replied.

"So, who will you be seeing today?"

"I would like to see Tony Blanco."

"Okay, check in your briefcase, and go to room 34. We'll send him up."

"Thank you very much." Mr. Holt replied as he let the other guard check his briefcase. Then, he walked to room 34.

"Yo, I bet five with your five. My hand is made, bruh, fold that shit." Tony said while throwing his chips on the table.

"Fuck that shit, I call. I'm made to." Hit replied, throwing his chips in.

"Turn out and win." Tony said.

"I got a straight." Hit replied, turning over his cards.

"Well, you lose. I gotta boat, kings over tres." Tony said as he gathered up his winnings and gave the house man his cut.

"I told y'all you couldn't fuck with me. I'm done, cash me out."

"Come on man, why you quitting? I ain't shit else to do." Quincy replied.

"Yeah, you heard the youngin', give me a chance to get my money back." Hit said.

"If I sat here all day, you still wouldn't be able to get your money back." Tony replied.

"I'ma get mine back though." Quincy said.

"Yeah, I bet."

"Tony Blanco, you have a legal visit." A guard stepped in the dorm and hollered.

"Who is it?" Tony asked back.

"A legal visit, get ready." The guard replied with a scowl.

"I'm ready now."

"Well come on, let's go then. Your lawyers waiting."

"Grab my chips, Quincy."

"A'ight, big bruh." Quincy replied.

Tony followed the guard out to the hallway to get patted down, then he followed him to room 34.

"Your lawyer is in here. Go in and have a seat. Mr. Holt, will you be alright by yourself? The guard asked.

"Yes, of course, I'll be fine. Just wait outside." Mr. Holt replied.

"What's going on Holt?" Tony asked as he sat down.

"Hey Tony, how are you doing today?" Mr. Holt replied.

"I'm here Holt. Did you find out anything new yet?"

"Yeah, I did. For one, I know that you are telling the truth about what happened. Because if you weren't, they would have never offered you a plea deal."

"A plea deal? What did they offer?"

"Life without parole, but I told her we are going to trial."

"You are damn right we are."

"Well, I just wanted to stop by and let you know the latest."

"We thank for your help, Mr. Holt."

"No problem." Holt replied then shook Tony's hand and walked out the door. Then the guard walked in.

"Alright Mr. Blanco, let's go." The guard said.

*3 months later at the United States Federal Penitentiary in Coleman, Florida. *

"How are you today, Damien? I am Agent Hurns, and this is my partner Agent Pennell."

"Ok, that's nice to know, but how about you tell me what you are doing here." Damien replied.

"Okay Damien, I will cut to the chase then. Agent Pennell and

I have come to offer you a deal if you give us information about Tony Blanco. Damien, you have a chance to walk away a free man today, right now. I checked your time; you still have twenty years left. We need your help."

"What do you want to know?"

"We want to know about Tony Blanco's cocaine empire."

"Mr. Hurns and Mr. Pennell, Tony is a hardworking man. I have never heard of him selling drugs. All of this is news to my ears, but even if I had, that's a bad deal."

"Why do you say that? I'm offering you your freedom. What better deal is there to offer?" Agent Hurns asked.

"Because, Mr. Hurns, I can only do one deal, and that's to never be a rat. So, if you would excuse me, I have twenty more years to do." Damien stood up and walked out of the room.

The agents were back in the car.

"Hurns, we can't get anything. What if someone saw those agents jump out of the SUV with their guns drawn? Damn, the plan was to kill his Black ass. We have to find something." Agent Pennell said.

"I know, you're right. If someone saw what really happened, we're fucked and he'll end up walking. I'm taking this personally. I'm not going to let Tony Blanco beat this." Hurns replied.

"Hurns, how do you go from $200,000 at age 33 to $5 million in 18 months, legit paper. Tony Blanco is the man, and he's the boss. I just have that feeling deep in my bones. He's 50 years old now and his net worth is over $70 million dollars." Pennell said.

"Pennell, I feel the same way as you, but haven't gotten one piece of information on him. Not one piece. Nobody is talking." Hurns replied.

"We gotta figure this out, and I mean fast."

Coleman Florida Penitentiary

"Yo Dre, I just left visit. Two federal agents from Raleigh came to see me about Tony." Damien said.

"What did they say?" Dre asked.

"If I gave some information about Tony that's helpful, I could have left prison today. I told 'em to fuck that shit. I'll see them in 20 years." Damien replied.

"Man, who the fuck do they think they are, marching up in here trying to get you to snitch on family?"

"It ain't nothing, man, fuck them pigs. They're calling chow, you trying to go?"

"Nah, I'm good. I got my coffee, plus, I'm about to hit the yard and run."

"A'ight, I'll holler at you later then."

"A'ight, later." Dre said while dapping Damien up, then headed to the yard.

As Dre walked out to the yard, he turned his radio on and began to stretch. He thought, "Damn, I can't believe those feds offered Damien that deal, and he didn't take it. Tony does send us a thousand dollars a month. But I need my freedom back." He began to jog. Lap after lap, crazy thoughts entered his mind about turning on Tony. "Damn, Tony is fam; fuck that shit." Dre stopped jogging and walked back inside the prison. Instead of going back to his block to take a shower, he walked to the back office to see his case manager.

Ring-ring-ring.

"DEA office of Raleigh, how can I help you?" Some lady asked when she picked up the phone.

"Hello, my name is Dremond Blanco. I'm calling to speak with the two agents who came to visit with Damien Blanco today. I have some important information for them."

"Hold on one second, sir." the secretary replied.

A cell phone rang.

"Hello, Agent Pennell speaking."

"Sir, I have a Dremond Blanco on the other line wishing to speak with you. Should I connect the call?" the secretary asked.

"Yes, please do." Agent Pennell replied. "Hurns, we might have something here. Tony's cousin Dremond is on the other end.”

“Good, good. Play it out for what it’s worth.” Hurns replied. The line then got connected.

“Agent Pennell speaking, how can I help you?”

“I was told that you visited Damien today, is that true?”

“Why you ask, and who am I speaking with?”

“I am Tony’s cousin, Dremond Blanco.”

“His cousin, huh?”

“Yeah.”

“So, what is your reason for calling?” Agent Pennell asked.

“I want to know if I could be offered the same deal that you tried to give to my brother.”

“That depends on you, Dremond.”

“Okay, come and get me out of this hell hole tomorrow, and I will help you with whatever you need.”

“Are you sure about this? Because once we start, it’s no turning back.”

“Yeah, I am sure. Just come get me out.”

“Well, we have to make some calls to get this approved, because the deal was for your brother, not you. I’ll tell you this though, if me and my partner, Agent Hurns, come to visit you tomorrow, you’ll never see the yard again.”

“I’ll be waiting.”

“I’m sure you will Dremond.” Agent Pennell replied, then hung up. “I think we got us one Hurns. Dremond sounds like he’s ready to work a deal.”

“We might end up getting Tony after all.” Hurns replied.

“Let me call the prosecutor’s office.” Pennell said as he picked up the phone and started dialing numbers.

Ring-ring-ring.

“Hello, this is the District Attorney’s office. How may I help you?” The secretary asked.

“Hey, this is Special Agent Pennell. Could you put me through to Mr. Robert Lockline, please?”

"Yes, please hold."

"Hello Pennell, what's going on? Is everything running smooth?" Robert Lockline said.

"Well, yes and no."

"What do you mean by yes and no? Tell me what you have."

"Well, Damien Blanco turned the deal down. Hours later, we get a call from his brother, Dremond Blanco, and he is willing to help us take down Tony Blanco, his cousin, only if he's allowed the same deal." Agent Pennell replied.

"For full cooperation, I can arrange for him to get the same deal." Lockline replied.

"That is good to hear Mr. D.A. I believe this is a sure shot."

"It better be, Pennell. I want to bury this Tony Blanco. I'm faxing the papers now for him to be released. I'll have Judge Covington sign it today. And I want you to text me the fax number to your hotel room and let's get our boy out."

"Mr. Lockline, as soon as I get the release papers and have him in the car, I will call you."

"Okay, you and Agent Hurns better not screw this up."

"We won't sir." Pennell replied before hanging up.

24 hours later at Coleman Florida Penitentiary

"Dremond, I'm Agent Pennell, the person you spoke to over the phone, and this is my partner Agent Hurns. Those stacks of papers you are currently flipping through are your release papers and your new plea agreement. I want you to fully understand that if you attempt to run, we are ordered to shoot to kill. When we leave here, we are going back to Raleigh, North Carolina to finalize everything. When we finish getting all of your statements, we will put you in a safe house in Colorado that you may leave daily. But you will have an 8pm curfew. Once you testify, we will buy you a house and get you a job. We will explain that in more detail later. Are you ready to go, Dremond?"

"Yeah." Dremond replied.

"Sir, state your names." The warden said.

"Agent Pennell. Agent Hurns."

"Okay. Inmate, state your name." The warden said.

"Dremond Blanco, 07636619."

"Thank you, you are free to leave." Dremond and the two agents got up and began to walk outside. Dremond could smell his freedom.

"Can I get something to eat?" Dremond asked.

"Yeah, as soon as we get on the road." Agent Hurns replied.

When they got outside the prison gates, Dremond was in the middle of two agents as they walked towards the agent's black suburban. Agent Hurns opened the driver side door and got in. Agent Pennell and Dremond walked to the opposite side. Just as Dremond began to open the back door, a grey minivan pulled up at blazing speeds, and stopped right behind the agent's black suburban. The mini van's side door swung open and chopper rounds rang out.

Round after round rang out through the air as bullets rippled through the black SUV. Agent Hurns and Agent Pennell tried to return fire. The chopper rounds were coming too fast, and the agents had no choice but to duck for cover or die.

Dremond's body lay on the ground rippled with bullets. When the gunmen in the minivan were sure Dremond was dead, they sped off. Guards rushed out of the prison, but by this time though, it was too late, and Dremond Blanco was dead.

"Fuck, Hurns are you okay?"

"Yeah, I am good."

"Are you hit?"

"No." Hurns replied.

"Dremond's gone."

"I know, but who the fuck could have done this? Who knew that he was leaving? I want his cell searched, all his phone calls rewound." Hurns screamed at the guards.

"I know Dremond didn't say shit. Agent Hurns, put a APB out on that van, find them now. I gotta call Lockline and let him know about this."

"I'll put the APB out, you call Lockline." Hurns replied.

Ring-ring.

"Hello, District Attorney's office."

"This is Agent Pennell. I need to speak with Mr. Lockline."

"Hold, please."

"Pennell, tell me you have good news." Lockline said.

"No sir, I don't. Dremond Blanco is dead."

"Dead? How? What happened?"

"As we were leaving, someone was in the parking lot waiting. They shot him multiple times. It was a hit, I am sure of it." Pennell replied.

"Are you all okay?"

"Yes, Agent Hurns and I are okay. He's putting a APB out on the van as we speak."

"I want these people found and locked away. And I want to know who sent this hit." Mr. Lockline said.

"We will sir, we're working on it."

"Well work harder." Lockline said and then hung up.

CHAPTER 4

6:00 pm later that afternoon, C-block, Florida Coleman Penitentiary. Damien Blanco stood in front of the television as Channel 5 News came on.

"Hi, I'm Louise Westbrook. Earlier today, a cocaine king pin was shot multiple times after he tried to escape from Florida Coleman Penitentiary. Dremond Blanco was pronounced dead on the scene."

When the news showed Dremond's mugshot, tears fell from Damien's' eyes, and he felt the pain of losing his brother. Damien couldn't believe that Dremond was going to lie on Tony just to be free. He knew after he told Dremond about the two agents coming to visit him and the offer that was made, that Dremond was going to try to rat. Dremond asked too many questions, red flags went up. Dremond was his brother, but he had to be taken care of. All rats had to die, even Master Splinter. Damien wiped the tears from his face.

"Yo D, what up?"

"What up, Glizzy?" Damien replied as he dapped Glizzy up.

"Sorry about your brother, man."

"Don't be, he deserved it."

"Why you say that D, that's your brother man."

"What goes around comes around." Damien replied then he turned and walked away.

Back at the Wake County Jail, after watching the news, Tony Blanco was deeply hurt at losing a family member. He laid on the bunk and gathered his thoughts together. Quincy walked into the cell after seeing his attorney. Tony wanted to say something about his cousin, but instead of saying something, he decided to keep his mouth shut and just listen to what Quincy had to say.

"Yo, big bruh. I seen my lawyer, and my bond got dropped. So, I'll be getting out today. Thanks for the love you showed me. If there's anything I can do for you, just give me a call."

"No problem, bruh, you are a good dude. So, what are you going to do when you get out?" Tony asked.

"I don't know really. My money is a little low. I gotta try to find me a connect; do you know anybody?" Quincy asked.

"Like I said, I smoked a little weed here and there."

"Do it be that gas or some bullshit?"

"Youngsta, do I look like I smoke bullshit?"

"Can you give me his number?"

"Youngster, the person I get my gas from is my family. If something happens to him, it's my fault."

"Tony, my word is all I have. I'll do good business with him."

"Quincy, I am going to trust you, don't let me down. My family are not the type of people that you cross. Let us be clear on that."

"We're clear, big bruh, you are like a big brother to me. I enjoyed being here with you. I know what I want out of life. I see how important family is now."

Quincy and Tony talked for a few more hours before one of the guards came in.

"Quincy Capps, pack up. You've made bond."

"Tony, I am gone man. You stay up." Quincy said while

dapping Tony up.

"Youngster, the phones are no good. Here's my family's number. His name is Stone. When you call him, let him know I gave you the number. And Quincy, Stone will kill you if you cross him, kids and all."

"I got you, big bruh. I told you, you can trust me. I am out, bruh."

"Okay, stay up fam."

When Quincy walked out of the jailhouse, his wife, Toya, and his kids were outside waiting for him. Quincy and Toya have been together now for 13 years and married four.

"Hey baby." Toya said as she ran up to Quincy and gave him a hug.

"Hey baby, I missed you so much."

"I missed you too. Don't ever leave us again. The kids are in the car."

"I won't baby." Quincy replied as he walked around the car, opened the door, and gave his two kids big hugs and kisses.

After Quincy finished hugging his children, him and Toya got in the car and drove home. When they got home, the first thing that his wife Toya did was take the kids to her next-door neighbor's house so that they could watch them for a couple hours. Quincy hopped in the shower so he could freshen up and wash away that jail feeling. When Quincy walked out of the shower after drying off, he walked into his bedroom, only to find Toya laid out on the bed with nothing but her panties on. Toya was five foot three, 135 pounds, and sexy as fuck.

"You like what you see, baby?"

"Of course, I do. I have been pining for you the whole time I was away."

"Well, the kids are next door with Keisha, so why don't you come over here and show Mommy how much you missed her."

Quincy dropped his towel to the floor, letting his wife see his erection as he walked towards the bed. Toya sat up on her knees,

Quincy began tongue kissing her, slowly moving to her neck and then to her breast.

"Oooh baby, you make me feel so good." Toya moaned.

Quincy continued to nibble on Toya's nipples. Toya reached her hand down and began to stroke Quincy's manhood.

"Lay down, baby." Toya whispered.

Quincy laid on the bed as Toya crawled on top of him and began to kiss him from his lips down to his stomach. Then, she slowly placed his penis in her mouth and Toya started sucking him slowly, then sped up and repeated, taking every inch of Quincy in her mouth. Quincy's toes curled.

"Aaah baby, you're going to make me bust a nut. Come get on this dick, I wanna feel that pussy."

At Quincy's command, Toya crawled on top of him.

"Aahh." Toya moaned as she took all of Quincy inside of her.

"Ride that dick, baby."

Toya began throwing that pussy, riding him faster and faster.

"Aaaahh, Quincy, I'm coming baby."

"Cum on this dick." Quincy replied as he gripped Toya's butt cheeks, slamming her pussy onto his penis. Toya screamed as she came.

Quincy sat up and flipped her over to doggie style. Toya, knowing how her husband liked to fuck, placed her face on the pillow and then spread her ass cheeks so he'll have full access to her kitty. Quincy slapped her butt cheeks with his manhood and then he entered her.

"Aaah aah aaah!" Toya screamed as Quincy began to pound her from behind.

"Damn, I love this pussy."

Toya began to get her energy back and began to throw her ass back at him. "Aahh, Quincy, fuck me Daddy. I missed this dick." Toya said while looking back at Quincy.

"Yeah baby, I am about to bust."

"Cum for me baby, cum for Mommy."

"Aaahh, damn, aahh!" Quincy grunted as he let his seed spill inside his wife. After Quincy nutted, he pulled out, but Toya wasn't finished. She turned around and started sucking Quincy's manhood, making his knees buckle as she sucked all of the cum out of him. When she was finished, Quincy laid back on the bed spent.

"Baby, I love you."

"I love you too." Toya replied as she cuddled with her husband. "Quincy, don't leave me again."

"I won't baby, I love you too much."

"Yeah right."

"I really do. Plus, I don't want to kill nobody for trying to take my pussy."

"Quincy, it's been hard paying these bills while you were away."

"Toya, don't worry about that no more. I got us."

"You promise baby?"

"I promise." Quincy stared at his wife as she fell asleep. Realizing that she is the real deal, he kissed her on the top of the forehead. Then, he fell asleep himself, hoping that Stone would come through for him.

The next day when Quincy got up, he and his wife played with the kids together. The kids were so happy that he was home, and he was happy that he was here with them. A few hours go by of Quincy enjoying his family, then he picked up the phone and called Stone.

"Ring, ring."

"Damn Stone, pick up."

"Hello." Stone said when he answered.

"Yo Stone, this is Quincy. Tony gave me your number and told me to call."

"What's up with you?" Stone asked.

"Bruh, can we meet some place? I don't like talking over the air waves." Quincy replied.

"Yeah, be at KFC over on Newbern Ave in 30 minutes."

"I'll be there." Quincy said and then hung up. "Hell yeah, damn I hope this works out."

"You hope what works out baby?" Toya asked.

"Nothing love, I was just talking to myself. Look though, I am gonna run out for a few. Do you need me to do anything while I am out?"

"No, but I would like to catch a movie tonight."

"Alright baby, be ready at 6:30pm. I'll come back and pick you up, then we can go see whatever movie you like."

"Okay baby." Toya said as she walked over and gave her husband a kiss.

Quincy walked out the door, got inside his black Charger, and pulled off. Thirty minutes later, he arrived at the KFC. Then he picked up his phone and called Stone.

"Ring."

"Yo." Stone said.

"I'm here." Quincy replied.

"What are you driving?"

"Black Charger."

"Park beside the red 760 BMW and get in."

Quincy parked beside the BMW, then he got out of his Charger and got inside the BMW.

"What's good Stone?" Quincy asked.

Stone didn't say a word, he just raised his finger to his lips, indicating for Quincy to remain silent. Then, Stone began to pat Quincy down. When he was satisfied that Quincy wasn't wearing a wire, only then did he speak.

"So, what's up Quincy?" Stone asked.

"What was that all about?"

"I had to make sure you weren't wearing a wire. Can't trust people these days. Feel me?"

"Yeah, I feel you, but you can trust me, though. Tony, that's my people."

"That's good to hear Quincy, but tell me, what can I do for

you?"

"I need a weed connect bad, but cocaine is my real hustle."

"Bruh, I only fucks wit weed, so what are you trying to do?"

"I got like four thousand saved up right now."

"Keep your phone on, I'll give you a call later."

"A'ight, Stone that's what's up, fam." Quincy replied, then exited the BMW and got back in his Charger and drove off. "I hope this nigga don't be on no bullshit." Quincy thought to himself as he sped down the road, Yo Gotti blazing through his car audio system. He was headed to see his brother, Tech, down in Burlington. It took him 45 minutes to get there from Raleigh. Then he got off the exit and traveled down Maple to Petersburg Apartments. Quincy turned his music down right before he pulled into the parking lot. The police stay posted over here and he didn't have time to be getting no useless tickets. Quincy threw his Charger into park, then got out and walked to the door. Tech was so paranoid, Quincy didn't even have to knock on the door; Tech opened the door as soon as he walked up.

"Yo, what's up, big bruh." Tech said as soon as he opened the door.

"What's good man." Quincy replied while he stepped up and gave his little brother a hug.

"Good to see you out of that jail."

"I'm glad to be out."

"So, what brings you down to Burlington?"

"Damn, I can't just come see my brother?"

"Of course you can, but I know you like the back of my hand, Q."

"So, are you going to let me in or are we standing outside all day?"

"Oh, my bad Q. Come on in."

Both brothers went inside. Tech put the TV on and turned it to ESPN, and they watched as the sports commentators gave their opinion about the Lakers trading with the Pelicans for a big man to go down to LA and play with Lebron James.

"You know if we get AD, that's a ring right there." Tech said.

"LA still trying to stack their team." Quincy replied.

"Bruh, I can't help it that your Chicago Bulls are sorry."

"Shit, we might be a'ight this year. Being that we just got Cody White out of the draft."

"White has got to prove himself first. Plus, y'all need some more help down there, y'all need a veteran to lead all them young boys ya got down there."

"I can go for that, you're right, lil' bruh."

"I'm 'bout to go get a beer out the kitchen, you want one?"

"Yeah, as long as it's not a Miller Highlife."

"Lord no. You know I only drink Bud Light's." Tech said as he walked to the kitchen and grabbed two beers. "Here, bruh."

"Thanks. Look bruh, I wanna talk to you about something."

"What's good?"

"When I was in jail, I shared a cell with Tony Blanco."

"The rich nigga that killed the two feds?"

"Yeah, that's him."

"What about him?"

"Well, me and Tony got pretty close when we were together. Before I left, I told him that I needed a weed connect, so he hit me with one of his people's numbers. To make a long story short, I called them and met them today. I mean, this dude patted me down and everything."

"What, he thought you were working for the police?"

"Let me finish."

"Go ahead."

"After he patted me down, and I was clean, he asked me what I needed. I told him a weed connect, but coke was my real hustle. When I said coke, he pumped the breaks ASAP, and said he only fucks with the gas. I believe this guy is the real deal, Tech."

"So, what's the plan?"

"I plan on getting close to him by moving that gas. But I know he fucks with the coke. I just gotta get him to trust me."

"So, what do you need me to do?" Tech asked.

"I need you to help me move whatever I get. I believe the faster I move it, the more he'll throw my way."

"I'm down for whatever, especially when it comes to getting that paper."

"Okay, that's all I needed to know." Quincy replied as he sat back and finished off his beer.

When they finished drinking together, Quincy and his brother, Tech, dapped each other up. It was mid-afternoon, and Quincy had to get back to Raleigh so he could pick his wife Toya up for the movie date tonight.

"I'ma get with you, stay by the phone." Quincy rolled his window down and said.

"I gotcha." Tech replied while watching his brother pull away.

CHAPTER 5

When Quincy got back to Raleigh, he swerved and picked up his wife. She was outside sitting on a lawn chair when he pulled up. Watching his wife walk to the car was like watching America's Top Model glide down the runway. His wife was that bad, and he felt blessed to have a woman like her by his side. Beautiful, strong, loving, caring, and most of all loyal. When the passenger door opened and his wife got in, only then did Quincy snap out of his little daydream.

"Hey baby." Toya said as she leaned over and kissed her husband.

"Hey sexy, I like your outfit." Quincy replied.

"Thanks, I figured you would."

"How you know?"

"Because I know my husband, that's why."

Quincy smiled, then put the Charger in drive and pulled away, headed to the movies. When they got to Blueridge Road, Quincy pulled into the parking lot of the movie theater, parked, then got out and helped his wife out of the car.

"So, what movie are we going to see, baby?" Quincy asked.

"I want to see that new Avengers movie, End Game." Toya replied.

"I heard some people talking about that movie; they said it was pretty good."

"Well, we are about to see."

Quincy and Toya walked into the movies and bought their tickets, then went to their seats. The theater was so slammed, you could barely move around. Quincy and Toya went and sat at the very top so other people's heads wouldn't block their vision. The movie was a long movie; it lasted three hours. Well worth the money though, because the movie was good. When Quincy and his wife got back to the car, Toya was hungry, so they decided to go to Outback Steakhouse on Capitol Boulevard. Quincy continued to check his phone because Stone still hadn't called. By the time Quincy and Toya got back home, it was 1:30 AM. Toya was horny as soon as she began to undress. Quincy's phone rang.

"Ring, ring."

"Damn, what perfect timing." Quincy thought to himself as he looked at the caller ID.

"Hello." Quincy said when he picked up.

"Ayo, Q, come to the car wash on Rose St. And Q?"

"Yo?" Quincy replied.

"Come by yourself."

"I gotcha. I'm on my way." Quincy said and then hung up.

"Baby, I gotta make a run real quick. I'll be back."

"It's 1:45 AM. You've got to be kidding me. What you mean you going out?" Toya asked.

"It's business, I'll be back."

"Well, when you get back, I'll be asleep. Be careful, because I ain't doing that jail shit no more."

"Baby, I'm not trying to argue with you." Quincy replied as he grabbed his keys and walked out the door.

It took Quincy 15 minutes to get to the car wash. When he

pulled up, he saw Stone and three other dudes wearing ski-masks. Before Quincy could get out, one of the masked men walked to his car with a finger to his mouth and tossed a duffle bag in the window. Quincy opened the bag and saw it was the green. Then, he handed the masked man four-thousand dollars. When the masked man counted the money, he didn't say a word. He only pointed his finger, motioning for Quincy to leave. "Damn, these dudes acting like they are selling ten keys or something." Quincy thought as he looked at Stone before he pulled off. Stone stuck his hand to his ear in the sign of a telephone and mouthed, "Call me." Quincy nodded and pulled off.

When Quincy got back to his house, he opened the bag and counted seven pounds. "I can take the weed game over with prices like this. Four thousand dollars for seven pounds, it can't get no better than this." Quincy thought to himself. When Quincy was satisfied with the product, he took the duffle bag, threw it over his shoulder and got out of the car and walked behind his house until he was in the woods. He walked over to a huge rock, sat the duffle bag down, then lifted the rock up. Under it was a drain. Quincy grabbed the duffle bag, quickly stuffed it inside the drain, then rolled the huge rock back over it. When he was sure no one saw him, Quincy walked out of the woods, and inside his house through the back door. When he got inside, he walked to his bedroom. True to her word, his wife Toya lay in their queen-sized bed asleep. Quincy removed his clothes down to his boxers and he slid in the bed right beside her.

The next day at 8:30 AM, Quincy had gotten up early and went to the woods to retrieve the duffle bag and threw it in the trunk of his Charger. Toya was still sleeping and there was no need to wake her, so Quincy wrote a note telling her that he was going to Burlington to see his brother Tech, and that he will be back in a couple hours. When he finished the note, he sat it on the dining table and then he walked outside and called his brother.

"Ring, ring, ring."

"Yo." Tech answered the phone in a sleepy voice.

"Bruh, what up?" Quincy asked.

"What's good Q, its 8:45 in the morning. What you want man?"

"I'm on the way over there man, I got something for you. You know, what I spoke to you about yesterday."

"A'ight, come on. I'm getting up now. Meet me in the Burlington Coat Factory parking lot. You already know how the police are over here in Peterburg."

"Okay, I'll call you when I get there." Quincy replied and then hung up.

One hour later, Quincy backed his Charger in a parking space in the back of Burlington's parking lot. Then, he pulled out his phone and texted his brother, "I'm here."

Tech's reply read, "I am on the way, be there in 5 minutes."

Quincy stuck his phone back in his pocket and waited. A couple minutes later, Tech was pulling up in his '89 Caprice Classic. He backed in the parking space right beside Quincy's black Charger. Tech cut his engine off and got out of the car, Quincy did the same.

"What up, Q."

"What up, Tech."

"The work is in the trunk, seven pounds." Quincy replied.

"What do you want back for it?"

"I need eight grand back."

"What kind of weed is it?"

"It's that come up, you could sell it for $170-$200 a zip easy."

Tech remained quiet for a moment, doing the math in his head.

"Okay, let me get it. I gotcha." Tech replied.

Quincy pulled out his keys and pushed a button on his key ring and his trunk popped open. Tech motioned to his girl who was in the passenger seat. She got out of the car as if on cue and walked to the rear of Quincy's Charger.

"Get the duffle bag." Quincy said.

The girl reached in and grabbed the duffle bag and then shut the trunk and walked back to Tech's Caprice and threw the duffle bag in the back seat. She then got back in the passenger seat and waited for Tech.

"Good. Look, big Bruh, I'll get back with you in a couple days." Tech said.

"That's what's up. Call me when you're ready." Quincy replied while dapping his brother up. When they both finished their embrace, they went their separate ways.

Two days later, Tech called and met up with Quincy and paid him the eight thousand dollars that he owed. Quincy had made a four thousand dollar profit that quick. That was the kind of flip that he had been looking for. A steady connect that would allow him to make some money. Quincy wasn't going to forget who put him on, so he sat down and wrote Tony Blanco a letter letting him know that he had met up with Stone. He also sent Tony some legal books to help him fight his case.

Three weeks had passed, and business was good. Quincy had been meeting up with the Mask Men on the regular. Quincy went from getting seven pounds to getting 20 at a time. Quincy's brother Tech stayed busy down in Burlington. His clientele was steady too so that was a good look for Quincy. He had thirty thousand in the stash, not counting his re-up. Quincy was feeling good about himself. He was starting to see the difference in his life. The respect that he was getting from everyone now that he was getting money.

He went and put eight thousand dollars down on an Escalade for his wife. He caught it for a good number, so he had to get it; plus, his wife Toya deserved it because she was his backbone in life. Months later, Quincy was still coping from Stone and them every three days. Stone didn't come no more though so he just dealt with the three Mask Men. That didn't bother Quincy, as long as the work kept coming, he was good. He had saved up close to $150,000.

Tonight, Q was going to take his wife and his homies out to have a ball, even though he didn't like going out because something always happened. Toya worked part time at the water department, so she stayed low key. Toya was the house type, the kind you love. That was one of the main reasons he fell in love with her.

11 PM, Saturday night. Quincy, Angel, Money, and Dreko all took their wives out to chill and have a good time. By now, they all had new whips. Quincy had a S550, Angel had a Camaro, Money drove a suped-up Charger, and Dreko pushed a Tahoe on 26's. Quincy and his boys hit club Next Level. When they pulled up in the parking lot, that bitch was packed. All eyes were on Quincy and his team as they walked in the club. They had a ball dancing the night away. Quincy took a break and walked to the bar to order his wife a Long Island Iced Tea. When he turned around, he saw this nigga named Wicked in his wife's face. Quincy couldn't believe what the fuck he was looking at. Wicked was Raleigh's most notorious gunslinger. Quincy didn't give a fuck, though. Toya was his wife, and he wasn't having that shit. As he walked over to them, he could tell that his wife was brushing Wicked off. Even though Wicked was drunk, he knew that Toya was Quincy's wife. Quincy pulled right up on Wicked.

"Did you lose something, what the fuck you got going on?" Quincy asked, stepping up in Wicked's face. Now the whole club was watching.

"Yeah, my bitch." Wicked replied.

Instantly, Quincy stole off on his ass, dropping Wicked to the floor. Wicked stood back up quickly and began reaching for his hammer. Shots rang out.

"Bloc, bloc."

Everybody in the club takes off running, Quincy grabbed his wife's hand and bounced out the side door. The same night, he got calls that his homie Angel pushed Wicked's cap back. Quincy pulled out his phone and got Angel on line one.

"Ring-ring."

"Yo." Angel said.

"What up, fool?" Quincy asked.

"Not shit."

"I'm hearing things."

"Like what?"

"That you let off."

"I was in the process, but somebody dropped Wicked before I pulled out."

"A'ight, I'ma bark back later."

"You good Q?"

"Yeah, I'll hit you later."

"Bet." Angel said then hung up.

"Who the fuck shot Wicked? I know it's going to be a war between us and them Haywood niggas." Quincy thought to himself.

CHAPTER 6

The next morning, Quincy heard that Wicked was hit twice by a 40 cal. It couldn't have been none of his people, because they all carried nines.

A week went by, and Quincy couldn't believe nobody was arrested yet for Wicked's murder. Word on the streets was that it was Quincy's people that killed Wicked, but nobody could prove it. Quincy wrote Tony a long letter after he received a letter from Tony saying that their friendship was over because he was a drug dealer, and Tony wanted no part in that life. It hurt Quincy that Tony was cutting him off, but he knew he was knee deep in the game now and it was no turning back. Quincy had mad respect for Tony, so after this letter he wouldn't write him anymore. This would be his last one.

Tonight, Quincy set up a meeting with the connects. Quincy felt it was time that they supply him with some coke. The weed money was good, but Quincy was trying to go to the next level and selling weed alone just wasn't doing it for him. The Westend crew were selling bricks for 27. When you could easily sell them for $30,000 all day, it was no doubt that them niggas were eating.

After the meeting was set up and hours had gone by, Quincy pulled up at the car wash to meet the three Mask Men. He parked his S550 Benz and got out of the car.

"What's up?" One of the Mask Men asked.

"The reason I asked you to meet me, well, the business is good, but I need a coke connect." Quincy replied.

As soon as Quincy said the word coke, the Mask Men backed up and got in their truck and left. "What the fuck, damn, I must have scared them off." Quincy thought to himself as he stood in the middle of the stall looking stupid. As he watched the truck pull out of the car wash parking lot, Quincy turned and got back in his Benz and pulled off. After that meeting, shit started getting crazy. A whole week had gone by, and Quincy couldn't reach the connect because the phones were disconnected. He couldn't supply Tech, or any of his other customers. Quincy was beginning to lose money, and just the thought of losing money was driving him crazy. He decided to take a vacation.

DEA Office

"Pennell, do you know in 15 years' time, we have come up with absolutely nothing on Tony Blanco." Hurns said. "Have you ever thought that maybe Tony Blanco is not who we think he is?"

"Hurns, Tony Blanco is more than who we think he is. We just have to put the pieces of the puzzle together." Pennell replied.

"I understand all of that, but the only witness we've had in 15 years got murdered in less than 24 hours after he spoke to us. They killed Dremond Blanco while in our custody, on prison grounds. Tony didn't know we talked to Dremond, no one did. I think it's a bigger player out there, someone we're not looking at close enough." Hurns said.

"I have a gut feeling it's him, I want Tony Blanco locked away forever. I want to see him lose everything." Pennell replied.

"If we really want to nail him, we have to turn his wife against him."

"How do we do that?"

"I have the perfect plan."

"Let me hear it."

"Okay, this is it. I'm going to take five thousand dollars and find a hooker, then have her set up a meeting with Tony Blanco's wife, Jessica Blanco. I will have the hooker tell her that Tony used to have an affair with her. I will coach her on everything to say before hand. I know Tony has some houses that his wife doesn't know about. I'll make it look like that's where they stayed when he went out of town on business trips. Hopefully, she will feel betrayed and want revenge." Hurns explained.

"I have to give it to you Hurns, you are on you're A game." Pennell said.

Hawaii International Airport

"Toya, wake up baby. We're here." Quincy said.

"Quincy, look how beautiful this place is." Toya replied.

"Yeah, it's nice." Quincy said.

"Welcome to the Island Resort, how may I help you?" The hotel receptionist asked.

"We have reservations."

"Name please."

"Mr. And Mrs. Capps."

"Four days and three nights, sir. That's a total of $3,700. Will you be paying cash or credit?"

"Cash."

"Okay sir, thank you. Your room will be on the 5th floor, room 362. Have a great stay."

Quincy took his key cards and him and his wife headed to the room.

"Quincy, this place is amazing." Toya exclaimed.

"Yeah, for $3,700 our room should be too." Quincy replied as he and his wife got on the elevator. When Quincy and Toya reached the 5th floor, they both got off the elevator holding hands, publicly expressing their love for each other. As soon as they walked into their hotel room, they were amazed.

"Quincy, baby, look how big this room is. The Jacuzzi is bigger than our bathroom back home." Toya said.

"Yeah, you're right. This room is huge." Quincy replied.

"Q, come to the window. They even have a big pool outside. Let's go swimming."

"I have a better idea, baby." Quincy said as he walked up to his wife and grabbed her around her hips.

"So does the idea you have in mind involve me riding that?" Toya replied while she squeezed Quincy's erection through his pants.

"I believe you hit the nail right on the head. Plus, we are in Hawaii, baby, with no kids. We gotta break the room in first."

Toya chuckled, stood on her tip toes, and kissed her husband. Quincy bent down and scooped his wife into his arms and carried her to their king sized bed. He laid her down softly and started kissing her with extreme passion.

"I love you, Toya." Quincy whispered.

"I love you too."

Quincy unbuttoned Toya's blouse, then unhooked her bra, slowly kissing her as he removed her panties. Quincy stood at the head of the bed, taking in the sight of his wife's nakedness as he removed his own clothing. When he was fully naked, he stroked his nine-inch erection until he was as hard as a rock. He smiled then, and slowly spread his wife's legs. He began kissing between her thighs until he reached his destination.

"Oohh baby." Toya moaned. "Eat that pussy, aahh, get that kitty wet." Toya whispered.

"You like that?"

"Yes."

Quincy stopped and started kissing her belly button, moving up to her titties. He stroked his manhood then inserted himself in her love box.

"Damn baby." Toya moaned as Quincy pounded her

missionary style.

Quincy spread her legs, pinning them behind her head as he continued to pound.

"Aaah."

"Oooh, shit."

Q flipped his wife over, pulled her to her knees, and then entered her from behind.

"Damn baby, that pussy feels good."

"You like it?"

"Yeah, I love it." Quincy replied, gripping her ass cheeks and pulling her close.

"Aaahh, I love this dick."

"You love it?"

"Yeah, I love it."

"Damn Toya, I'm 'bout to cum."

"Cum for mama."

"Aaahh shit!" Quincy grunted as he jerked back and forth.

After Quincy busted his nut, he pulled out. But before he could wipe himself off, Toya turned around and grabbed Quincy's dick and began sucking him, making his toes curl and draining him of what was left of his energy.

"Aahh, Toya, that's enough." Quincy said, tapping out.

Toya removed her mouth from his penis but continued to stroke him with her hand.

"Are you sure you don't want mama to finish?" Toya asked, smiling, knowing good and well what the answer would be.

"Yes baby, we are good. We can finish later."

"Okay, I'm going to go get in the shower, and then we can go get in the pool."

"That works for me."

After Quincy and Toya showered and got dressed, Toya in a black bikini and Q in a pair of Gucci swimming trunks, they both took the elevator down to the bottom floor. They walked out of the hotel headed towards the ocean holding hands.

"Quincy, thank you for this trip." Toya said.

"Nah baby, thank you for being my wife." Quincy replied.

Quincy and Toya sat in front of the ocean and talked for a while, just having a good time enjoying the moment. Just as things began to heat up between them, a couple came up and laid their towel in the sand beside them.

"Excuse me, are these seats taken?"

"No, no. Go right ahead and sit down." Quincy replied.

"I apologize for not introducing ourselves. I'm Mike, and this is my lovely wife, Weslyn." Mike said.

"I'm Quincy, and this is my wife, Toya." Quincy replied.

"Nice to meet you both." Weslyn said.

"So, Quincy, where are you from?" Mike asked.

"Raleigh, NC. Yourselves?"

"We live right here on the island."

"Must be nice living out here and getting to see the ocean every day."

"Yeah, I guess it has its perks. So how long do you plan to stay?" Mike asked.

"We're here for four days." Quincy replied.

"That's a nice vacation."

"Yeah, we're loving it so far."

"Toya girl, they must not think we are here. Mike can be controlling sometimes." Weslyn remarked.

"Yeah girl, I know the feeling. Quincy can be the same sometimes." Toya replied.

"Baby, come on, you know you are the boss." Quincy said smiling at his wife.

"Yo Quincy, Weslyn is too." Mike said.

They all started laughing.

"Quincy, I'm about to grab some drinks; You mind helping me?" Mike asked.

"Sure, we can let the bosses talk." Quincy replied as he took a talk with Mike.

"So, what brings you to the island?"

"Well, I needed some time to clear my head. What type of work do you do on the island?" Quincy asked.

Mike laughed, "I own this hotel."

"Yeah, right."

"I'm serious."

"Damn, you must be a millionaire."

"What type of work do you do Quincy?" Mike asked while ignoring his question.

"I run a clothing store."

"So, how's business?"

"It's good. I'm here."

"And what do you have on the agenda for you and the wife tonight?"

"I was thinking of taking the wife for a stroll on the beach and go sight-seeing. Just enjoy the moment with her."

"How about you and your wife attend the dinner that I am having tonight? You and the wife will be our personal guests. What do you say?"

"Sounds fun, I'm with it."

"Okay, well it's settled then. Let's go tell the girls that we are double dating tonight."

Quincy and Mike walked back inside to tell their women of their new plans.

"Weslyn, baby, Quincy and Toya will be our guests tonight. That's if Toya would like to come." Mike said.

"Splendid, sounds good. I was just telling Toya about the dinner." Weslyn replied.

"If Q wants to go, then we will be there." Toya replied.

"It's fine baby, sounds like we will have a good time." Quincy said.

"Okay Q, here's two invitations. The directions are on the back of the cards. We will see you both at 8pm." Mike said.

"8 it is, see you then." Quincy replied.

CHAPTER 7

Quincy and Toya spent most of the day shopping. When they finished, they returned to the hotel for a little wild sex, until it was time to attend Mike and Weslyn's dinner. *7:40pm*

"Come on Toya, we are running late. Let's go." Quincy hollered.

"Okay Q, I'm coming." Toya replied as she finished putting her make up on.

Toya stepped out of the bathroom knowing that she was a diva.

"So, Q how do I look?" Toya asked.

"You look beautiful, baby, but not as good as you look with your clothes off."

"Shut up Q." Toya replied as she lightly hit Q's shoulder. "For real, how do I look?"

"You look good, baby, for real. It's time to go, you're ready, right?"

"Yeah, let me grab my purse." Toya grabbed all her things, then her and Quincy headed to the elevator and then to the car.

"Q, all this traffic. How far is it?"

"The GPS says two blocks away, up on the right."

"Q, you need to slow down."

"We're good, bae."

Suddenly, sirens came blazing out of nowhere.

"Fuck we're getting pulled." Q said while slamming his hand on the steering wheel.

"I told you to slow down." Toya whispered.

"Come on, bae, don't start that."

"Driver, turn your engine off now, roll your window down, and put your hands out the window!" The officer shouted. "Okay, open the door with both hands, and let them remain on the door handle!" The officer continued to shout instructions.

Quincy made no sudden moves, afraid that he would be mistaken to have a gun, and then be shot down in the streets, like so many Black men before him.

"Now, walk backwards, keep your hands up. Keep coming. Stop. Quincy Capps, put your hands behind your back." The officer shouted.

One of the officers ran up and cuffed Quincy. "Who else is in the car?" The officer asked.

"Just my wife. Officer, what is this all about?" Quincy asked.

"You'll find out when you get down to the station." The officer replied.

Another officer walked to Quincy's car.

"Ma'am, your husband will be taken down to the station for questioning." The officer said.

"Excuse me, sir, what for?" Toya replied.

"Mr. Capps will let you know once he's downtown. Mrs. Capps, follow us please."

15 minutes later, they pull into the bottom of some building. Quincy was thinking hard about what this could be about. When

they came to a stop, they pulled Quincy out of the back of their squad car. They walked inside the building and got on the elevator. Quincy still couldn't figure out the reason why he was there. The elevator took them to the 21st floor. Then, they took him down the hall to some glass room.

"Have a seat, Quincy."

"Where's my wife?"

"She's in another room on this very same floor."

"Who are you and why am I here?" Quincy asked.

"I'm Agent Handeland and this is my partner, Agent Prince. Quincy, we have been watching you for months. We know about your weed business, and the new Benz you just recently bought. So tell us how many pounds of weed you are buying from Stone?"

"Who the fuck is Stone?" Quincy asked.

"Let me refresh your memory. Your weed connect; the one who drives a red 760 BMW."

"Like I said before, who the fuck is Stone?" Quincy replied.

"Let me keep it real with you Quincy. Did you know the FEDS picked Stone up? By the look on your face, I can tell you didn't know that. The word has it, Stone gave you up. Quincy, Stone is saying you killed Wicked, you do know him, right? Oh, I forgot, I have to refresh your memory. Wicked used to run with the Westend crew. Don't tell me you still don't remember? Wicked is the guy you were arguing with at the club Next Level about your wife Toya. Didn't you punch him or something, then you shot him with a 40 Cal?"

"I don't know what you're talking about." Quincy replied.

"Quincy, I have statements young man. This is your only chance to talk. If you love your wife and kids, give us something about Stone and you'll never do a day in prison. If you should refuse when we come again, I will make sure you do no less than 30 years."

Quincy laughed.

"What's so funny, Quincy?" Agent Prince asked.

"You pick me up on my vacation, threatening me with prison time, and threatening to take me away from my family. Agent Handeland, whatever your name is, you don't have nothing on me. I don't know the people you speak of. If you did have something, I'm sure you would have put me in a jail cell and not this glass room. If you don't mind, if I'm not under arrest, I would very much like to continue my vacation with my wife. As of now, I'm late to a very important dinner. So, if you don't mind, I would like to be released." Quincy replied.

"Very well Quincy, you are free to leave. But before you go, just know I will be seeing you again real soon." Agent Handeland replied.

Quincy got up from the table and walked out of the room to retrieve his wife.

"Baby, let's go."

"Q, what's going on? Who are these men?" Toya asked.

"They're federal agents."

"Who?"

"I'll tell you in the car, bae." Quincy replied.

When they got to the car, Toya told Quincy, "Q, let me drive. You speed too much, and finish telling me what's going on."

"Okay, okay. I was buying weed from this guy. They say he's given me up and someone gave a statement that I killed Wicked over you."

"But why are they following you?"

"I guess because I am being investigated. I don't know Toya, let's just drop it for now and get to the dinner. We are already late."

"Okay, we will talk about it later Q." Toya said.

Ten minutes later, they arrived at the Hawaii Coliseum.

"Babe, there's a parking spot beside the Lambo."

"That's a nice car." Toya said.

"Yeah, that's my dream car." Quincy replied.

The two parked and got out of the car. They then walked up

to the front entrance.

"Name please?" the hostess asked.

"Mr. and Mrs. Capps."

"Yes, we have you right here. We have been waiting on your arrival, your table is over here. Please follow me."

"Mrs. Capps, what will you have to drink?"

"A Hawaiian Cooler would be nice."

"And you Mr. Capps?"

"A Henny and Coke on the rocks."

"Very well, I will be right back. Enjoy the party."

Mike walked over to the table. "Quincy, Toya. Glad you could finally make it. We were expecting you over an hour ago." he said.

"Yeah, we got pulled." Quincy replied.

"Is everything okay?" Mike asked.

"Yes, we are good."

"Weslyn will be over here in a few minutes. I have some people that I need to attend to. I'll get with you in a little while. Enjoy the party, it's on me." Mike said.

When Mike left, Quincy was in deep thought over the current events that happened in the last two hours.

"Q, baby. Enjoy the party, don't let what happened today bother you." Toya said.

"I'ma try, baby, but know I am not feeling 5-0 running down on us during our vacation." Quincy replied.

"I know, I know, but let's just enjoy the rest of this time that we have together, in peace. Stress free."

"Okay, baby, let's do this then." Quincy said as he grabbed Toya's hand and led her to the dance floor. When Quincy and Toya finished dancing, they went and sat down at their table and ordered some food. By the time the waitress brought out the food, Weslyn had walked over and joined the couple. Weslyn and Toya sat at the table and had what you would call girl talk. Quincy sat attentive, taking in his surroundings. He observed Mike move around the party and noticed that he fucks with a lot of old, rich, white people, and everyone respects him.

"This nigga got it going on." Quincy thought to himself.

Raleigh, North Carolina 11pm

Angel and Money riding.

"Yo Angel, hit this gas station so I can grab some blunts." Money said.

"A'ight, bro, I am 'bout to pull over."

Angel pulled up to the pump. Him and Money both got out of the car and walked inside the store.

"Grab some skittles, bro." Money said.

"I gotcha, I gotta put thirty in the tank, too." Angel replied as he handed Money the blunts.

"I'ma go to the car and pump the gas." Money said.

"A'ight."

When Money got to the car, he opened the passenger door and threw the box of blunts inside, then walked to the gas pump and began pumping gas. "It feels good out here tonight." Money thought to himself, as he closed his eyes and enjoyed the breeze. Just when he opened his eyes, Money saw a blue sedan pull into the parking lot with four people inside. Money stared at the sedan and the three guys that got out of the car. Money recognized one of the guys as being from Westend. "Shit, Angel." But before Money could get the thought out of his head, the stores front door swung open.

"Fuck you niggas." Was all Money heard right before he saw Angel reach in his waistband to pull his 40 Cal and let it ring out.

Blue fire spit from Angel's forty as he ran out of the store firing behind him.

Money pulled his 9mm Beretta and pulled the trigger, aiming at the front door.

Angel ducked for cover behind a parked car. He looked over the hood of the car he was hiding behind. One of his attackers hit the ground as he heard gun fire coming from the opposite direction. Money, it had to be him. Angel turned his head and saw Money running across the parking lot.

Round after round hit the car, causing Angel to duck for cover again.

Money ran across the parking lot, trying to get as close to Angel as he could. He saw bullets ripple the car Angel was hiding behind causing him to return for cover. Angel was pinned down and Money had to find a way to get him out of there. There were only three Westend goons left. One was down, Money had hit him in the stomach. Out of nowhere, Angel was running across the parking lot towards him. Bullets were being slung at his heels as he sprinted for dear life. Money began to fire back.

As Angel ran past him headed towards the car, Money fell in right behind him. When they both reached the car and got inside, Angel pulled off, letting his tires burn.

"Money, one of them Westend niggas stole off on me in the store. Bruh, I'm going to kill them niggas." Angel said as he continued to speed down the street.

"Angel, you are slipping homie. You know they think one of us killed Wicked. I am surprised they didn't stop your clock while you were in the sto'." Money replied.

"I know, bruh, I know. Good look on holding me down."

"Bruh, what's understood don't need to be explained."

"That's facts, bruh. But look, we need to stash this car. Know 5-0 heard the shots."

"Yeah, you're right."

"Ring, ring."

"Hello." Angel said as he answered his phone.

"What's up Angel, this is Annie. You know Black Tone just got shot."

"So what, Annie, fuck him." Angel said right before hanging up.

"Yo, who was that, bruh?" Money asked.

"Annie." Angel replied.

"Ain't she from Westend?"

"Yeah, I was her first, so she always keeps me in tune wit what's going on. Yo, Money, text Dreko and let him know what happened."

"Bet." Money replied.

"Bruh, his phone must be fucking up because he ain't hitting back."

"We got to find him, but first we gotta find Lotto."

Money and Angel drove out to the country and stashed the truck that they were driving. They hopped in a crackhead rental then shot straight to the block to find Lotto. Money and Angel were both relieved that Lotto was in the hood.

"Yo Lotto, where's Dreko?" Money asked.

"He just went to the sports bar." Lotto replied.

"Let's go." Angel said.

"Welcome to Hams, may I take your order?" The waitress asked.

"Yes, let me have a turkey salad." Dreko replied as he pulled out his cell phone.

"Damn, my phone been fucking up all day. Twenty texts, let me see here." Lotto said to himself. Then he began to read his messages. The first one he read said, "Yo Dreko, leave the bar. We just hit Black Tone."

"Oh shit, excuse me ma'am. Here's $20, keep the change." Dreko said as he got up and headed out the door.

"There's Dreko coming out the door right now. Wait until he hits the parking lot then light his ass up." Killah said to his soldier that sat next to him.

Dreko came strolling out of Hams, moving fast. After he viewed the text from Angel, he knew he had to get the hell out of there. As soon as he hit the parking lot, all hell broke loose.

"There he goes, get his ass!" Killah commanded his soldier.

Killah's soldier jumped out the car and ran towards Dreko, firing two shots.

The first shot grazed Dreko's neck, causing him to spin around.

He then took off running straight for Ham's front entrance. But then he was hit in the ass by the soldier's second shot. Dreko fell to the ground, crawling on his hands and knees. Dreko felt helpless as this strange man closed in on him, walking slowly, savoring his kill, knowing he was about to earn some rank by killing Dreko.

When Dreko realized it was over, he dropped his head to gather his thoughts. Then, he looked up to stare his killer in the eyes, only to see a red Honda speeding into the parking lot. Dreko could see the driver, it was Angel. Next thing he knew, Money is out the window with some monster fire power. Killah's soldier shot back, but he was no match for whatever Money was shooting. He took off running behind the building. Seeing this, Killah pulls off. Angel and Money hopped out of the fire red Honda and rushed to Dreko's aid.

"Bruh, I'm hit." Dreko said to Angel.

"You good, bruh, get in the car and let's go."

CHAPTER 8

Back in Hawaii, 2:30AM

The party is closing, and Toya and Weslyn are tipsy. Just when they were saying goodbye's, Mike showed back up.

"Quincy, I'm sorry. I didn't get a chance to talk with you. As you can see, hosting takes up a lot of my time. I hope that you enjoyed the party. Let me make it up to you, say I pick you up tomorrow morning around 10 AM. We'll send the wives shopping while we go golfing." Mike said.

"In that case Mike, I'll speak for my husband. We will see you at 10AM. Weslyn girl, I'll see you in the morning." Toya replied.

"Okay, you have a good night, Toya." Weslyn said.

While driving back to the hotel.

"Baby, how you know I wanted to go golfing?"

"I didn't, I just know I wanted to go shopping. Weslyn, she is nice and come on Q, Mike seems like a nice guy too." Toya replied.

"I guess."

"I think it's good that we are meeting new people that are

doing things with their lives Q. I just want us to be happy."

"Ring, ring, ring."

"Toya, answer that phone, please."

"Okay, baby, okay." Toya replied. "Hello."

"Toya, I'm sorry to bother you, but I need to speak with Q." Angel said on the phone.

"Hold on."

"This better be good, bruh." Q told Angel.

"Bruh, we are at the hospital. Dreko got shot."

"What? Who did it?" Q asked.

"Them Westend niggas."

"I'm on my way." Quincy hollered before hanging up.

"What's wrong baby?" Toya asked while placing her hand on her husband's chest.

"Dreko got shot."

"Oh my god, is he okay?"

"I didn't even ask."

"So, we're leaving tomorrow?" Toya asked, dreading to hear his response.

"Baby, I don't know."

"Q, baby. If you need us to leave, I understand. I support you one hundred percent."

"Toya, baby, that's why I love you so much." Q replied as he rolled over and kissed his wife.

"Good night, love."

9AM the next morning

Room service knocked on the door of Quincy and Toya's hotel room.

"Okay, okay, I'm coming." Toya said.

"Here's breakfast. Is there anything else I can get you?"

"No thanks." Toya replied as she grabbed the cart and handed the room service lady a tip.

"Well, thank you. If you need anything else, just call the desk. Enjoy your breakfast, honey."

"Thank you." Toya pulled the food inside just as Quincy was coming out of the bathroom with a toothbrush in his mouth, brushing his teeth.

"What is it?" Q mumbled.

"It's breakfast baby. Mike and Weslyn had it sent up to us." Toya said as she lifted the tray to reveal its contents. "Oh baby, its turkey sausage, scrambled eggs, pancakes, toast, and orange juice!" she exclaimed.

"Yeah, that sounds good." Quincy replied. He grabbed a plate and sat it on the table. He then rinsed out his mouth and sat down with his wife to eat.

45 minutes later, they were about finished eating.

"Q, I am full, so I'll go ahead and hop in the shower and get dressed."

"I'm coming with you." Q said with a grin on his face.

"Make sure you keep your hands to yourself bad boy." Toya replied in a low tone all the while knowing she wanted some dick this morning.

The two of them both took a long shower and shared a morning of passion, bringing each other to a satisfying climax. When they were finished exploring each other, they completed their shower and got dressed. Now they were prepared for today's events.

"Baby, we are running late again. Toya, are you ready?" Quincy hollered.

"Yes, I am ready, but you're not." Toya replied.

"It's five minutes to 10. I'm moving as fast as I can. If I wasn't so drained, I could move faster."

"Oh hush, you're the one that wanted some of this booty."

"I couldn't help myself. It looked so fat and juicy. I couldn't help myself, baby. You know you liked it though."

"Yeah, it was a'ight."

There was then a knock on the door.

"Baby, someone's at the door!" Toya hollered.

"See who it is."

"I'm coming, I'm coming, give me a second. Who is it?" Toya asked before opening the door.

"It's Weslyn."

"Oh, one second. Hey Weslyn." Toya said as she answered the door.

"What's up girl, are you ready?" Weslyn asked.

"Almost! Hello Mike, how are you doing?" Toya asked.

"I am good Toya, where's Quincy?" Mike asked back.

"He's coming. He likes to take his time getting dressed."

"Well, baby, me and Toya will see y'all later." Weslyn said right before she kissed Mike's cheek.

"Okay, have a good time." Mike replied as he walked inside.

"Mike, what's good. You ready?" Q asked as he dapped Mike up.

"I am waiting on you."

"Say no more."

Once outside, Quincy spotted the exact same Lambo that he'd seen the night before.

"Yo, Mike, who's whip is that?" Q asked pointing at the Lambo.

Mike laughs as he pops the locks.

"Go ahead, get in." Mike says.

"Oh shit, this you?"

"Yeah, this me."

"Your wheels are crazy, dude. I gotta give it to you."

"Thanks!"

Just when they were about to get inside, Weslyn and Toya rode by in a Bentley coupe, waving. "Damn, this dude got that bread." Q thought to himself.

"So, Quincy, what do you think about the island?" Mike asked.

"It's perfect. When I was in the county, my cell mate told me about this place. He said it was a must-see. So, when I got myself together, I came out here."

"What you go to jail for?" Mike asked.

"A shooting charge."

"How are things looking for you?"

"Well, my lawyer says he can beat it, and my cellie told me not to take a plea."

"Sounds like a smart fellow."

"Yeah, but he's in deep shit."

"What do you mean?"

"What I mean is he's the one all over the news for killing those two federal agents."

"I don't think I heard about that. Matter of fact, I think my wife mentioned something about that a while back. I'm so busy, I hardly keep up with anything. Tell me, Quincy, on average, how much does a clothing store gross in a month's time? Not to be in your business or anything."

"It really depends, Mike. Some days we may do up to five thousand a day. On a good Saturday, five to ten thousand." Q replied.

"That's a good living, Quincy. So why do you sell weed?" Mike asked.

"What you say?"

"You heard me. I did a background check on you last night. You know, when you have millions, information is easy to come by."

"Man, whoever you getting your info from, you need to fire them."

"Quincy, the only way you get ahead is to be honest. I'm not the police, so please don't treat me that way."

"You shouldn't be asking personal questions."

"I didn't ask you about your wife."

"Watch your mouth, Mike."

"See Quincy, that's personal, so let's try this again. How's your weed business?"

Quincy just sits and thinks to himself on whether or not to

answer the question.

"I just lost my connect. Last I heard, the feds had him."

"That's deep. Is he snitching?" Mike asked.

"I don't know."

Mike laughs.

"What's so funny?"

"Listen Quincy. When you hustle, do it big. So when you are sitting in a cell, you're not wondering how your family is going to eat. A few hundred thousand, that's bill money."

"Damn, whose house is this?" Q asked as Mike pulled up in a driveway that resembled an air plane landing field.

"Quincy, that's personal." Mike replies. Then they both begin to laugh.

"Mike this is really nice. It's like a dream house."

Elsewhere, back in North Carolina (Raleigh)

"Agent Hurns, will you ride with me to meet someone?" Pennell said.

"Of course. Where are we headed?" Agent Hurns asked.

"Cary, North Carolina." Agent Pennell replied.

"What for?"

"I found a woman who's willing to take the money, and she's beautiful. Plus, she's a stripper." The two agents made the ride to Cary where they would meet the stripper at her house.

"Knock, knock, knock."

"Who is it?"

"Mr. Pennell."

"How are you? Glad you made it."

"Kristan, this is my partner, Mr. Hurns." Agent Pennell said.

"Come on in, make yourselves at home." Kristan replied, stepping to the side to let the two agents in.

"Would you like something to eat or drink?" Kristan asked.

"No, thank you." Hurns replied.

"Okay, Kristan, let's get down to business. Tony Blanco takes trips to Florida once every month. He has a condo on Rich

Fort Lane down in South Beach. Every other month he goes to California. Mr. Blanco owns two houses there; one in Beverley Hills and Malibu. What we need is for you to set up a business meeting with Tony Blanco's wife, Jessica Blanco. When the meeting takes place, you have to let Mrs. Blanco know that you and her husband were having an affair. The reason you're telling her this, is because Tony misled you into thinking he wasn't married. Also, that you believed him until you saw him on the news with her, leaving the hospital." Pennell said trying to put his plan into motion.

"Okay, Mr. Pennell. This is all I have to do for five thousand dollars?" Kistan asked.

"Yes, that's it. Oh yeah, before I forget, tell Mrs. Blanco that her husband has a tattoo of her name in the middle of his chest, but he said it was his late grandmothers name." Agent Pennell replied.

"So, when am I supposed to do all this?"

"We will let you know when."

"Well, just call me when you're ready."

"Okay, we will keep in touch." Agent Pennell replied, then he and agent Hurns got up and left.

Back in the car, Hurns asked, "Where did you find this woman?"

"I went to the strip bar."

"What?! Pennell, if your wife knew that, man, your ass would be kicked.

Back in Hawaii

"Quincy, I brought you here so we can talk. When I met you, I thought you was a good young fella. I see a lot of potential in you. And the fact that you don't like to do a lot of talking, that's the best part about you. So what are your plans now, since your weed business has fallen apart?" Mike said.

"Gotta find a coke connect, the weed game is good but it's nothing like coke money." Q replied.

"Quincy, I've done a thorough background check on you. I know where your wife works. I know where your pops lives. I really like you Q, so I'm going to front you fifty keys at fifteen thou' a piece. At that pace, you will be a millionaire in one month."

"Damn, I know he didn't say what I think he said." Q was nervous, thinking to himself.

"So, Quincy, can you handle it?" Mike asked.

"Yeah, yeah."

"Q, I hope I can trust you, for your sake that is."

"Mike you can trust me, but I have a problem."

"And what is that?"

"My friend was shot last night, and I need to get back to Raleigh soon."

"When are you leaving?" Mike asked, genuinely concerned.

"I'm planning for tonight. Okay, I'ma give you the run down, so I don't have to do it twice."

"Listen, Q, each month I'll hit you with 50 keys until you need more. Don't worry about getting them back to N.C., I'll take care of that. I'll call you one day this week. You have to stop whatever you are doing, when I call, and come to the pick up. One more thing Quincy, if you fuck me over, I'll kill your whole family and then feed you to my sharks." Mike replied.

Mike and Quincy headed back to the hotel. Quincy was still in a state of disbelief over the current events. He didn't know whether to jump for joy because he was finally about to get all the way on his feet, or keep the see-it-to-believe-it attitude. What he did know, was that he hadn't received one brick, but he was happy as hell. He had a feeling in his gut that Mike was for real. He lived like a drug lord, drove a Lambo, and his wife drove a Bentley coup, and at $15,000 a key, the game would be his in no time. He could buy a house, buy his grandma a house. There wouldn't be anything that he couldn't do. Mike dropped Quincy off at the hotel where he waited for his wife, Toya, and Mike's wife, Weslyn, to arrive back from their little shopping spree.

"Baby, I'm back." Toya said as she walked into the hotel suite.

"Hey, baby." Q replied, as he walked up and gave his wife a kiss. "Hey, Weslyn. How are you?"

"I'm good, Q. Me and Toya had us a good ol' time. Hold, Mike just texted me and said if you're leaving tonight, the limo will take you to our private jet at 9pm."

"Well, Toya, I have to run. I have your number; I'll keep in touch." Weslyn said.

"Okay, take care Weslyn." Toya replied and then shut the door.

"So, how was the golf game?"

"It went great."

"See, I told you Mike was a good person."

If only she know who Mike really was.

"Baby, I'm sorry that we're leaving. I promise we'll be back real soon. This place is a gangsta's paradise."

"When?" Toya asked.

"Soon, real soon, baby."

CHAPTER 9

Tony Blanco, Wake County Jail

It's crazy how things happen in life. Here I am with two murder charges, facing a life sentence, or even the death penalty. Things happen for a reason though. My old cellmate, Q, sent me $1,000. I appreciate the fact that he thinks so highly of me. I like Q, but he's involved in the wrong game for me to be his friend. When Q left and went home, of course they gave me another cellie. They call him 2K. He also has a capital murder charge. Since me and 2K became cellmates, I realized that he was a good dude. I seen him lose his mother since we've been cellmates, and it crushed me to watch him have to go through that. We all lose loved ones, it's all a part of the natural circle of life. I lost mine when I was 16. During that struggle I became lost for a long time. The streets showed me love until I seen the light. 2K, he's young, and just going through the motions of becoming a young man. Yeah, he's a little wild, but, nowadays, who isn't. My lawyer, he's still not talking 'bout shit. I'm bored as hell, it's never nothing to do here. I go outside from time to time to play a lil' basketball and workout. You would be surprised how much doing push ups, pull ups, and dips relieves stress. It's no cable, so it's never shit on T.V, and on top of that, it's always loud as fuck so it's hard to get some decent rest.

My wife and kids are doing okay. Some days she's frustrated, but that's normal for a woman who's man is in prison; most lose theirs. I'm blessed to still have my wife; she's my rock. I wish I could lay in my own bed; this small bed is killing my back. I often wonder what will happen to me, I think about escaping. I'm sure I could pull it off. Shit, for a million dollars, who wouldn't help me? I know I wouldn't be able to sleep if I escaped.

"Yo, 2K, what you doing?" Tony asked.

"Reading this book, 48 Laws of Power." 2K replied.

"Word. Did you talk to your sister today?"

"Yeah. That made me feel good to hear her voice."

"I'm glad you spoke to her. How's your kids doing?" Tony asked.

"Tony, they are getting big. My son asked me to come to his school and play. Tony, that brought tears to my eyes."

"I understand exactly how you feel. My girls do the same to me. Have you heard anything from your lawyer?"

"Yeah. But he ain't talking about shit. 25 to life is the best he has on the table right now, and I'm not about to take that."

"I feel you, but stay positive, lil' bruh. Think about your family and your freedom. I don't know what your religious beliefs are, but make sure you stay prayed up. And no matter what, never give up." Tony said, kicking 2K a little wisdom.

"Tony, thanks for the support, man. For real, for real."

"No problem, lil' bruh."

Quincy and Toya flying from Hawaii

Mike and Weslyn's private plane was laced. It looked like a house inside. Quincy was starting to believe that Mike is part of the drug cartel. While on the flight to North Carolina, Q texted his homies and ordered them to be still until he came home. He didn't need any extra problems to occur. His soldiers weren't rookies. He was just crossing his T's and dotting his I's. After a couple of hours, Quincy and Toya finally landed at the RDU Airport in Raleigh.

"Yes, I've come to pick up a rental." Toya said while digging in her purse for her I.D.

"Name please?" The receptionist asked.

"Toya Capps."

"One moment please, Mrs. Capps." The receptionist said reaching under the counter to grab a set of keys. She matched Toya's face to her I.D. then handed her the keys.

"Drive safe now."

"Will do. Thank you."

Toya headed out of the car rental to the parking lot where Quincy was waiting.

"Everything go well?" Quincy asked.

"Of course, baby." Toya replied as they both got in the car.

"Q, do you wanna pick the kids up first or do you wanna wait until later?"

"Yeah, let's go ahead and get them now, so you can carry them to church tomorrow."

"What you mean "me"? Ain't you coming to church with us too?"

"Not this Sunday, baby. I'm sorry, I'll make it up to you."

"I know you will."

On the way to Toya's mothers' house to pick the kids up, Q called the hospital to check on Dreko. The receptionist patched him through. Dreko was good. Q knew he was a live wire, so he mentally prepared himself for the war that was to come between his crew and the Westend crew. He didn't need to talk to everybody else to know that. "Blood was shed so it's no turning back from that." Q thought to himself. After Q and Toya picked the kids up, they went home to get settled. They did the family thing for a while and just enjoyed playing with the children, until it was time to put them to bed. Once the kids were sound asleep, they played with each other.

Trap house

"Yo, Boss Jones, it's 'bout time to pass the sticks, 21 skunk."

"Man, fuck that shit. Run it back, double or nothing." Boss Jones replied.

"Say no more."

"I'm picking the Ravens this time. I'ma smash you with that fire power defense they have."

"Oh, like you did with the Cowboys."

"Forget you fool."

"Nah. Don't forget this ass-whooping I'm 'bout to give you."

"We'll see." Boss Jones replied. "You talk to your brother?"

"Yeah, I spoke with him. He should be on his way back by now. He shot me a text 'bout an hour ago. He wants us to chill until his plane lands."

"Man, that shit crazy how them Westend niggas popped off on Dreko like that. You know he'll be out for blood when he gets out of the hospital."

"I already know, and Q knows it too. But Q, that's the big bro. If he says stay put, then we stay put. It has to be a reason that he wants us to wait."

"I know, bruh, but I'm ready to pop."

"In due time, fam. In due time." Boss Jones replied. "Yo Spook, go outside and check and see how the runner's doing."

"I gotcha boss. I'm wit the homie on the Westend situation. When I lay eyes on 'em, I'm popping bro."

"Not until Q gives the green light. You got that Spook?"

"I gotcha." Spook said, adjusting his tool in his waistband." Then headed out the door to check on the runners.

As soon as Spook stepped on the porch, he noticed a beat up mini-van speeding down the street. When Spook's instincts finally kicked in, it was too late. Shots rang out.

"Ooh shit." Spook jumped off the porch, while ducking for

cover. He pulled his tool from his waist and proceeded to fire back. The mini-van was out of range for his shots to do any real damage. Boss Jones and Richie ran outside after hearing the shots, guns in hand. But it was too late. Chicken George, the neighborhood crackhead, lay dead on the sidewalk.

"It's on, muthafuckers!" Boss Jones screamed at the fleeing mini-van.

"Damn, Spook, are you hit?" Richie asked.

"Nah, I'm good. We seriously have to finish this Westend crew before we get caught slipping and end up on the sidewalk like Chicken George." Spook replied.

"That ain't going to happen. I'ma get with Q. Right now, we gotta get the hell outta here and off this block. I know you already hear the police sirens.

"Yeah, lets get the fuck outta here."

Boss Jones, Richie, and Spook hopped in Richie's baby mama's Altima and fled the scene.

*Gangster's Paradise, Hawaii

Mike and Weslyn lay in beach chairs, enjoying the sun.

"Baby, what do you think about Q?" Weslyn asked.

"I think he's solid, and maybe a potential asset. Only time will tell." Mike replied.

"Do you think he can handle all that work?"

"Yeah, I think he can handle it. It may take him over a month, though. I expect a delay."

"I like his wife, Toya, she's cool. If Q messes up, don't kill him like you did that last one. I wanna keep Toya as a friend."

"We'll see how he does. You know I love you, right?"

"Yeah, I know, baby. Because you have a fabulous way of showing it." Weslyn replied.

"Anything for the queen of my paradise."

"Aah, baby, don't you think we should reach out to Tony?"

"No. not right now. It's a lil' hot and he has plenty of money, so really it's no need. He'll reach out to us if he needs us."

A Day Later

"Trevone Capps, I'm Detective Gammon. I need to ask you some questions."

"About what?" Trevone asked.

"About the drive by shooting, and the death of 46 year old George Martain. That happened right in front of your home."

"Mr. Gammon, first off, I've already told the police what I know. And second, I wasn't home when the shooting took place."

"Where were you."

"With my girl."

"Did you know the victim?"

"Yes, sir, I did. He usually comes by and mows my grass."

"Was he part of a gang?"

"No."

"Are you a part of a gang?"

"No. And why is that relevant?"

"It's relevant, because it's not like it's a drive by shooting everyday. Do you know Dreko?"

"Who's that?"

"Your homie that got shot at Hams Sports Bar?"

"Sir, I didn't see the shooting. I wasn't home, and I don't know nobody named Dreko."

"I'm sure that part is true."

Just when Tech was about to say something smart, his brother Quincy was pulling in the driveway."

"Yo, lil' Bro, what's up? Why he here?" Quincy said, as he nodded his head at the detective.

"So, Quincy, this is your brother, huh? Now I get the picture. You two both know whoever did this will be back. I'm sure you will see them first. I'ma be sure to keep my eye on the both of you. I have no more questions." Detective Gammon replied, and then got in his cruiser and left.

"Bruh, what happened?" Q asked.

"Them Westend niggas did a drive by and killed Chicken

George. Boss Jones, Spook, and Richie were holding the trap down at the time."

"Chicken George, that was my dude, yo. I've known him since I was 14. He was like family." Q replied.

"I know, bruh. We gotta crush these guys, Q." Tech said.

"We will, lil' bruh. Where's Money and Angel?"

"Boss Jones sent them over here to get the work. They picked up and left."

"Okay, bruh. I gotta put some pieces of the puzzle together. Then I'ma get back with you in a few."

"A'ight, cool. What's up with them Westend niggas, though? The homies out for blood and this drive by didn't help the situation."

"We move em', that's what we do. Tell the bro's it's on site."

"I got you."

"Peace, bruh." Quincy said, then dapped Tech up and walked to his car.

When Quincy left his brother Tech, he had to put some things in motion. If Mike was going to be fronting him 50 bricks every month, he has to make sure he had a way of moving them. So, Quincy hopped on the interstate, and went and hollered at one of his partners. A dude named Hell Rell from Burlington. Hell Rell was a big time baller and a local club promoter. He also owned a small trailer park at the end of Apple Street extensions., where his brother Capone moved weight.

After about a 30 minute ride, Quincy got off on the Burlington exit and headed to Apple Street. Quincy didn't have Hell Rells' number so he had to pull up on Hell Rell's brother, Capone, so he could link up with Rell. Quincy didn't have Capone's number either, but everybody knows Capone don't ever leave the trailer park, and that was Q's destination. When Q pulled into the entrance of the trailer park, he saw two abandoned cars and a group of bums huddling around a fire barrel. Q continued driving. When he passed the bums, they seemed to be mean mugging him. He continued, paying them no mind, knowing that he didn't have his heat on him. He wasn't trying to spark no drama. Q finally reached the bottom; what they call the Dead Ends. He parked his car and walked to Capone's doublewide and knocked on the door.

"Who is it?"

"Q."

"Quincy?"

"Yea."

"Hold up bro, I'm coming." Capone said as he walked to the door and opened it.

"Damn, homie, long time no see. What brings you here?" Capone asked.

"I need to speak with your brother, I don't have his number, and even if I did, what I need to speak with him about, I cant talk about over the phone." Q replied.

"Come on in then, make yourself at home."

Q followed Capone inside the doublewide. When he walked in, the first thing he saw was the three naked white girls sitting in the kitchen, cutting, bagging, and cooking dope.

"Nice, right?"

Q laughs and smiles.

"You can take one home if you like." Capone said.

"No thanks, Capone, I'm good. I just need to holler at Rell."

"A'ight bruh, I'm 'bout to go get him on line one now."

"I'll be outside."

"Don't be like that Q."

Door slams

Ten minutes later, Capone comes outside.

"Damn bruh, you don't have to be so uptight."

"I'm not."

"Look, Rell said that he will be here in 20 minutes. He's at Pumpkin Pack, grabbing some fried chicken and potato wedges."

20 minutes flew by, then Q spotted a black Cadillac sitting

on 24's creeping down the Dead Ends. The black sedan came to a stop, Hell Rell got out, dressed in all Prada, with a big cross encrusted with diamonds hung around his neck.

"Yo, Q, what up partner?" Hell Rell said as him and Q shared a brief embrace of brotherly love.

"What's good bro?" Q replied.

"So what's so important that made you want to come see me? What you need some work, you having problems?"

"Nah, nothing like that. I wanted to see you in person because I need your help."

"Just say the word bro, I gotcha."

"Nah, it ain't nothing like that. What I got in mind will help me and you both. I just came across a sweet connect." Q replied.

"Connect?"

"Yeah."

"I gotta connect already."

"What's the numbers on your keys?"

"I get 'em for $32,000. Pure cocaine." Hell Rell replied.

"32,000, huh. Let's say I could sell them to you for $28,000."

"Then that means you're my new connect. Just like old times when we were selling loud."

"How many can you handle?" Q asked.

"At $28,000, I can handle 15 pretty easy." Hell Rell replied.

"Okay, say no more. I'll be in touch." Q said and then dapped Hell Rell up and headed back to Raleigh.

CHAPTER 10

Back in Raleigh

When Q came home, he kicked it with his wife and kids for a while.

"How was your day, baby?" Toya asked.

"Everything is crazy right now."

"What happened?"

"Westend crew did a drive by on Tech's trap house and Chicken George ended up getting hit."

"How's your brother?"

"He's good, but hurt. You know George didn't have a home. Tech had been looking out for him for the last five years now, so he's upset."

"Are you going to church with me and the kids tomorrow?"

"Yeah, baby, I believe I will."

Quincy and Toya chilled for the remainder of the night and made passionate love with each other until the wee hours of the night.

Church service the next day

"There's been a lot of shooting going on here lately. It has gotten so bad, people will shoot you at the gas pump or even the restaurant. Will somebody tell me why we can't love each other. Why do we destroy our own people? I praise God and sleep at night in peace. I praise God that I'm not on the corner selling drugs. See the ones that's riding around in their fancy cars and wearing nice jewelry; they are the ones at fault. It's their drug houses that people are dying at. They buy the guns and give them to their buddies, then they act like they really care. God see's everything. It's okay if you lie to me, but you can't lie to God. George Martain was shot dead last night. Somebody did a drive by on one of them dope houses, and he was an innocent by-stander. A victim murdered for nothing. When does it end? The sad thing about it is the ones who have the power to stop it don't care. Bow your heads, take a few seconds. If there's one person that's here today that wishes to help make a change, please step forward."

"No one knows I'm selling weed but Tech, so why do I feel guilty?" Q thought to himself as he sat in church with his family.

When church let out. Q had his wife, Toya, drop him off at the hospital to see Dreko.

"Baby, do you want me to pick you back up?" Toya asked.

"Nah, love. I'm good. I'll get a ride back from one of the fellas." Q replied, then shut the door and walked over to the driver side, kissed his wife, then walked inside the hospital to see Dreko. He took the elevator to the fourth floor. When the elevator stopped, Q got off and walked to Dreko's room, where he knocked on the door.

"Come in." Dreko hollered.

"How's that ass?" Q asked while laughing.

"This shit hurts."

"I bet it does."

"Look, big bruh, this some personal shit. When I get out of here, I'ma handle it."

"Who did it?"

"Wicked's punk ass cousin. I guess they think we killed Wicked."

"I know they do, and it's nothing we can do about that."

"We can send 'em all to meet God." Boss Jones said.

"Fellas, we have to take our time, and move right. I know I told Tech that it was on-site. I've been thinking, I want the moment to be right when we hit 'em. I wanna make it count." Q replied.

"I hate to say it, but you're right." Angel said.

"Listen up though. I got us a new connect on the coke." Q said.

"Bruh, yeah right. We've been scraping a whole month now." Boss Jones replied.

"I understand, and that's exactly why we are about to take over these streets."

"So when do we get the work?" Spook asked.

"I'll have them any day now. I'm letting them all go for $23,000 a brick. Tech will supply everybody. I don't want anybody calling me for work. Am I clear on that?" Q replied.

"Bruh, $23,000 at a time like this, be for real. Where did you get that connect, Mexico?" Dreko says.

"I'm dead serious, guys. We are no longer in the weed game. At 23 a brick, y'all should lock the streets down in no time." Q said.

"Tech, I need you and Angel to take me somewhere. Dreko, we'll be right back."

"A'ight, we out homie. Dreko, take it easy." Tech replied.

"A'ight fool, I will." Dreko replied.

While riding, Q let his bros know that they would be changing traps. Matter of fact, he was moving it completely out of the city limits. He didn't want to be in the public eye, because of all the extra problems they were dealing with. Q was determined to play it safe, handle his problems, and run that check up like never before. While riding, Q's phone began to vibrate.

"Hello, this Q. What's up?"

"Where you at?"

"Who the fuck is this?"

"Mike, are you by yourself? If not, whoever you are with, drop them off right now; unless it's your wife and kids."

"Okay, Tech, I need y'all to get out at this store and wait for me in McDonalds. I'll be right back."

"Man, you must have lost your damn mind. How you gonna put us out of my car, with no guns, while we're in the middle of a war?" Tech replied.

"Hey yo, pull over and take my gun, bruh."Quincy said frustrated while still on the phone with Mike. Tech pulled over, and him and Angel got out. Not before taking up Q's offer to take his gun.

Q also got out and jumped in the driver seat and pulled off. He felt bad leaving them. Q knew he couldn't live with himself if something happened to them.

"A'ight Mike, I'm alone. Where am I going?"

"Come to the car wash on Steel Street." Mike replied.

"I'll be there in five minutes."

"When you get there, pull to the back, beside the white truck. Grab the duffel bag off the back." Mike replied.

Q pulled up and hopped out of Tech's car and grabbed the extra large duffel bag, threw it in the back of his brothers ride, and pulled off. Headed back to McDonalds with 50 keys. Q sweated bullets as he drove to pick up Tech and Angel. When he pulled up at McDonalds, Tech and Angel came out eating, like always.

"Yo Q, what's in the bag?" Angel asked.

"Our dreams is in that bag." Q replied.

Angel open the bag. "Oh shit, Tech, you have to see this."

Tech looks. "We're rich, bruh."

"Hey, yo, Angel. Hand me that paper inside the bag." Q asked.

"Bruh, I don't see no damn paper, wait, here's an envelope." Angel replied.

"Let me see it."
Westend Crew
Killah and Mad Max gathered their soldiers and planned out the next set of events to occur.
"We going to sit back and let them think shit cool. Then we're going to blow their soft asses off the map." Killah said.
"Its time we hit Quincy up." Mad Max replied.
Wake County Jail, Tony Blanco
Today has been crazy as fuck. This white boy got fucked up. One of the lil' bros in here was pressing him for his food. The white boy didn't give in, so they fucked him up. Tony hated seeing that. This was jail, things happen and every beef wasn't his. He just prayed that he wouldn't have to hurt anyone, because given the circumstance he would not hesitate. 2K was no longer his cellmate. He started running with the wrong people on some tough man shit. They really weren't trying to do anything for real, mainly fronting. Tony had heard that Q and his crew were beefing with Westend. He wished him the best with that. Tony Blanco was nowhere near to being a broken man. He had money, and family support, so he intended on staying strong until the end. He had met some really good people that he wished could get another chance.
"Ring, ring, ring."
"Hello, Agent Pennell speaking. How can I help you?" Agent Pennell asked.
"Agent Pennell, this is Kristan. I need to speak with you now."
"Okay, what's up?"
"No. Not on the phone, and not in front of anyone.
"Kristan, I'm really busy. Is this important?"
"Yes it is."
"Where are you?"
"I'm home."
"I'll be there in an hour."
An Hour Later

"Knock, knock."

"I'm coming, I'm coming." Kristan hollered as she came and opened the door. "Please come in and have a seat, make yourself at home."

"Kristan, I only have 20 minutes. I have work to take care of. What's on your mind?" Pennell asked. Damn, he had to admit, she had his dick hard, coming to the door wearing them boy shorts that were sticking in her ass. Pennell thought to himself as Kristan bent over to pick something up off the floor.

"Agent Pennell, I called you because I need your help." Kristan said laying on the charm. "I need help with my rent, you know. You can take it out of the five thousand you were going to give me to talk to that guy Tony's wife."

Kristan was one bad stripper. She was 5'5", 140 pounds, thick and sexy, with caramel skin. She laid her charm on Agent Pennell, then she went the extra mile and sat on his lap, leaned over and whispered in his ear.

"Do you think you will be able to help me, Agent Pennell?" Kristan whispered?

"I don't know, I have to see."

Kristan then leans over and kisses Pennell on the ear and begins to stick her finger in his mouth. Pennell try's to speak, but couldn't get any words out. He pushes her back, but Kristan stands up and pulls her shorts down. "God help me, I'm married." Pennell thought to himself. Kristan unzipped Pennell's pants and pulled out his small dick to suck it.

This girl was a champ, Pennell wanted to push her off but the head was too good. So he laid his head back and enjoyed himself. Kristan then pulled out a rubber and slid it on his dick with her mouth.

"You like that, baby?" Kristan whimpered.

"Yes." Pennell replied.

Kristan stood, walked closer, and sat on Pennell's lap. Letting her wetness consume his small penis. She rode him until he nutted. When he finished, she pulled the rubber off, and sucked him dry until his knees buckled.

When Kristan finished laying her charm, Agent Pennell was exhausted but his senses came back.

"Kristan, don't ever do that again. I'm married."

"So why didn't you stop me?"

"You know why I didn't stop you." Agent Pennell replied reaching in his pocket, grabbing a few hundred.

"Because my head and my pussy is too good."

"Why you say that?"

"I got my money."

"Bye Kristan, I'll call you when we're ready." Agent Pennell said as he pulled his pants up, fastened his belt buckle, and headed for the door.

"I'll be waiting." Kristan replied watching the pig slam the door.

"I can't believe I had sex with her. I've never cheated on my wife." Pennell thought as he walked to his car.

CHAPTER 11

After Quincy recovered the 50 bricks, him and Tech dropped Angel off. Angel was Q's man, but he only wanted to deal with his brother Tech on that level. They drove to Cary to Tech's house, where they busted the bricks down. Q took 100 grams of coke off every brick and cut it with 100 grams, then re-compressed it. That's five free bricks. Q gave Tech one free off top. Once they got all keys re-compressed and bagged up, Tech drove Q back to Raleigh and dropped him off at home.

"Yo, be careful who you fuck with, bruh. If I was you, I would give that shit to the bros on the block, and let them move it." Q said.

"Big bruh, you just keep the work coming. I got this. Tech replied.

On the block, Westend

"Yo, Mad Max, what's good. Let the homies know that we're going out of town to party tonight." Killah said.

"I gotcha, I'm on it." Mad Max replied, then walked in the

trap house to call the crew. By the end of the night Mad Max had rounded everybody up.

When Quincy left Tech, he went straight home, feeling so good he wanted to take the kids out. When he got there, the kids were hyped up for ice cream. Q told his wife that he would take the kids to the dairy.

"You spoiling them." Toya said as she watched her cheerleaders run out the door to the car.

"I know, they're daddy's little girls. I cant help it, baby." Q replied closing the door behind him.

Q and his girls ordered ice cream sundaes. While he was ordering, he heard someone ask one of his daughters her name. When he turned around to see who it was, it was Killah and a couple guys from his crew.

"What's good, Quincy?" Killah said.

Q didn't say a word, he just looked at Killah. Trying to feel what his next move would be.

His daughter turned and asked. "Daddy's who's these men?"

"Some nobody's." Q replied.

Killah bent down. "Lil' princess, I'm the man that's gonna kill your daddy." Killah said.

"No you ain't. Get away from my daddy." Q's girls began to cry.

Killah ignored Q's daughters cries as he stuck his hand in his coat pocket. Q thought to himself, "Not here in front of my kids."

"That money you're making, put some up for your family." Killah said, then him and his boys walked away. After Killah left, Q calmed his girls down, and they left Baskin Robbins. Q called Tech and let him know what had just happened.

"Yo, bro, I'm gonna kill them niggas. They pulled up on me in front of my girls."

"Yo, Q, this Dreko. Be easy homie, we gonna handle it."

"I know, that's a fact." Q replied, then hung up the phone

angrily.

The next day was even worse. Spook and Boss Jones both were in the Raleigh mall, shopping for what has seemed like hours of being dragged along, store to store, by their girlfriends. Tired and irritated, they both took off to the food court to grab some pizza and some homemade fries. As they were walking to sit down, Boss Jones spotted a guy he knew from the Westend crew, named Famous. Famous was an okay dude. Right now, Famous was at the wrong place at the wrong time. Spook and Boss Jones sat down at the closest table and ate their food.

"We need to get at him. He out here like shit sweet." Spook said.

"I feel you, bruh. But here?" Boss Jones replied.

"Why not here?" Spook replied.

"The ladies, remember?"

"What that mean?"

"What that means is, we don't want them to get caught up in our mess."

"Boss, you're getting soft on me." Spook replied, then got up from the table and began to walk towards Famous. When Spook got close to the dude, he punched him slap dead in his nose, and before Famous could hit the ground, Spook yoked him up in a mean choke hold. The girl Famous was with took off after seeing her man get choked out. While Spook was choking Famous, Boss Jones walked up and stabbed Famous four times in his stomach. Spook smiled at Boss Jones, then released his hold, and let Famous fall to the floor, dead before his body hit the ground. Spook and Boss Jones then walked away like nothing had just happened.

Over the next 3 months, Q's crew and Westend had been going to war. Houses were getting shot up, stash houses robbed, innocent people killed in turf war crossfire. The murder rate was up, and so was the price of keys. During that same period, Q and his crew had been moving kilos all over North Carolina. Dudes were buying birds like fried chicken in a drive-thru. Q was up to 75 keys a month, and he was feeling himself. Over the months, getting money and beefing became second nature to him. He had over a million and all his homies had Benz', BMW's, or drove Escalades. When you rode through their spot in the country, you would think you was at a car show. Getting the type of money he was getting, Q enjoyed seeing everyone around him smile. He was cruising down the road in his Maybach 557 when he looked in his rearview mirror and he recognized that he was being followed. Blue lights came on.

"Damn this looks like Detective Richmond. Yeah, he's puling me over." Q thought to himself and pulled his Maybach over.

"License and registration, please." The detective said.

Q reached in his glove compartment and handed the officer his paperwork.

"Nice car. How much does a car like this run, $250,000? Quincy, I'm hearing your name a lot these days, I'm sure the feds do also. You have a good day now." Detective Richmond said, then he handed Quincy back his paperwork.

Later that day, on New Years Eve, Quincy and Toya went to Toya's mothers house for a BBQ. When they got there, they both ate, then Toya's mother wanted to stand up and speak to everybody.

"This is a nice day and I'm happy to have my family here. You know, in life, you can have so much money it kills you or even your loved ones. I pray that my son-in-law and his family have a safe year. They're involved in a lot of violence that happens in this city. I go to bed at night fearing the phone call that someone has broken into Toya's home and killed her and the kids."

"I can't keep listening to this shit, I can't believe she put me on the spot like this." Quincy looked at Toya, then signaled for them to leave, right before he got Techs' attention. When they left, they looked like something off a mafia movie; pulling out eight cars deep.

Q's phone rang, and he saw that it was Toya calling, but he didn't answer. Q and the bro's went to the car wash, where they cleaned their cars and smoked an un-numbered amount of blunts. They decide on going to club Next Level tonight.

"You know Wicked was murdered the last time we went to club Next Level." Tech said.

"I know, but we good, though." Q replied.

Night of New Years Eve Party

"Yo Money, this bitch is jam packed." Tech said.

"Yeah, it's going down in here."

"Yo, Q, I love you, big bruh. Happy New Years." Tech said hugging his brother.

"I love you, too." Q replied. Then Tech stood up and started making it rain.

Q looked in the opposite direction and saw P. A dude from Durham that he knew. P was that dude in Durham he couldn't front.

"Hey, yo, Money. Them Westend punks just came in, bruh. I'ma ice one of them fools now." Dreko said.

"Nah, Dreko. Macks fam." Money replied.

"Fuck that Money, they shot me." Dreko said.

"Not here though, bruh." Money said. Then as soon as he turned to holler at Angel, he heard shots ring out. Dreko had walked away and blacked out. So now they were in the heat of a shoot out. As soon as the homie Fab stands up, he's hit once in the chest. Q grabs him and then pulled him out the side door, the Westend goons go out the back. The bros give chase, more shots ring out. As Q is holding Fab, Fab begins shaking trying to talk. Tears fall from Q's eyes because he raised Fab, and he hated to see him hurt like this, and in so much pain. Fab starts coughing up blood as he lay in Q's arms and took his last breath. All the shooting has stopped, people are shot inside the club. Q looked around and saw bodies all over the floor.

"Sirens."

Within minutes, cops are pulling up. Tech and the rest of the bros have already left. Q stayed back to be with Fab; Angel is also with him. The cops are everywhere as they watch as their friend is zipped up in a black body bag and carried off. Two of the Westend soldiers also got sent out in body bags. It wasn't about them though, it was about Fab right now. Q and Angel both went to the hospital. They were the first ones there, then Fab's family starts pouring in.

Deep down, Q hated to face them. Fab's mother broke down, his sister and grandma are taking Fab's death hard. "Damn, why didn't Dreko listen to Money; this is his fault. Fab's death is on his hands." Just as Q was thinking to himself, Fab's mother screams out.

"God, why my baby? Why did you have to take him? Why, God, why?"

Angel and Q got up to leave the hospital. But as soon as they got outside, the FBI were waiting.

"We need you both to come downtown." One of the agents said.

Wake County Police Department

"Gabriel Akins, or should I call you Angel. I'm Agent Pennell and this is Agent Hurns. I'm sure you know Detective Richmond."

"What is it you want?" Angel asked.

"Franklin Lawson, he's a friend of yours right?" Pennell asked.

"Yeah, that's my man."

"Do you know who killed him?"

"No, sir. I was in the bathroom at the time of the shooting."

"Angel, you have to help us here. I mean, Christ, he was your friend! Just give me one name."

"Like I said, I was in the bathroom when he died."

"I heard this happened over a drug war. Is that true?"

Angel laughs. "Agent whatever-you-say-your-name-is, am I under arrest?"

"No, you're not."

"Then may I leave?"

"Sure."

"Quincy Capps, I'm Agent Hurns, this is my partner, Agent Pennell. Detective Richmond will be joining us. I won't ask who killed your friend. I know that will be a waste of time. That's a $250,000 car you're driving. When I heard about you and your clothing store, I was planning on leaving the Bureau and opening me a clothing store myself, or better yet, I could work for you. How's that sound?"

"I don't hire police officers." Q replied.

"Q, I can see you paying $3,000 a month for your car. How your friends afford to pay is the million-dollar question."

"I think you should ask them. Look, my friend just died. Is there anything else you want to ask, if not can I leave?" Q said.

"Q, you're not under arrest, yet. I got a close eye on you though."

"Well, I'm leaving, go get your warrant." Q said as he got up from the table and headed for the door.

"Hey, Q!"

Q turned around.

"When I do, my friend, you won't like it." Hurns said.

Q just smiled. When he walked out to the lobby, his wife, Toya, came up and hugged him.

"Baby, are you okay?"

"I'm fine, Toya."

"Don't let these assholes get to you, Q."

"I'm not, baby. Where's Angel?"

"He's waiting in the car. He didn't want to stand in the police station."

"I feel him, baby. Let's get out of here."

Q and Toya took Angel home, Toya had rode with her sister to come check on Q, since Q and Toya's sister didn't get along too well. The ride home was quiet. All Q could think about was Fab and his family. He was only 21 years old; he had his whole life ahead of him. Q hated to see Fab's mom going through all this pain. He knew how much she loved Fab. "When I get home I have to hit the homies up for a session. Lord knows I need it." Q thought to himself.

When they got back, Q hopped in his car.

"Please don't do anything stupid, Q. Me and the girls need you." Toya said as she bent down and kissed her husband.

"I won't."

"Promise?"

"I promise, baby." Q replied with a smile.

Q met his bros 30 minutes later in the country.

"What's good? Who we missing?"

"Angel and Dreko." Spook replied.

"Okay, it's time we take this shit to the next level. If you ain't wit it, now is your time to leave." Q said as he looked into the eyes of his soldiers and felt nothing but love and loyalty.

"Good. Everybody's down. Gutter, I need you, Spook, and Tech to go over to Mad Max's house and kill him. Then go to Killah's crib and dead him too. No survivors." Q said.

"Say no more, big bruh. We got this." Gutter replied as he turned up his shot glass.

CHAPTER 12

The next day, Gutter, Tech, and Spook go and get the stolen whips that they had put up for times like these. When it was time to get your hands dirty.

"Hey, yo, we do this quick and we get rid of the guns asap." Tech said.

"Facts." Spook replied.

They arrived close to Mad Max's house. They got out of the car and walked up the block. They pulled their ski-masks down and cocked their guns.

"Spook, you and Gutter hit the back; I'ma hit the front. We go on my signal." Tech said.

"And what is that?" Spook asked.

Gunshots rang out.

They spilt up. Gutter and Spook went around back. Tech crept up to the front door of Mad Max's house. The barrel of his 40 cal leading the way.

Tech shot the lock off and stormed inside. Once inside the house, he didn't see anybody. He only heard Spook and Gutter coming through the back door. Next thing he knew, glass shattered and he heard bullets being fired.

"It's a set up!" Gutter yells and then a flame of fire came through the window.

"Duck, its cocktails!" Spook hollers.

Glass is being shattered, bullets are shooting through the walls.

Tech jumps out the window. Spook and Gutter are still pinned down, and the house was burning up, smoke is everywhere. "Think, think." Tech thought to himself. Then he ran up the side of the house firing his 40 cal. Spook and Gutter still couldn't get out of the house, because the Westend crew were hiding in the woods, waiting for anyone that came running outside. Tech thought all was lost until he heard shots coming from up the street, He looked around the corner of the house and saw that it was Angel and Dreko. The distraction gave Spook and Gutter a chance to escape, and they took it. When the bullets stopped hitting the house, both of them dove out the window.

More bullets rang out. It was a mass shoot-out.

"I'm hit!" Spook hollered as he grabbed his stomach and fell to the ground. Gutter ran to his side and helped him back to his feet.

"We gotta get outta here!" Tech said almost on the verge of panic.

"We can't see right now." Spook replied through a whisper, still clutching his 9mm, firing round after round at the enemy. Tech, Spook, and Gutter, after heavy determination, they finally made it to the car, and pulled off.

"Let me out, stop the car!" Gutter hollered.

"What the fuck, bruh?" Tech said as he stopped the car.

Gutter hopped out of the car with two pistols in his hands. "I'm going back."

"Bruh, you trippin. Get the fuck back in the car."

Gutter ignored Tech, and continued walking back down the block. As he got closer, Gutter could see the house burning and a bunch of people standing out front. Killah, Mad Max, and a few others went inside to put the fire out. Gutter cocked his 9mm, and continued to slowly gain ground. When he got closer, he noticed Mad Max's two brother's and Killah's little brother standing out front. "I got those muthafuckas now, I'ma checkmate these fools." Gutter thought to himself. Then he made his move.

"What's up now!" Gutter hollered then he pulled the trigger.

Shots sounded off. All these Westend boys are hit bad. Killah's lil' brother is crawling on his hands and knees, begging for his life, as he sees his friends lay dead beside him.

"Don't kill me, man. Please."

Gutter didn't say a word, he just walked right up and shot him square in the head. Then walked over to the other two and did the same to them, just to be sure.

Hearing the shots, Killah and Mad Max came running at the house. It's too late. Gutter was making his escape. Killah and Mad Max sent shots aimed at Gutter back. It did no justice; Gutter was gone.

*Breaking news, Tamara Lane

"There was a triple homicide at club Next Level. 21 year old Franklin 'Fab' Lawson, and the Wright brothers have been shot dead. Rumor has it the shooting took place inside, and then outside around back, where the Wright brothers were murdered execution style. Four people were also shot. Sources say that the Westend crew and Money Mafia was involved in the shoot out, that stems from almost a year ago. The FBI has been called in to help put a stop to this war, right here in our capitol, Raleigh, North Carolina. I'm Tamara Lane, reporting live."

Back at Mad Max's house, Max and Killah saw the brothers laying dead on the pavement. Gutter dropped his phone during his escape. Max picked it up, thinking it belonged to his brother. Killah is furious and in a fit of rage. The police and the fire department are all over the place. The police are walking around asking questions, but no one will talk. After hours, the police are still on the scene. The news crew pulled up.

"Breaking news. I'm here in front of Jeremiah Sparks' house reporting live. Three more are dead. Tonight, the violence is at an all time high. How can six people die in a weeks time and no one see a thing? This has to end. Parents are losing children. I'm sad to know that I live in a city that doesn't care. Reporting live, I'm Tamara Lane."

After everything settled down, and the police, news crews, and fire department were gone, Mad Max sat with his family as his mother mourned the death of her two sons. Killah went home and came back. Max and Killah were outside talking. When Max's mother came outside.

"I want whoever did this, dead. I mean it." Then she walked back inside.

"How's your family?" Max asked.

"They're taking things hard. Lil' bruh was mom's heart." Killah replied.

The phone in Max's pocket rang. He reached in and grabbed it. Before he answered it, he looked at the screen. He didn't see his brothers picture; he saw Gutters.

"A, Yo, be quiet. This is Gutters phone. He dropped it." Max said.

"Quincy is calling Gutter's phone." Killah replied.

"Hello." Max said in a low tone.

"A, yo, bro, where you at?" Q barked.

"Tell Gutter he's a deadman." Max says then hangs up.

"What the fuck. Let me call Dreko."

"Ring, ring."

"Hello."

"Dreko, where y'all at?"

"The hospital Q."

"Spook was hit in the stomach."

"Is he alive?"

"Yeah."

"Leave right now. They have Gutter's phone."

"Q, I got a call that Mad Max and Killahs brothers were murdered."

"Dreko I'm out. I have to find Gutter before they do."

Q hung the phone up, jumped in his car, and spent most of the night driving around the city looking for Gutter. When he realized that he couldn't find Gutter, he decided to head home.

When Quincy walked through the door, as soon as he looked up, Toya is pointing a gun. When she saw Q, she broke down crying.

"Q, I'm so scared, baby." Toya said while hugging Q.

"It's okay, Toya."

"No, it isn't, Q. Fab is dead and you're out for revenge. The streets are crazy. So you listen to me Quincy Capps. You're going to die if you don't end this war." Toya replied.

"What do I tell our kids? What do Fab's girl tell their daughter?" Toya asked. "It's bigger than me, Toya."

"Q, what's bigger than a drug king pin? Yeah, I know that you're a drug dealer. What? You thought I was dumb? You blow $50,000 like its five dollars. Q, I know how much you make at the clothing store, I stayed because I love you. Fab is dead, Spook is hospitalized, so talk to me, please. I don't want to lose you, baby."

"You won't lose me." Q replied.

A week has gone by, and everybody has been laying low. It's been a lot of funerals this week, but Fab's funeral is tomorrow.

Westend crew meeting

"I got a call that Gutter is at some chick named Becky's house, on the South side. I have soldiers on the way over there now. Gutter is not to make it out alive." Killah said.

"Are you sure he's there?" Zoe asked.

"Yeah, I'm sure, Zoe. I went there last night to sell Becky some loud. I seen him in the kitchen hiding through the living room mirrors that's on the wall."

"It's on then."

Killah and his team took three cars and rolled out. When they got close to the house, Killah pointed out, "That's it, right there."

They parked the cars on the other side of the block and walked back. When they got to the house, Killah ordered three to go through the front and three to through the back.

Killah walked around the house and he sees Gutter sitting on the couch. Killah becomes angry, then informs everyone that it was a go.

"This is where you earn your stripes. On my signal, hit the front door." Killah held up his hand, and then closed it into a fist.

Zoe hit the front door. Kicking it off it's hinges. Zoe entered the house, Mac-10 leading the way. A startled Gutter raised up off the couch. "Bloc, Bloc." Firing rounds like he was 2Can Sam. He hit Zoe in the shoulder and face. Boom! The back door crashes in, Gutter turns to run, but he meets Big Robs' 45. "Bloc." Gutter is dropped to the floor. His gun flew from his hand from the impact. He tries to reach for it, Killah walks up and kicks the gun away.

"I gotcha now."

"Fuck you, pussy."

"Nah, fuck you. Say hello to my lil' brother." Killah says then pulls the trigger. "Bloc." Right in front of Becky.

Becky hollers.

"Bitch, shut the fuck up." Mad Max said grabbing hold of Becky's hair.

"Aaaah, I'm pregnant, my baby." Becky screamed.

"That baby is what's saving you're life right now. If you say a word about what happened here, I'll come back. When I know that baby dropped, we clear. Nod your head."

Becky nodded.

"Oh yeah, let Quincy know Westend did this." Killah said, then slung Becky to the ground.

"A'ight, let's go." Mad Max said.

"911, how can I help you?"

"Two guys are dead in my house!" Becky hollered on the phone.

"Ma'am, where do you live?"

"412 Professional Boulevard."

"Ma'am, are you ok? Are you hurt?"

"No."

"The police are on their way."

Becky hangs the phone up and calls Dreko.

"Ring, Ring."

"Hello." Dreko said, answering on the second ring.

"Dreko, this is Becky, Gutter's girl."

"What's up, shorty?"

Becky breaks down crying. "Dre, they made me watch."

"What? Where's Gutter?"

"He's gone, they killed him Dre, right in front of me. What am I supposed to tell our baby? When he asks for his   father."

"Becky calm down, I'm on the way." Dreko replied then hung up.

When Dreko got off the phone, he called all the homies and let them know what had just happened.

Becky's House

Everybody arrived in full force. Police, ambulance, and of course, the news crew.

"Breaking news, I'm Tamara Lane, reporting live on Professional Boulevard, where two men were gunned down in cold blood. Justin Favors and Travis Starback are victims of an ongoing drug war that has terrorized our triad. This is sad that young men are still dying. It's been confirmed by reliable sources that a female was made to watch while masked men killed her friend. Travis Starback was one of the intruders in the invasion. I'm Tamara Lane, Reporting Live."

"Mrs. Becky Willis, I'm Detective Richmond. May I speak with you, please."

"Yes."

"I know this is a difficult time, but whoever did this needs to be arrested. Did you by chance catch a glimpse of any of their faces?"

Becky just sits and cries. "No, sir, they were all wearing masks."

"Ma'am, do you have any kids."

"No, I'm pregnant with Justin's baby."

"I'm sorry to hear that. Any help you could give would be appreciated."

"Sir, I didn't see anything. If you would excuse me, this conversation is over."

"Okay, ma'am, if you remember anything, anything at all that may help us, please give me a call. Here's my card."

"Detective, I told you, I'm not any help."

"Ma'am, I'm just trying to help."

Becky smiles and walks away. Agent Pennell then walks up.

"Detective Richmond, how's it going?" Agent Pennell asked.

"Not too good. Two dead, the female saw what happened, but is too afraid to talk."

"I see."

Quincy, Angel, Dreko, and the rest of Money Mafia pulls up.

"Q, when are you going to end this war of yours?" Pennell asked.

"Agent Pennell, why don't you go on a doughnut break." Q replied as he walked right past the agent to comfort Becky.

After leaving Becky's house, Q went home. This time, Toya didn't say a word. Q rolled a blunt and sat and relaxed on the couch all night long in a daze. Fab's funeral was in a couple days, so he was super stressed.

The next day, Tech called up the team to let the bros know to lay low for a while until shit cools down. Q had Tech close all the trap houses and give the order to sell nothing until they heard from him. He felt that shit was getting too hot and it wouldn't be long until the FED's came knocking. He needed to be on point. When the FED's came, they didn't come playing games.

Fabs Funeral

Everybody came out to show their respects. Q and Toya sat in the fourth row. He couldn't bare to look at Fab's mother. It hurt as the preacher began preaching the word. Something he said hit Quincy square in the chest. He began to cry. The realization really set in that Fab was gone. After the preacher finished his winded sermon, all of the family and then friends got up and lined up so they could view the body and pay their final respects. When Q and Toya got their chance to view the body, Q broke all the way down. He was trying to stay strong, but he had reached his breaking point. The loss of Fab really hit home. After viewing the body, Q and Toya walked over and hugged Fab's family, then headed for the exit behind Dreko. As soon as they stepped outdoors, the police and the FBI rush them and inform Dreko that he's under arrest for the murders of the Wright brothers, that took place on New Years Eve at club Next Level. Q couldn't believe what he was seeing. Dreko was his main man; he was all Dreko had.

Dreko was causing a scene, talking shit. Telling the police they didn't have shit on him.

"Jeremy Howell, I'm Detective Richmond and this is Agent Hurns and Agent Pennell. I'm tired of you punks running around acting like y'all tough. We have an eye witness, your ass is finished."

"Man, I have nothing to say. I want a lawyer." Dreko replied.

"Agent, get this punk over to the jail."

"Will do, Agent Hurns."

When Agent Hurns got Dreko to the county jail, he stood before the magistrate. Being that he was charged with double homicide, he was denied bond. Things were looking on the down side for Dreko. He will have to sit in jail until he gets a bond. After the funeral, they all went to Fab's mother's house. Q spoke with Fab's brother Power. Power is in Miami doing five to seven. I know when he touches, whoever is alive will be dead. Power and a few of his homies upstate were known as the murder cartel, because they drop bodies like drug lords move keys. Once they left Fab's mom's house, Q went to visit Gutter's mom.

"Knock, knock."

"Who is it?"

"Quincy."

"Hold tight, I'm coming." Mrs. Favors replied as she opened the door.

"Hey Quincy."

"How are you holding up Mrs. Favors?"

"I miss Justin so much, sometimes I don't know what to do. How are you?"

"I'm just so stressed out, Mrs. Favors. I feel like it's all my fault."

"Don't think like that. Justin passing, that was God's plan. God wanted him up in heaven with him. It's not for us to understand why." Mrs. Favors replied.

"I know, Mrs. Favors."

"I know you do, baby."

"Mrs. Favors, I knew Justin was helping you out with the bills. If you need something, I can help."

"Thank you, baby. I always liked you the most, but Justin had a habit of saving every dime he made. So Mama Favors is okay."

"If you need me, let me know."

"I will Quincy." Mrs. Favors replied as she walked up to Quincy and gave him a hug. When she released him, she looked in Q's eyes. "Quincy, baby, get away from here. Take your family and go enjoy your life."

"I will Mrs. Favors, as soon as it's finished."

"I see why my son loved you so much. Loyal to the end."

"He was my friend."

"I know, baby. I know."

After Q spoke with Mrs. Favors, he went outside. When he got to his car, his phone started to vibrate.

"Hello."

"You have a collect call from Dreko. Thank you for using Globaltel Link."

"Dreko, what's good fam?"

"Not shit. These muthafuckas won't give me a bond."

"I heard, bruh. Keep your head high, though. We're working on that bond situation. Monday I will holler at the lawyer to see if we can get you out. Look though, you know this phone call is being recorded, so I'm going to holler at you."

"Later, bruh."

"Love you homie." Q replied and then hung up.

Monday morning, Wake County Jail

"Order in my court. Jeremy Howell, I've looked over your charges, I'm denying your bond. Mr. Howell, you are a major threat to society and people like you belong right here, where you are in jail. Bailiff, please take the defendant away."

"Fuck you, bitch!" Dreko yelled as he was escorted out of the room.

A few weeks have gone by and there haven't been any murders, nor shooting. Even though Q closed all his trap spots, he was still moving 100 keys a month with no problem. Quincy was the new Boss in the triads, but little did he know the FED's were on to him.

Dreko's bond still hasn't gotten dropped. Q had gotten a letter from him yesterday telling him that he was locked up with a guy named Tony Blanco and that he sends his love. Q couldn't front he felt good knowing that Tony cares about him. When Q finished reading the letter from Dreko, he set it down and decided to take his girls out to get ice cream. On the ride to the ice cream parlor, Q gathered his thoughts. The last few months had been kind of overwhelming. The plug, the war, Fab's death, a lot of weight weighed on Q's shoulders. He just needed a moment to get his head straight, and quiet time with his girls always did that for him.

Q pulled into the ice cream shop, made a round in the parking lot just to be on the safe side. He parked and got his girls out of the car and went inside.

"Welcome to the ice cream parlor, may I take your order."

"Yes, I would like three bowls of ice cream."

"Will that be all, sir?"

"Yes."

"Your total is $8.75. I'll bring it right out to you."

"Thank you." Q replied, then turned to find a table for him and his girls. When he turned. He saw this big, Black, dude that had to weigh 360 pounds with long dreads. He was clean as fuck, and Q could swear the guy looked familiar, but he wasn't sure. Paying it no mind, Q continued on to the table in the back. When Q and his girls sat down, the Black guy came and sat at the table next to them. Q became nervous thinking the guy was a hitman for Westend. He pulled his Glock and placed it on his lap, just in case.

"Sir, here's your order." The waitress said as she placed the ice cream bowls on the table. "I'll be back to check on you."

Trying to focus on his kids and this strange guy, Q noticed that he pulled out a news paper and sat it on the table. As he drank his coffee and gets his food, he never touches the paper. Q keeps a sharp eye on him as his girls finish their ice cream. When they finished, Q left a tip for the young waiter, then led his girls back to the car. After he loaded his girls in the car and shut the door, Q turned around and immediately noticed the fat man standing at the door of the ice cream parlor, smiling at him. As Q got in the car, the fat man pointed his finger at him and flicked his finger like it was a gun. Q got in his car and pulled off, realizing this was the wrong time to beef, and also happy that he had his kids with him, because if he didn't, he might be dead. That guy was a hitman, just as Q had sensed, and it was no telling how long or when he was being followed. Quincy dropped the girls off with his wife, Toya. He wanted to take a drink, so he headed to the liquor store. Cruising, bumping Young Dolph. Q stopped at a stop light. A grey Benz pulled up beside him with a snow-bunny driving. Q didn't pay her no mind. He was too busy, lost in his tunes. He turned his head, then glanced back at her. When he did, a man that was hiding in the passenger seat of the Benz popped up with a Mack-10.

"Thratt, thratt, thratt."

Glass shattered. Bullets hit the side of the car. Off reflex, Q hit the gas and ran the light. The Benz gave chase, Q swerved through traffic.

"Thratt, thratt."

The back glass shatters. Q almost lost control. As he saw bullets hit the dash. Panic is taking over. Q tries to figure out what to do. Hand on the steering wheel, drenched in sweat, maneuvering through traffic. Q made a left turn on Benbow and headed for the safest place he could think of at the moment, Black Jesus' Chop Shop. Black Jesus was a longtime friend that made a career out of stealing cars. He was from Jersey so that's all he knew. Pedal to the floor, pushing the Maybach to 160mph. Q calls Black.

"Ring, ring, ring."

"Hello?"

"Black."

"Q, is that you?"

"Yeah, it's me. I got trouble. Westend on my tail."

"Come to the shop. Bumpy and the boys are here."

"A'ight, I'm five minutes out." Q says then hung up the phone.

Shots are still being fired from the Benz. Q pulls in the junk yard, sped down the dirt road, crashing through the gate. The grey Benz following behind him. Bumpy and his crew hid behind the old, crushed cars. As soon as Q beat the corner with the grey Benz behind him, Bumpy and his crew opened fire on the Benz. Bullets tearing through the car like paper. The two inside were tore to shreds, instantly killing them. Q hit the brakes on his Maybach and slowly got out. 40 cal in hand, taking in his surroundings. The first thing Q saw was the two bodies slumped inside the Benz.

Bumpy slings his AR-15 over his shoulder and walks up to Q.

"Nice to see you partner."

"Yeah, you too Bumpy. It's been a long time. Where's Black?"

"He left right after you called. You know he couldn't be here for all this."

"Facts, we gotta clean this up, Q."

"Nah, bruh, we got this. Black told me to give you these." Bumpy said as he handed Q the keys to Blacks 745.

"What these for?"

"Ain't no way you're driving that shot up Maybach outta here."

"Yeah, you're right." Q replied as he tucked his 40 cal in his waistband, grabbed the keys from Bumpy and headed towards Blacks 745.

"Yo, Bumpy, come by the hood later and see Tech. I'll have him give you a paper bag."

"Not necessary."

"I insist."

"I gotcha bruh, I'll see Tech later." Bumpy replied.

"Good, good, and thank you, Bumpy."

"No problem, Q."

CHAPTER 13

Another month has went by, Dreko is still locked up. Money and Angel opened up new trap spots. A lot of people have died since the failed hit on Q by the Westend crew. Business was still good. Q has gone from thousands to millions. It seemed like the more beef that popped off, the higher the coke prices went. Q had people from the Villa, Gboro, Bull City all the way to Atlanta coming to get keys like they're free. He was getting so much coke and money he was growing paranoid. He spoke to the owner of Piggly Wiggly about stashing his coke in the stores basement for $10,000 month. The drop no longer comes to Raleigh. Q had to go to Detroit, Michigan to pick it up. Mike has them shipped in through general motors. So he had to get more involved with the daily operations. Mike was dropping 200 keys a month for $10,000 a key. On a fishing vacation in Detroit one day, Q met a pig farmer, named Jake, who said that he transported pigs to a Virginia four times a month. Since the recession his business has slowed up. Q made him an offer of $50,000 a month to ship drugs inside his pigs.

Jakes biggest concern was, would it work? Q eased Jake's nervousness by explaining to him that all he had to do was drive the pigs to Virginia and someone will pick them up. After all the details were worked out, Q and Jake agreed to a deal that would bring Q millions over time.

Kristan

"Let me call Agent Pennell and see if I can get me some more money outta him."

"Ring, ring."

"Pennell."

"Hello, Agent Pennell, this is Kristan. How are you today?"

"Oh, hey, I'm fine. How's everything with you?"

"Good. Are you by yourself?"

"Yeah, why, what's up?" Agent Pennell asked.

"I have something important I would like to speak with you about. Could you please come to my house?"

"Okay, yeah. Give me a couple of hours."

"Come whenever you're ready."

After a couple hours of paperwork, Agent Pennell was pulling his police cruiser up at Kristan's house. He got out and walked inside.

"Agent Pennell, how are you?" Kristan said laying on the charm by placing her hand on his chest.

"Like I said on the phone, I'm okay. What is it that you want to speak to me about, Kristan?"

"Well, I was wondering, when do you want me to speak with this Jessica girl?"

"I told you, Kristan, I will let you know about that."

"I know that, but I have some bills that I need to pay." Kristan replied making her voice sound seductive then sticking her tongue in Agent Pennell's ear.

Agent Pennell backed away surprised.

"Kristan, what are you doing? I told you I was married."

"I'm trying to make you feel good." Kristan replied moving a little closer.

"I don't like cheating on my wife, Kristan."

"We don't have to have sex. I can think of something else we can do." Kristan said, then began to unbuckle Agent Pennell's pants. Pulling them down to his knees. She slid his underwear down, letting his four inch penis free. She reached her hand up and stroked him until he was at his full five inch length. Kristan pushed Pennell in the chest, causing him to fall back on the couch. She walked up closer, then bent down on her knees, and took Agent Pennell's penis in her mouth. She sucked him and listened to him moan, over-come with pleasure. After about two minutes of giving him oral, Agent Pennell jumped up. Kristan saw the lust in his eyes and began to undress. He stopped her; placing both of his hands on her shoulders. He lowered her back down to her knees, then he rammed his small penis back in her mouth.

Agent Pennell fucked Kristan in her mouth until he began to jerk from climaxing, shooting his seed in her mouth. It turned Kristan on to have control over a federal agent. Even if she had his dick in her mouth, it got her pussy wet. "Too bad he had a lil' dick." Kristan thought to herself, as she sucked Agent Pennell dry.

"Aaah, damn, Kristan. That was good."

"Really?" Kristan replied, wiping her mouth.

"Yeah."

"You know what I need, baby?"

"How much?"

"$300, I have a couple bills I need to pay."

Agent Pennell pulled his pants up, and reached for his billfold, and pulled out five crisp hundred dollar bills, and handed them to her.

"Five hundred dollar bills, for five inches." Kristan thought to herself as she grabbed the money laughing.

On the way back from Raleigh, Agent Pennell got a call from

Detective Richmond. He wanted him to meet him at Crabtree Valley Mall parking lot. Agent Pennell pulled in, heading around the back of the mall. When he got fully around the front parking lot, he saw Detective Richmond's police cruiser backed in at the far end of the parking lot. Agent Pennell pulled in beside him and rolled his window down.

"Detective Richmond."

"Agent Pennell."

"Glad you could make it. I need your help putting Quincy Capps behind bars. Something has to be done about him and this guy I keep hearing about from Westend."

"Killah." Agent Pennell interrupted.

"Yeah, that's him. I know you want to put Tony Blanco behind bars. He's already there."

"He won't stay, and I know he's the source of the cocaine coming in the Triad. I think Quincy's connected to Tony Blanco. I don't have any proof it's just a hunch."

"Hunch's lead to convictions." Detective Richmond replied.

"I'ma follow it wherever it leads me."

"Quincy is getting major drugs from somewhere, and we need to know where. I want to put a GPS on his car."

"I'm with that, but we don't have a warrant."

"We don't need one, we gotta get dirty on this one."

"Okay, I'll get it done on my end, that should give us a lead on his operations." Pennell replied.

"Thanks a lot Agent Pennell. We'll nail this one for the good guys."

"You're welcome Detective. I'll be in touch."

Quincy Capps

Gutter's girl moved to Seattle, so Quincy gave her two-hundred thousand to start over. Plus, he put seventy thousand in a second account for the baby when it's born, but she can't touch it until the baby is 21 years old.

Over the past few months, people have been coming forth about the incident that took place with Dreko at club Next Level. Some said the Wright brothers shot first, others say Dreko shot first. Right now, his case is at a stalemate, but his lawyer says he might get him a decent plea deal worked out. Q let Hell Rell from Burlington take over the operation in Greenboro. Dollar was being too careless with his money. With Hell Rell taking over, it cut down traffic, and raised profits. Quincy was kind of beside himself because he hasn't written Tony in a while, so he figured he would take some time out and write him.

Killah and Mad Max are at each others throats over 30 keys Killah's lil' partner took. "I hope they kill each other." Q thought to himself.

Later that night

"Toya, school is out next week. Let's say we get up and pack up right now, and take the kids to Disney World."

"Q, it's 9:30 at night."

"I've already made reservations, the plane leaves at midnight."

"Stop playing games, Q."

"A'ight, watch this." Q said as he got up and gathered his girls.

"Amanda, Destiny, get up. We're going to Disney World."

"For real, daddy?" Destiny asked.

"Yep, for real, princess. So come on, lets go get dressed so we can go." Quincy said while he walked his little Destiny back to her room to get dressed.

"Q, you're serious?"

"Toya, you need to pack some clothes so we can make our plane."

"Okay, bae."

After everybody is packed and ready, Q and his family leave the house, not knowing that Detective Richmond was following them. After the plane lands, Toya is happy for once and the kids are amped up about seeing Mickey Mouse. Q is happy to see his family happy.

The next day at Disney World

"Daddy, Mommy, there's Mickey Mouse! Amanda said.

"Go, give them a hug princess. Take Destiny with you." Q replied.

"Okay, Daddy."

"Yo, this is a beautiful sight." Q said to his wife while he watched his girls play with Mickey Mouse.

"Quincy, I love you so much."

"I love you too, baby."

"Q, I think it's time we pack up and leave Raleigh."

"And go where, baby?" Q asked.

"Anywhere, Q. We own houses, stores, and a car lot, all in one year. It's time to leave. Q at least think about it."

"Okay, if that will make you happy, then I'll think about it." Q replied.

"Excuse me, sir. Do you know how to get to the ghost house?"

"It's straight up the walkway." Q replied to the strange guy. "A, yo, have we met before?" Q asked the guy.

"Nah, I'm from Kansas city."

"Bruh, I swear you have a twin back in Raleigh."

"Nah, as far as I know, it's only me, but thanks. And you all have a good day."

"You too."

Q watched as the guy walked off. "I'm tripping, but he has to be that guy I seen at the Ice Cream Parlor." Q thought to himself as he re-joined his family and enjoyed the rest of their day at the park. When night fell, Q and Toya took the kids to see the fireworks show. After the show ended, they returned back to their hotel.

Back at the room, Q is rubbing his wife's feet. The kids are sound asleep from all the running they did today.

1:30am. "Ring, ring."

"Hello."

"Q, I hate to call you, but the bro, Remy from the Villa, I

heard them boys picked him up for selling to the FED's." Tech said.

"I'll see you when I get back." Q replied and hung up. "Damn, it's always something."

Fayetteville, North Carolina

"Chris, I'm Agent Reese. If this guy is as big as you say, I can almost guarantee that you won't see a day in jail."

"Okay, but you have to understand. Right now, I'm locked up and nine times out of ten, he knows it." Chris replied gearing himself up to snitch.

The agents laughed.

"Do you want to go home or not. If so, who's your connect?"

"His name is Angel. He's from Raleigh. Have you heard of Money Mafia?"

"Nah, that name doesn't ring any bells."

"Did you hear about the six Black guys getting killed a few month's back?"

"Keep talking, Chris."

"Well, they're controlling not only Raleigh, but North Carolina."

"How much do you get a week?"

"I buy three and they front me three."

"How much do you pay?"

"$23,000 a key."

"Agent Brown, can I speak with you outside?" Agent Reese asked one of his head agents in charge. They walked out, spoke briefly, then walked back in.

"Okay, Chris, we just talked. We're going to call Raleigh PD to see what info they have on this guy named Angel that you speak of."

"If everything is as you say it is, you will walk today. But you will have to call Angel and make a controlled buy from him or Money Mafia soon."

"I'm with that, I understand. I'm just trying to get back home to my girl."

"Ring, ring."

"DEA office."

"Yes, this is Agent Brown from Fayetteville, North Carolina. Could I speak with someone that's handling the Money Mafia crew."

"Hold one second."

"Agent Pennell speaking."

"Agent Pennell, this is Agent Brown. I'm calling you today to inform you that I picked up a Chris Tilman, aka Remy, on federal drug and gun charges. He claims to buy drugs from a Gabriel Atkins, whom he calls Angel, supposed to be a part of this Money Mafia team."

"Yes, Agent Brown, I know Gabriel. He's a mid-level dealer who works for Quincy Capps, who we believe is the biggest drug dealer in North Carolina." Agent Pennell replied.

"Well, Agent Pennell, our boy Chris has agreed to make a controlled buy from this Gabriel guy in a few days."

"Agent Brown, I haven't been able to get one thing on Money Mafia, so this is definitely good news."

"Agent Pennell, I have your number. As soon as the buy takes place, I will inform you. Also don't tell anyone, not even you're partner or boss. Some of you may be on the payroll. We'll talk later."

Back in the Ville

"Okay, Chris, let's make that call to Angel, and let's see if he even knows you."

"Ring, ring."

"Yeah."

"What it do, Angel?"

"Bruh, I heard you were in jail."

"I was on probation violation, that's why. What's up?" Chris said trying to hide the nervousness in his voice.

"I got a few calls that the FED's had scooped you up."

"Angel, I'm good dog. I just called to let you know what happened. I'll call you later."

"Yo, Remy, you sound down."

"Nah, just a lil' pissed with this PO."

"Well, bruh, hit me up."

"That's whats up."

Click.

"Good job Chris, go home and get you a good night's sleep." Agent Brown said.

"Okay."

"And Chris, if you run. I will personally make sure you die in prison."

Raleigh, North Carolina

"Shit, I'm going to get straight down to it and let Angel know what I heard about Chris." Money thought."

"Ring, ring."

"Yo."

"Bruh, what's goodie."

"You already know, Money Mafia."

"Yo, Angel, I heard Chris got picked up by the FED's today, and I hear he's snitching."

"Nah, Money, that young goon goes hard. The lil' homie got picked up on a probation violation. Thats all he had on it."

"A, yo, Angel, if this bitch wasn't so ugly, I might fuck her.

"She don't look all that, but the whore is thick."

Wake County Jail

"Tony, word is the FED's are onto Quincy. One of the inmates informed him."

"Dreko, let me holler at you for a sec."

"What's up?"

"Have you heard from Q lately?"

"Bruh out of town right now. Why you ask?"

"Well, I heard from some guys coming through that the FED's are on to him. Plus, them dudes y'all beefing with found out where he lives." Tony Blanco replied.

"Oh word. I gotta get in touch with bruh, asap. I'm going to make a call and I'll be right back."

"Dreko, keep my name out of it."

"Ring, ring, ring."

"Damn, bruh, pick up."

"Hello?"

"You have a collect call from Dreko. Thank you for using Globaltel Link."

"Yo, Tech, they know where Q lives. Put him on game."

"Bruh, say no more." Tech hung up.

"Yo, Tony. I just spoke with Tech, Q's brother, he's going to let him know what's what." Dreko said as he walked up to Tony.

"How's your case looking?" Tony asked.

"Well, its 50/50 right now, hopefully it works out. I'll be here a while though."

"We both will."

"So, Tony, how's you're family?"

"They're good, you know how that can be; when your woman thinks you're never getting out."

"Yeah, my woman, she thinks the same thing. But I have to think positive, no matter what."

"Be patient, it will work itself out. Patience, Dreko."

"Thanks, Tony."

Agent Pennell

Finally, he may get something on Quincy Capps Black ass. Pennell wondered who could be working for Quincy inside the Bureau. Remy wouldn't say that, it wasn't true. His main focus was keeping Tony Blanco behind bars. What he needed to do was get Kristan to meet with Tony Blanco's wife. Matter of fact, let me text Kristan now.

"Kristan, how are you today? This is Agent Pennell." Pennell texted.

"I'm waiting on you, since you got me on standby."

"Give me a few more weeks and you'll have your money."

"Okay, a few weeks and that's it. Bye."

This bitch was getting on his nerves, Pennell thought.

Angel texted Q over and over, but didn't get a response, so he texted Q's brother, Tech, and told him to put Q on game and to let everyone know what's going on. "These fools tripping hard if they go at my brother. They touch him, I'll kill their whole family." Angel thought. Besides his baby mama and kids, Q was all he had. On the way to the trap to meet the bros, when he pulled up everybody was outside and Tech was talking to the homies. Angel parked his Benz, got out and joined his team.

"I'm glad everyone made it. The Westend bitches are plotting to hit Q at home." Tech said.

"How you know?" One of the little soldiers asked.

"Dreko hit me from the county and put me on game."

"How the fuck he knows from jail?"

"All I know, is he called me, so we gonna see what's up. Tonight we're going to lay in the woods. If we see them, no shooting at his crib. Got it?"

"Gotcha Tech." Money said.

Tech gave his team instructions.

Detective Richmond watched the Money Mafia meeting through a set of binoculars. He had followed Angel to the meeting location, and was staking them out.

"I need backup. I'm on Black Church Road. I think we have a major drug deal in progress."

"10-4, back up is on the way."

Within minutes, backup arrives.

What do we have Detective?" An officer asked.

"The whole Money Mafia team is about to pull out. They are armed and dangerous. Watch yourselves. Rush them as soon as they get on the highway. We need road blocks in both directions. Let's do this."

"Put all the guns in the Escalade with Savage since they are in his name, then let's move." Tech said.

As soon as Tech and the Money Mafia hit the street. Blue lights came from everywhere. All cars stopped. It's about 30 officers and agents.

"I got Tech's car, y'all take the rest. Bring the dogs. Trevon step out the car."

"Sure."

"Do you have any guns or drugs in the car?" Detective Richmond asked.

"Search and see." Tech replied.

"Okay, smart ass. Bring the dogs, Sargent."

"Detective Richmond, he's clean." The K-9 officer said after a thorough search.

Tech smiles, then an agent yells, "We have guns!"

"Watch him." Detective Richmond said as he pointed at Tech, signaling to another officer.

"Oh yeah, jackpot. You're in some deep shit now."

"Whose guns are these?" Detective Richmond asked.

"They're mine." Mark said.

"Fifteen guns."

"Yeah, fifteen guns."

"Run the guns." Detective Richmond said.

The officer complied. After running the guns, they all came back clean. The dogs searched every vehicle and came up empty handed.

"Detective Richmond, since we're clean, can we go? We have somewhere to be. Oh yeah, this won't look good for you." Tech said laughing.

"We'll see." Detective Richmond replied.

When the police released them, Tech texted Angel and let him know the plan was still in motion. Once they reached Q's housing complex, they parked and walked through the woods until they reached Quincy's house. They sat in the woods for hours, locked and ready for whatever. Just when they were beginning to leave, Money spotted some of Killah's crew ride by and another pulls off.

"They're casing the house out." Tech said.

"Fuck, boys, get out that car. I'm spraying." Money replied.

"Get down, relax. Let's see what they do." Angel said.

Tech and the rest of the team laid in wait, ready to pop off. But the Westend crew never stopped, they only rode through. After hours of laying in the woods, Tech and his team picked up and left. Tech let's everyone know he will meet them tomorrow. When Tech got back inside his car, the first thing he did was call his brother, Q.

"Ring, ring, ring, ring."

"Yeah."

"What up, big bruh."

"What's good."

"Them Westend fools know where you live, bruh. They been outside you house waiting for you to come home. Me and the boys laid in the woods. Wanted to see for myself, and I seen it." Tech replied.

"Who told you about it?"

"Dreko called me, bruh."

"Dreko? Where in the fuck did he get that info?" Q asked.

"Q, I didn't ask." Tech replied.

"I'll be home in two days. Keep your phone on. Later."

When Q got off the phone with his brother, Tech, he was mad as fuck. He couldn't believe that his problems were beginning to turn up on his door step. If they want war, then a war is what he would give them.

"Toya, baby, wake up."

"What is it, baby?"

"We need to talk."

"It can't wait until morning?"

"No baby, right now. Toya. I've been thinking, tomorrow we are going to find us a home here in Orlando."

"What made you decide this?"

"We need a change. Plus, it's something different for us, away from everyone. I want you and the kids to stay here, find the house. I'll send some personal stuff of ours through the UPS."

"Ooh, baby, thank you so much. I love you." Toya replied.

"I love you too, baby."

Two days later

"Toy, I'ma take a plane back to Raleigh tonight. I'll be back in a few days. I'll go ahead and put the house on the market, and take care of some more business. I'm selling everything that we own in North Carolina." Q said.

"Baby, be safe." Toya replied.

"I will." Q said, and then walked to the children's room, and read them a bed-time story. Frozen Princess were his girls' favorite cartoon, so he read them a Frozen Princess book. They were both asleep before he could finish. He kissed them, then went back into the room with Toya.

"Baby, find a house that you like, and dress it up. Make sure it has a car garage and a high tech security system."

"Okay, baby. What time does our plane leave?"

"At 3AM"

"That means we have a little time, to, you know." Toya said, sticking her finger in her mouth and sucking it like a lollipop.

"And you know it." Q replied, then began to pull his shirt off. Then he unbuckled his Gucci belt, and let his pants fall. He stood in front of his wife completely naked, then he began to stroke his manhood until he was fully erect.

"Damn, baby, that's what I'm talking about! You so nasty."

Toya replied walking towards her husband. When she got up close, she took her hand and began to stroke his bulging penis. Q dived in, tongue kissing Toya.

"I love you, baby." Q said through a whisper then he loosened her bra and let his wife's D-cups fall free.

"I love you, too."

Q began to kiss Toya from her neck to her nipples.

"Aaaah!" Toya moaned as she continued to stroke Q's penis.

Driven to consume his wife sexually, his passion taking over, he scooped his wife in his arms, slowly laid her on the hotels king size bed. He kissed her from her neck to her navel. Sliding her barely-there panties off. Q kissed between her thighs. Toya whimpered and moaned. Q tasted his wife's love box until her kittie flowed with wetness like a river.

"Aaaah, baby, stick it in. I wanna feel it."

Q stood up, rubbed his wife's pussy with his dick, driving her crazy, just before he slid it in. An hour went by until Q and Toya laid on the king-sized bed tired; spent from their love making. They cuddled until it was time for Q to get ready for his flight.

CHAPTER 14

Once on the plane, Q was deep in thought. It was game time; time to get dirty. The Westend crew was a potential threat to business, and a threat to business was a threat to his family's lifestyle, and he couldn't have that. Too much has been going on these last couple months, and he needed to put the breaks on it and that was exactly what he was planning to do.

Raleigh, North Carolina 5:30AM

The plane landed and Q stepped off with a mission. The first place he went to was the car rental place to get a car. He needed to get some wheels but didn't want anyone to recognize him, with Killah trying to get at him. After he get the car, Q calls his brother, Tech, before he pulls off.

"Ring, ring, ring, ring, ring."

"Hello"

"Damn, it took you long enough to answer." Q replied.

My bad, bruh. Baby mama had me pent up."

"A'ight. Look, I'm back in town. Hit Angel, let him know. Then I want you both to meet me at the Hamptons in Durham on King Drive."

"I'm on it, big bruh." Tech said and then hung up.

Q meets them at 11:30am, and gives them the plan, and orders them not to say a word about it.

Mad Max's homies ride by Max's girls' house to make sure that everything is good. They notice Killah's white 760 BMW parked down the street from her house, so they park and wait.

"Yo Kev, can you believe this Nigga playing Max like this, man? Mad Max is going to kill his ass." Ice said.

Another hour went by and then a man came out from the back of the house with the same kind of hoodie on that Killah be wearing. Ice takes a picture with his phone.

The next day

"You have a collect call from Max. Thank you for using Globaltel Link."

"Ice, what's happening, bruh?" Max asked.

"Max, I'm glad you called, bruh."

"What's up?"

"I got some bad news." Ice said.

"Give it to me."

"Well, last night we rode by Sandra's house, to make sure she was good, like you asked. When we rode by, we saw Killah's 760 parked down the street from your house. We posted up to see why his car was over there. A few hours later, we saw Killah leaving out the back of your house. We took pictures."

Mad Max flips out.

"Yo Ice, who else knows?"

"Just me and Kev."

"Okay, keep it that way."

"I want you to go over there tonight, and see what happens. I'll call you in the morning around ten. I'll talk with you then."

Mad Max said then hung up.

When Mad Max hung up, he was sick as hell. He couldn't believe his girl was cheating on him like this; with his home-boy at that. "When I get out, I'm killing Killah. Let me call Sandra." Max thought to himself.

"Ring, Ring."

"You have a collect call from Mad Max. Thank you for using Globaltel Link."

"Hello." Sandra said.

"Hey, baby."

"Hey, how are you holding up?"

"I'm good." Max replied. "How are you?"

"I'm good, bae." Sandra replied.

"I bet you are."

"What's that supposed to mean?"

"Nothing. What you do last night?"

"Nothing, bae. Me and the baby went to bed as soon as we hung up with you." Sandra replied.

"Sandra, do you love me?"

"Yes, baby. You, and only you."

"Yeah right." He thought to himself then asked, "How's the baby?"

"Missing her daddy."

"Give her a kiss for me, I'll call you later. Love you."

"Love you too, Max."

Max hung up with his girl, not saying a word about what he knew.

Later that night, Mad Max's homies pulled up and parked down the road at the same spot where they had spotted Killah. After a couple hours, Ice and Kev spot Killah's Benz. This time he didn't park. Somebody else was driving his Benz and had dropped him off. Killah went in through the backdoor. Three hours later, his Benz pulled up and Killah comes out the backdoor. The same thing he did the night before. Then he got in the Benz and pulled off. Ice and Kev were ready to set it off after the sight they had just seen, but Mad Max said he had something in store for Killah.

Riding down 85, headed to Burlington, Dollar puffed on a blunt of gas as he took the exit. The hottest young rapper, Lil' Baby, blasting through his audio system. Dollar knew he was out of order. Blowing gas while transporting 20 keys. He was on his way to meet Hell Rell to drop him his re-up. Headed down Maple Ave, a blue and white police cruiser jumped in behind him. Dollar checked his rear-view mirror, and immediately recognized who the officer was. Blue lights flash, Dollar slowly pulls over, but doesn't put out his blunt. The officer gets out of the car, and walks to the driver side of Dollar's Ford F-350 and tapped on the window.

Dollar rolled the window down.

"Officer Thompson, how are you today? Did the wife like that trip to Jamaica?" Dollar asked.

"Yeah, she liked it. Hell Rell sent me to follow you to the spot." Officer Thompson replied.

"Where's Shawn?" Dollar asked.

"Rell sent him on another run."

"Okay, let's get with it then." Dollar replied.

"I'm right behind you. And Dollar, put that shit out. And Tell Quincy that my son has a birthday coming up."

"I gotcha." Dollar replied, then he rolled his window back up and pulled off. Officer Thompson following close behind.

Ten minutes later, Dollar pulls into a old abandoned warehouse. The windows were all boarded up and there were old car parts an motors laying around in different section of the property. Dollar pulled around back where Hell Rell was waiting with a couple of his goons. Rell signaled for him to pull into the garage. Dollar backed in, then hit the button on his dash board for the motor on his truck bed cover to lift up, exposing the keys for Rells inspection. After the truck bed was lifted up, Hell Rell and two of his goons began to unload the keys and stash them in the back of the warehouse.

"All done. Tell Q I'ma give him a call. Same time as always." Hell Rell said.

"I gotcha, bruh." Dollar replied while hitting the dash button lowering the truck bed cover and pulling off, headed for the interstate. For the past couple weeks, Dollar had been kicking it with this hot college chick that was a senior at A&T University. She lived in the Ville, which was where Dollar was headed. After 45 minutes on the road, he pulled his truck over to the nearest gas station to get gas. While pumping gas, a black Aspen pulls up to the pump that was in front of him. Whoever it was, had that Aspen on 26's. When the guy got out of the car, Dollar could have sworn that he recognized him.

"A yo, you ever been to Raleigh?"

"Yeah, I think I've seen you at Angel's crib."

"Word! I knew that I had seen you before. What's your name?"

"Bullet." The guy replied.

"Oh, I thought you were Remy."

"Nah, I heard he got caught up."

What dollar didn't know, was that Bullet was really Remy, but since Dollar didn't recognize him, Remy said his name was Bullet.

"So what's good?" Remy asked.

"I'm Gucci, bruh. In a rush, that's about it." Dollar replied.

"What's your digits, bruh, I'll hit you sometime?"

Dollar gives him the number not knowing what's up!

"You still good?" Remy asked.

"Yeah, hit me tonight around nine."

"That's what's up. I gotcha."

Dollar paid for his gas and pulls off. After about an hour or so, Dollar pulls up as Tasha's house. She runs out to greet him, jumping in his arms, happy to see him. They go inside, and enjoy the dinner that Tasha had prepared for him. Then they chill for the rest of the evening.

"Baby, I've been doing a lot of thinking. What do you think

about moving in together?" Dollar asked.

"Are you ready to be in a serious relationship?" Tasha asked.

"Yeah, I'm ready to settle down. What about you?"

"Sure."

Dollar was excited about Tasha's answer. After they finished dinner, they made love and enjoyed each others company. After a while, Dollar's phone had went dead, so he ran out to Walmart to buy a charger. After he gets it, he heads back to Tasha's house. When he pulled in her driveway, his phone rings.

"Hello." Dollar said.

"Yo, what up? This Bullet."

"You tell me."

"Bruh, I'm trying to get some work." Remy said.

"What happened with you seeing Angel?"

"Man, bruh went up on the price."

"What?!"

"Yeah, that's why I hollered at you."

How much he charging you?"

"Shit, $24,000 a brick."

"Damn. Look you can get them for $23,000 if you buy a few at a time. The numbers drop if I do this, you can't say a word to Angel or anybody else." Dollar replied.

"Say no more. Where can I get at you?"

"You gotta come to the boro. That's the only way I can serve you."

"Just say what time and I'll be there."

"Be in the boro tomorrow at 4pm. I'll meet you. Give me a call when you get there."

"I'll holler at you tomorrow."

"Yep, make sure you do that." Dollar said, then hung up and walked back in the house for another round of lovemaking with his girl, Tasha.

Three hours later

"Ring, ring, ring."

"Hello."

"Agent Brown, this is Chris. I hate to call you this late, but I have a buy set up for tomorrow in Greensboro, North Carolina."

"Chris, I want Angel or someone that's a part of Money Mafia." Agent Brown replied.

"He's one of them. I have it set up for tomorrow at 4pm. So I'll leave here tomorrow around 1pm."

"Chris, good job. I'll see you tomorrow." Agent Brown replied.

Raleigh, North Carolina

Killah's boys are sitting in a Caprice outside of the studio. Killah was inside working on producing his cousins album. Mad Max gets out tomorrow. Killah hasn't spoken to him since those keys came up missing and they never will. Now that Mad Max knows that Killah is fucking his girl, Sandra.

Quincy and Money Mafia are still making moves. Q has sent some things for the house to Toya through the UPS in a fake name. He was laying low, so Tech, Angel, Money, Dollar, and Hell Rell are handling the business. Money is up and retail was at an all time high. Which was good for business. A couple of days have gone by, Mad Max has just gotten released. As soon as he got home, he hit his homies up.

"Ring, ring."

"Hello."

"Ice, I need y'all to come through." Max replied.

"We're on our way, bruh." Ice replied.

A half hour later, Ice and Kev arrived at Mad Max's house. Ice gave him the pictures that he took of Killah sneaking around with his girl. When Max sees the pictures, he blanks out. Gathered his homies, and left, heading straight for his girls crib, not knowing that the FED's were following them. When they got to Max's girls house they went inside. Sandra was happy to see him, she ran towards him with open arms. Max smacks Sandra in the face, then accuses her of fucking Killah. Sandra cries, denying it. He then dragged her into their bedroom. Once in the bedroom, Max beats her some more. Ice and Kev, sitting in the living room, could hear her cries for help, but the sounds fell on deaf ears. When Max's anger had died down a little, he grabbed his baby and Sandra, and headed to the car.

During the whole drive, Sandra kept asking what he was talking about. Max didn't say a word; his anger was focused. He made a short stop to drop his baby off at his mother's crib. Then headed straight for Killah's house. On the way there, he got a call from one of his bros who informed Max that they were being followed by agents. Max, thinking on his toes like always, pulled into the pizza hut, and they all go inside. He pays the manager $1000 to go out the backdoor. They all go through the back and walked up the alley until they reached the bus stop. They take the bus to the car rental, rent three cars, and leave.

Mad Max calls Killah.

"Ring, ring, ring."

"Yo."

"What's up? This Max."

"What's good?"

"You home, I'm about to come through."

"Yeah, I'm here."

"See you in a few." Max replied then hung up.

When Killah placed his phone down, he picked it back up and called his homies. He had a feeling something was wrong, and he didn't want to get caught slipping.

15 minutes later, Mad Max and his crew pull up in front of Killah's house. Killah's homies pull up also and were all posted in the front yard. Max and his boys got out of their rentals and walked to the house with Sandra in tow.

Killah came outside and stood on the porch.

"Yo Max, why have you come to my home with all your homies and your girl?" Killah asked.

"I come to tell you, that what you did broke my heart, and

ended our friendship." Max replied.

"What are you talking about?"

"You fucking my girl, that's what I'm talking about." Max replied as he reached in his pocket to retrieve the pictures, then he threw them at Killah's face.

Killah looked at the pictures, but no words rolled off his tongue. He just stared at the pics. Max grew frustrated at Killah's facial expression, pulled his Glock, and pulled the trigger. Sparking a big war right on Killah's front yard.

"Bloc, bloc."

Killah is hit in the stomach. He turns to run, Max shoots him in the back. Bullets flying everywhere, Max is hit in the leg and the right side of his chest. Sandra gets caught up in the crossfire and takes a bullet to the head, falling limp on the ground. Max knew she was dead. It pained him because there was nothing he could do. He tried to get to his feet so he could help her, but her couldn't move. Seconds later, the shooting stops. Seven are wounded and one dead girl.

Calls go out over the police radios, the agents sitting across the street from the Pizza Hut couldn't believe what they are hearing. They run over to the Pizza Hut. Once inside, they realized that the criminals they were following were gone.

"Excuse me, I need to see the store manager." One of the agents said.

"I'm the store manager."

"I'm Agent Dawkins. About ten people came here about 20 minutes ago. Where did they go?"

"Sir, they said that some gang members were outside trying to hurt them. They asked if they could go out the backdoor."

"Fuck." Agent Dawkins said.

Within minutes, there are a dozen officers at Killah's house.

Channel 5 News

"I'm Rachel James, reporting live. There has been a deadly

shooting that left seven wounded and one dead. The incident took place at Keith Robinson's house. Who is a known leader of the Westend Crew. Sandra Rodgers, who was at the residence with her boyfriend, was shot and killed by a stray bullet in a massive shootout. There are no details about what took place. What we do know, is two of the victims are leaders of the Westend crew. I'm Rachel James, reporting live."

Quincy's Hotel Room
"Ring, ring, ring."
"Hello!"
"Yo, bruh, you watching the news?"
Tech, I'm watching Lebron & AD go at it with Kawhi and Paul George." Q replied.
"Well, turn the news on. Mad Max and Killah just went to war. Max's girl Sandra got killed."
"I'll call you back, lil' bruh." Q replied then hung up. Sitting down, Q turned to the news. A smile came across his face.

CHAPTER 15

Wake County Jail

Yo Dreko, you see this?"

"Yeah Tony, I'm looking at it now."

After watching the news, Tony saw that Sandra Rodgers has gotten killed. He knew her mother. She was an old girlfriend of his. He felt the pain of Sandra's loss. Everyday Tony wondered if he would make it home. He wondered if he would ever eat his wife's cooking again? Would he get to raise his two little girls? Deep down he felt like he wouldn't make it.

Since Tony has been locked up, he has met some good people. One of them was a guy named Carlos. Los was an old Indian that was kind of stuck in his ways. His wife had died since he had been in. Tony had seen him go through that pain, so they were kind of close. Whatever Tony needed, Los would make a way to get it. The brothers didn't know much about the legal system, so since Tony was new to this jail shit, he went through Los on that too. This experience has taught Tony a lot. The number one thing is to respect time, and to cherish your moments. Spend time with your family because we never know when it will be our last.

Police taskforce meeting

"I've talked with all the gun shot victims, no on is saying a word. I have no one to charge for Sandra Rodgers' murder." Detective Richmond said.

"I think you should hold on the warrants, so they can help us get Quincy." Agent Hurns replied.

"So do you think it was a drive-by?" Agent Pennell asked.

"Pennell, we've been partners for years. When have you ever seen a drive-by that ends like this? What we have is two leaders going to war. The reason is what we have to find out. When we do that, then we can figure out how to lock these hoodlums behind bars." Agent Hurns replied raising his voice to get his point across.

"Does anyone know where Quincy Capps is?" Pennell asked.

"Nah, no one has seen him or his family." Detective Richmond said.

"Okay, listen up. I'm going to speak with Sandra Rodgers' family, and let them know that we have a suspect in mind and we're exhausting our resources to locate him. I'm going to do this while you big boys work and find out who shot Sandra Rodgers and why."

"We'll work on it." Detective Richmond replied.

"Then what are you guys waiting for? It's time to punch the clock. Let's get to it." Agent Hurns commands as the rest of the agents and officers fell in line.

A week later

Mad Max was released from the hospital today, slightly still in pain. They all had told the police someone did a drive-by on them and killed his girl. Also, today is Sandra Rodgers' funeral. Killah is still hospitalized.

Quincy

"Yo, Tech, I'm going to Sandra's funeral. Are you going?" Q asked.

"I want to, but I didn't think it was safe."

"Well, we're going. I grew up with Sandra, plus, I got a lil' surprise for Max.

When Money Mafia arrive at Sandra's funeral, it had already started. So Q and his homies took their seats in the back. When the preacher began to speak, it hit deep.

"Today is not a sad day. Today is the homecoming of Sandra Rodgers. Praise be to God, Sandra was a daughter, a mother, and a productive citizen of our community. Gang wars of today have robbed us of our loved ones. The Killah's, the Quincy's, they are the reasons this type of violence happens. Is the beef that important that this woman had to die? That her daughter will never get to see her mother again? I tell you this. The Devil's happy. He's jumping for joy from all the souls he's receiving from all this violence."

The church choir sings, then people stand up and begin to view the body, paying their respects. Q gives Sandra's mother a hug.

"We grew up together, she was a good person." He said to her.

As the funeral is letting out, Max and his crew walk out behind Sandra's mom and the casket. When they get outside, Max see's Killahs' Benz and his 760BMW sitting straight across the street. The same ones that was at his girls' house. Max became furious, wondering who was driving Killah's car.

Just as his mind began to race, Quincy and a couple of his soldiers get out of the car. Max walks over to Q and asks.

"Where's Killah? And how y'all get his cars?" Max asked.

"Max, these are my cars. When I heard about y'all plotting on my house, I sent a White man to buy both of Killah's cars from him. I got a hoodie made to look like his also. I'm sorry about Sandra. I was hoping y'all killed each other."

"The last thing I do in this life will be watching your whole family beg for their life." Max replied then he walks off with tears in his eyes.

Everyone left the grave site, then Max called Killah's hospital room.

"Ring, ring, ring, ring."

"Hello."

"Yo, Killah, don't hang up, hear me out. I seen your cars at the funeral today. I thought your homies were plotting on me. Quincy got out of those cars, Killah. Quincy."

"Max, I sold those cars to an old, White, man."

"Yeah, I know. Quincy sent him to buy the cars from you." Mad Max replied.

"I had those pics you threw in my face blown up. And you can tell in the zoom that isn't me in those pictures. You seen the hoodie and the cars, but also in the pic's, you should've seen the red shoes on the guys' feet. You know I don't like red. They set us up, man, and they did it good."

"Killah, I know, bruh. That's why I'm calling you."

"I'm sorry about Sandra, and I ain't mad. I would've thought the same thing.

" I 'preciate it, bruh. How's your health?" Max answered.

"I'm a'ight. I'm moving around. I could be better."

"We all could. I'll hit you later. I have some business to handle."

"Make sure you do that Max. Call Loco and them to help you."

"I will." Max replied and hung up.

1:00PM Saturday

"Agent Brown, this is Chris. I'm on my way to Greensboro to pick up five kilo's from Dollar."

"I've already contacted the FBI there in Greensboro. I'll follow you. I'm leaving in five minutes. We will meet up at the Food Lion on highway 55. See you then." Agent Brown replied.

"Okay."

Within the next hours. Everyone was at Food Lion, and Agent Brown wired Chris up to make the buy from Donald 'Dollah' Newton, high level dealer of Money Mafia. 2:55pm they arrived in Greensboro and Chris called Dollar.

"Ring, ring, ring, ring."

"Hello." Dollar said.

"What's up? It's Chris. Remember, I saw you at the store and you tossed me your number."

"Yeah, I remember. Where are you?"

"I'm passing McDonalds, coming into Greensboro."

"Okay, meet me at the mall off highway 85."

"I'll be there in a few." He hung up.

On the way over there, Dollar called his girl, Tasha, and let her know that he'll pick her up in 30 minutes. Then he hangs up calls Chris back.

"Ring, ring, ring."

"Yo, Bullet, where you at?" Dollar asked.

"Over by Dillards."

"A, yo, come around to the JC Penny side, I'm parked in a blue, Honda Accord."

Chris pulls around the mall, and spots the blue Honda and pulled right up beside it. Chris gets out of his car and gets in the Honda.

"What up, bruh?" Chris said.

"Let's get this done." Dollar replied.

Chris tossed Dollar a small book bag. "All the money is there. $15,000."

"Yo, grab that bag in the backseat."

Chris grabbed the bag from out the backseat. Opened it up and tested the product.

"Damn, this shit strong."

"98% baby. Pure as you'll get."

"I feel it. Good looking on the work though. I'll hit you up in about a week."

As Chris was getting out of the car, Dollar noticed a White man talking into his shirt, and he became nervous. Thinking fast.

"Yo, Chris, here's my new number."

Not trying to bring attention to himself, Chris sat back down, When he was fully seated. Dollar stuck his 9mm in Chris' side and put his finger to his mouth. Dollar patted Chris down and felt the wire under his shirt. "Damn I can't believe I fell for this shit." Dollar thought to himself as he stared at Chris with his killer look in his eyes. He knew if he shot Chris, he would never get away. So he played it off, knowing the FEDs were close.

"Yo, since you paid cash. I'll front you five more. That a'ight with you?" Dollar said.

"Yeah, I can handle it." Chris replied nervous; afraid Dollar would pull t he trigger and end his life. It's a fact, he didn't want to go to prison. But going to prison sounded better than having a 9mm pointed in his face.

Dollar crunk up the old Honda, and pulled off having a normal conversation. His pistol still pointed at Chris' side, trying to buy himself some time. Dollar attempted to get on the highway. A patrol car sped behind him, and hit his blue lights. Dollar didn't stop. He put the pedal to the floor. Speeding up the exit, rounding the corner. He came face to face with two state trooper patrol cars. Slamming on the brakes, bringing the Honda to a rough halt, then his cell phone rings. Pistol still pointed at Chris, he answers.

"Hello."

"Hey baby, how much longer will it be?" Tasha asked.

"Baby, I caught a flat tire. Let me finish changing it, and I'll be right there." He said, then thought to himself, "Damn, if only I could get away." As he looks around, seeing he is surrounded.

"I love you, bae."

"I love you too, baby. What's wrong?"

"Nothing, I just wanted you to know is all." Dollar replied

then hung up.

Dollar turned back to Chris. "I should kill your punk ass." Dollar said and punched Chris in the face. "We trusted you."

Chris' phone rang.

"Hello." Chris answered.

"This is Agent Brown. Chris, put Dollar on the phone."

"It's for you." Chris said, as he passed his phone to Dollar with shaky hands.

Dollars' eyes got big as Chris handed him the phone.

"Hello." Dollar said.

"Don't do anything stupid. We know you have a gun and you just sold five kilos. Right now you're looking at twenty years. Let Chris go and help us get Quincy, and I'll make sure you don't do a day in jail."

"I ain't no snitch like this punk ass fool here."

"Listen to me, there is no easy way out of this, unless you help us. I know you love your girl and your kids. We're making a big scene. We need to end this before everybody knows. I give you my word we release you in two hours max if you co-operate with us."

Dollar dropped his head, knowing he was out of options. Then he folded.

"I need to pick up my girl from the beauty salon, and take her to school."

"We can handle that, as long as I can ride with you. Tell her we're looking at houses or something." Agent Brown replied.

"Alright." Dollar said, then he hung up and turned to Chris. "Get your bitch ass out of my car."

Chris slowly opened the passenger door, then sprinted towards the waiting officers. Agent Brown then began to wave his arms while he spoke through a bullhorn.

"Okay everybody. Let's clear out. I'm going with Dollar, he's in my care." Agent brown said, removing the bullhorn from his mouth. He leaned over to Detective Richmond. "Detective, take

Chris to headquarters, hold him there until I get there, then I'll release him myself after he's debriefed.

"I'm on it."

Raleigh's DEA Office

"Agent Pennell, I'm glad I could reach you. Chris was able to make the buy from Dollar. Now Dollar may be willing to make a buy from Quincy's number three, Gabriel Atkins, aka Angel." Agent Brown said.

"Good work, Agent Brown. Keep me informed on everything that takes place." Agent Pennell replied.

"Will do, sir. I'll call later." Agent Brown said then hung up.

"Everything is coming together nicely. It won't be long now." Agent Pennell thought to himself.

Wake County Jail

"Tony Blanco, you have a visit." The jailer announced over the intercom.

Tony got dressed and then walked around to the visitation room, where his wife, Jessica Blanco, was waiting.

"Hey, bae." Jessica said, excited to see her husband.

"Hey, baby. How are you doing?"

"I'm okay. Missing you. How 'bout yourself?"

"I'm fine."

"Have you heard from your lawyer?"

"Yeah, bae, but he ain't talking about shit."

"Today I got a call from the lady that bought the building from us. She told me while she was cleaning your closet, you had a private basement there. She said she went down there and found your security system and was wondering what you wanted to do with it."

"Baby, go get the recording tapes from her. It should have recorded the shooting. I'll call you later. I love you." Tony replied while he stood up to leave.

"I love you too, Tony. But why are we rushing when I haven't seen you in weeks?" Jessica said.

"Because this is my freedom that we are talking about. I need for you to go straight there and get that for me, please."

"Okay, baby. I'm going now. I'll talk to you later. Call me tonight." Jessica said.

"A'ight, I will." Tony replied, then he turned to leave. When he got back in the block, he pulled up on Dreko.

"Yo, Dre. Let me holler at you for a sec."

"What's good Tony?"

"I think I'm on to something, lil' bruh."

"Is it good?"

"I hope so." Tony replied.

"I spoke to my lawyer today, and they're coming at me with a plea, 13 to 18 for both bodies."

Dreko said, "That's a fast plea deal. It sounds good for two bodies. You should take it and run."

"You think so?"

"Yeah, lil' bruh. One week is a long time in prison, Dre. Take the plea, go to prison, get you a education. Have you heard from Quincy?" Tony asked.

"Not since the last call I told you about."

"I heard Q got them Westend boys to go at each other. I heard it was a hell of a plan, except for Sandra getting killed."

"Yeah, Q was fucked up about that. But now he has to be real careful, because Mad Max and Killah won't stop until he's dead."

CHAPTER 16

Quincy's House

"Ring, ring."

"Hello." Q answered.

"What's good Q? This is Mike. How you holding up?"

"I'm here, bruh. That's all I can say."

"Well, I'm hearing your name all the way out here. You're getting sloppy, Q. When you have problems, you get rid of them, you don't let them linger."

"Listen, Mike, they were plotting on me."

"That comes with the game. Somebody's always out to get you."

"I know that, bruh."

"You acting like you don't, though."

"I'ma tighten everything up."

"I hear you have a guy on your team that just got jammed up by the feds."

"Nah, bruh. I would know that." Q replied.

"Not when you're living two lives; you can't focus like that.

The drop is on it's way. After this, we're finished until shit cools off." Mike replied then hung up.

Quincy hangs up the phone, pissed off about the way Mike had just checked him. "Fuck him. When that work drops, I'm keeping everything." Q thought to himself while he punched in numbers on his phone.

Dialing Tech.

"Ring, ring."

"Yo."

"Tech, the shipment is on it's way. 400 blocks this trip."

"Say no more, bruh." Tech hung up.

Quincy calls Mike back.

"Ring, ring."

"Talk." Mike said into the receiver.

"My people are ready."

"Okay, like I told you before, it's on the way. I'll see you in two hours tops. Oh yeah. Some major dealer got busted today in Greensboro. They're not releasing any news, so y'all be careful."

"I gotcha fam. See you in a few one." Q replied.

Q hung up with his plug and called his bro's back and decided to get breakfast at Shoney's. Everybody met up at Angels crib and left driving the cars that Q had purchased from Killah through a third party. Once they are settled and breakfast was served, he let them know that a major bust went down in Greensboro. Angel calls Dollar to see if he's good.

Cell phone ringing.

"Hello."

"Yo, Dollar, you good? Heard something big went down your way." Angel said.

"I'm good, taking Tasha to school. Why, what's up?"

"Nah, I heard someone got hit down your way."

"I got like two calls saying some Mexicans got fucked up, but that's it."

"Ask Tasha, does she have a friend I can take out?"

"Yeah, her sister." Dollar replied.

"No, not my sister. So you can tell him to get that out of his mind. My sister doesn't have time for dogs." Tasha fired back.

"Bruh, tell Tasha I'll stay on the chain." They all laugh.

"Angel, I'll holler at you later."

"A'ight, then be safe homie." Angel replied then hung up.

"Yo, Q. Dollar said some Mexicans down his way got fucked up from what he heard."

"Where is he at?" Q asked.

"Taking his girl to school."

"After we leave here, we're selling these hot ass cars. I don't even know why we are still driving them, anyway."

"Q, it ain't like we drive a lot. This is the first time since the funeral."

"Yeah, but we should be pushing them to handle business. Not going out to eat breakfast."

"You right, bruh." Angel agreed, then they sat and talked for a while. After breakfast, Q had made up his mind. Fuck Mike. He was ready to war if he had to, but by no means was he paying for that work. Not knowing too much about Mike, Q had to tread lightly.

"Yo, Tech. You and Angel ride with me. Money and Flip, we'll follow you to Greensboro so we can sell these cars, We'll get a rental and come back.

They pull off, Money driving the Benz. What they didn't know was, Mad Max was following them in a black van. Quincy got in the 760, but realized he left his keys on the table. He runs back inside Shoney's to grab them. When he came back out, he saw the black van pull behind Money. He recognized Max as the driver. Immediately, Q pulls out his phone to call Money, but before he could pick up, the vans side door open. Money pulls off from the stop sign. The black van sped up beside Money, and then shot rang out like it was Desert Storm. Q watched helpless as the Benz Money was driving was rippled with bullets. Q tried to run towards the van. Angel started spraying his 40cal, his shots hitting nothing but air.

After the deed was done, Mad Max pulls off. Minutes later, the police came from everywhere. Q and Angel race up the highway, fearing the outcome. When they get out the car, it's a mess. Flip is dead, and Money is coughing up blood. The way it's looking, he won't make it. Money was shot five times. Wanting to come to Money's aid, Q pauses in mid stride as more police arrive on the scene.

He and Angel watched as the medics began to remove Flip and Money's bodies from the car. When they left the scene, they went straight to Angels' house. Two of their friends just died. The pain was devastating. They both rolled up a couple blunts and blew smoke the rest of the day until it was dark outside.

"We have to hit them right now." Tech says.

"They are waiting on us. I know how Max thinks." Angel replied, shaking his head. "Let's hit him Sunday at church, when it lets out." Angel said.

"I got this Q. Go home to your family. We'll move the work, and bring this beef to an end." Tech said.

"Lil' brother trying to be the big brother, huh?" Q asked placing his right hand on his brothers' shoulder. "I'll neva' leave your side, bruh."

"I know Q, but I want you to be with your wife and kids. I'll call you when it's done."

"Okay, lil' bruh. I'll take a cab to the airport. Be safe, y'all call me asap."

Once at the airport, Quincy calls Toya to let her know that he was on the way home. To Q's surprise, Toya had already known what had happened back in Raleigh with Money and Flip. Her mother had given her the news. Q's plane didn't leave for another three hours, so he walked in the RDU lobby, sat down and watched the news.

Channel 5 News

"Good afternoon, I'm Louise Westbrook. Today there was a deadly shooting on the beltway and two were found dead inside a Grey Benz. Dexter Berry and Felix Triendad. All rumor to be members of Money Mafia, a drug ring. Witnesses say a black van pulled up beside the Benz and let off 30 shots. Another sad day here in Raleigh, North Carolina."

Wake County Jail

Dreko sits and breaks down as he watches the news. Money was his best friend. All Tony could do was shake his head in disbelief at all this bloodshed.

Getting up and leaving the airport lobby, Q walks around emotional, trying to hold it together. He entered the Subway, sat down, and ordered a salad because he wasn't really hungry. Wiping away his tears. He began to reflect back over the past year, and somehow he went from dealing with three masked men to getting truckloads of coke. He was making millions, but now it's death on top of death and the toll was still rising. "Ever since I got this connect, my life has gotten worse." Q thought to himself. More money, more problems. He had thought this would be the life he wanted to live. Money, power, respect. Now he was thinking about getting out before he gets his family killed. He had thought that the money would make him and his family and friends lives better. How wrong was he?"

Last week, he sold all his businesses and deposited the revenue in his wife Toya's off shore bank accounts. 30 million; that was a hell of a lot of bread for someone with a background like Quincy's. He had about six million in cash that he could touch real quick for drugs or other businesses. Snapping out of his train of thought after hearing his flight called, he got up and headed to the tunnel.

2 Hours later, Florida International Airport, Orlando Florida

When Q's plane landed, Toya was there to pick him up.

Rushing to him with open arms. Love and joy could be seen in her eyes as her and Q shared a long passionate embrace.

On the way to the house, Toya lets Q know that she took out a life insurance policy on him and begins to cry.

"Baby, It's okay. You didn't have to do that. I have 30 million in a off shore account in your name, and ten more put up."

Toya's eyes lit up. "What did you say?"

"I'm saying, we good, baby. You can cancel the claim."

"The claim is for the kids, not me. I knew you had money put up. I didn't know that much, though. I knew you were selling drugs seven months ago. Angel's wife found a duffel-bag of money in their home while she was cleaning. She followed him to meet you with it. I was already thinking it, but that put the icing on the cake."

"Toya, baby. I'm finished. This whole war started when Wicked got killed, and it got worse over time."

While they were riding, Q could tell that it was time for him to get out of the game. An unhappy wife makes an unhappy man. After a 20 minute drive, they pulled up to a gated community, went through the gate, and drove for another two minutes. Then Toya pulls into the driveway of this beautiful seven bedroom, four bath, four car garage, a pool, a basketball court, and a movie theatre, you name it, the house had it.

"This is amazing, bae."

"You like it?"

"Of course." Q replied as he stepped out of the car and both walked inside.

When they got inside the house, the first thing Toya did was take Q's hand and lead him to his new office. She hits a button and the wall slides back. It was a hidden room and there was monitors for every room in the house.

"This is the security room that asked to set up."

"This is nice, bae. I really like this." Q replied as he played around with the controls; zooming in and out. Then she leads him downstairs to the basement, where there's an underground tunnel that leads to a storage house out back.

"The real estate agent told me this house was built by a billionaire drug lord from Columbia who died a few years ago." Toya said.

"Bae, I really like this house. You did a good job in picking it out." Q replied as he stepped closer to his wife and brushed her hair aside and kissed her on the forehead.

"I'm glad you like it, honey."

"The only thing that's left to do now is for us to break the house in." Q said as he began to kiss Toya's neck. "Baby, I gotta pick the girls up."

"We have time." Q said, unbuckling Toya's jeans. Sticking his hands inside her pants, fingering her love box.

"Baby, aaah, what are you doing to me?"

"What your husband is supposed to do." Q replied, peeling his wife's jeans off until they were around her ankles. Then he slowly pulled her panties down, squatted on his knees, bent his wife over, and ate his wife out from behind.

"Ooooh baby, that feels so good." Toya replied poking her butt farther out giving her husband total access to her love box.

Q released the grip he had on Toya's ass and stood up. He pulled out his wood and entered his wife from behind, feeding her every inch, bringing her to climax. Toya glazed his penis and stained the couch from her wetness. Several more pumps, Q was filling Toya with his seed.

"Aaah baby, I missed that pussy."

"I missed that Dick." Toya replied as she turned around and kissed Q and stroked his penis until it went limp in her hand. "Just a quickie baby?" Toya asked.

"You said you had to pick the kids up."

"I do. 45 minutes from now." Toya said, dropping to her knees as she inserted Q's penis in her mouth. She sucked him with perfection, causing his manhood to stand to attention. After a few minutes, Q released his seed in her mouth and his wife swallowed every drop of him.

After their little sex escapade, both being satisfied, they continued to look over the rest of the house. Quincy, being tired from a long stressful day, went to sleep after he viewed his new house.

CHAPTER 17

Next Day, Duke Medical Center

Today, Killah got out of the hospital. His wife and kids had picked him up. Since being shot, he looked at life differently. He realized that his family was the most important thing to him. When he got home, he called Mad Max and told him to have everybody at his house at 9:00pm. Once everything was put into motion, Killah played with his kids and talked with his wife. She was a faithful woman that has loved him since the 8th grade. Her name is Michelle.

"Bae, while I was hospitalized, I did some thinking. I'm through with the game. You and the kids mean the world to me. I wouldn't know what to do if I lost y'all. If it's okay. I would like to move away from here."

"Where do you wanna move to?"

"Anywhere, you pick the place."

"Are you sure?"

"Yeah, I'm sure, baby."

"Well, if you really wanna move, I've seen some nice places

out in Utah. I think it's nice and laid back. Michelle replied.

"You find the place that you are happy with, and I'm coming. I called a meeting with Max, they'll be here tonight around nine. Why don't you pack up a few things, and we'll catch a plane tomorrow to Utah and find us a home."

"Okay, since you're having this meeting, me and the kids will go to my mothers' house. I guess we'll leave around eight. Call me when they leave."

"That works for me." Killah replied as he got up and ordered pizza for his crew.

9:00pm rolls around.

Killah has a table set up in his house with pizza and plenty of Bud Light. His crew arrived car after car. Before you knew it, there was about 30 dudes in his house. Killah stepped up and faced his team.

"I called this meeting today, because I love y'all. I've grown up wit y'all, came up in the streets with y'all. I have one question to ask and that is will y'all let me move out West with my wife and kids? Before you say a word, I'm forever Westend. That's why I'm asking for permission to leave." Killah said.

"Bruh, I'm not voting yes." Mad Max said.

"Killah, you're all I got. How are you just going to leave us? You've been by my side since I was 15 years old. I can't vote yes to that either." T.Loc said.

Tears flowed down Killahs face, then he walked over to the bar, and grabbed a duffel bag and brought it back and tossed it on the floor.

"It's $200,000 in cash, and a map that will take you to 20 kilos. My plane leaves tomorrow, all who support my decision, show me your hands."

Slowly hands go up. Mad Max was the last to raise his, then walked over, and dapped Killah up.

"I can't say I'm your brother if I don't want to see you do good." Max said, then the rest was history.

They all drank and had a good time. After a few hours, everyone began to leave.

"I guess this was your going away party." Mad Max said, "So roll out, and never look back."

Q, finally on the offensive, sent Angel to put Killah in a pine box. Angel patiently waited in the woods, observing the Westend meeting, as Killah and Mad Max partied. Angel watched as every Westend members left Killah's house. He knew Killah was alone and now was the time to strike. Going on the move, Angel emerged from out of the woods, headed towards the house. He saw as Killah closed the side door. He reached in his pocket and dialed some numbers on his phone. Angel posted, hidden behind the trash next to the back door.

After all of his Westend members left, Killah called his wife Michelle.

"Hello."

"Michelle, what time are we leaving tomorrow?

"The plane leaves at four in the morning. I'm on my way back now so I can finish packing. How did it go with the fellows?" Michelle asked.

"It went great, baby. They understood where I was coming from and they gave me their blessings."

"That's good, baby. I'm on the way home. I'll be there in a few."

"Okay love." Killah replied then hung up.

When he got off the phone, Killah walked out the front door to get something out of his car. He heard his dogs barking around the back. As soon as he turned to head towards the backyard, he bumped right into Angel's 40cal.

"Don't move, motherfucka. Get on your knees." Angel said.

"I'll die on my own two feet like a man. Not on my knees like a bitch."

Angel shoots Killah in the knee-cap. Then pulls out his phone and calls Q.

"Yo." Q said.

"I got him."

"Good. Finish him."

Just when Angel walks closer to Killah, and kicks him in his face, he falls on his back. Angel points his 40cal down at Killah. Knowing it was over, Killah closed his eyes. Seconds from pulling the trigger, Killah's wife and kids pull up. Jumping out of the car screaming.

"Please don't kill my husband." Killah's wife hollered while their kids jumped on top of their father to protect him.

"It's your call, Q." Angel asked, still on the phone with his leader.

"Not in front of his kids." Q replied.

"I gotcha." Angel hung up, then patted Killah down to make sure he wasn't armed. Then he took off running, disappearing back into the woods from which he came.

This would be the last night anyone has heard from Killah.

Two days later, Flip and Money had a double funeral. During the service, Q kept imagining that that was him laying in that casket. He never thought it would get this bad. He was tired of losing friends. He couldn't face Money and Flips' parents, so him and Tech left.

A week has went by, Q still hasn't spoken to Mike. Today is the day that he usually makes his money drop. "Fuck him, I'm keeping the money." Q thought to himself. The FEDs were on his trail. They have been hitting all of his spots. A few of his bros got knocked, but with only small shit, mostly weed. So it was nothing for Tech to post their bonds. He had 200 keys left, then he was gone. But he knew he had to deal with Mad Max before he left.

Meeting between Agent Pennell and Agent Brown

"Agent Pennell, the buy went well. We'll have an indictment for Gabriel Atkins soon." Agent Brown said.

"What did Dollar say about Quincy Capps?" Agent Pennell asked.

"I asked, but no one has seen him with any drugs. He lets his brother, Tech, and Angel handle everything. Gabriel is the key to getting Quincy Capps."

"Gabriel Atkins is a mid level dealer. I don't think he will roll over on Quincy. We have to focus on Quincy. He's the big fish." Agent Pennell replied.

"Pennell, Chris informed me that Money Mafia has agents on the payroll."

"Not in this life time. You're giving them too much credit."

"No, I'm just being careful. I want them all behind bars."

"Agent Brown, we want something."

"Okay, well, let's keep this between me and you. I'll call you again in a week or so."

"Alright. Agent Brown?"

"Yeah."

"Good job."

"Thanks, I'll be in touch." Agent Brown replied then hung up.

Federal Building in Greenboro, North Carolina
The agents on Q's tail went to the Grand Jury to get warrants on Gabriel 'Angel' Atkins. If only Angel knew that Dollar has given him up. Dollar and Chris aka Remy charges were dismissed due to both being willing to help bring down Money Mafia.

Back at Wake County Jail
"Tony, I just spoke with my lawyer. I'm taking the plea. It's been dropped down to 10-12½ **years.**" Dreko said.

"That's good, Dre. I'm happy for you." Tony Blanco replied.

"I'm probably gone tomorrow. I'm going to miss you, bruh. You've been a blessing to me. I see things different now. The only thing that bothers me is I won't be able to be there for Q. I have a feeling he's going to die."

"It's Angel. He's talking too much."

"Why you say, Tony?"

"Angel told someone that he thinks Quincy beat his connect out of 8 million and I heard that it's the Columbian Cartel. If Q did what Angel is running his mouth about, the Columbians will kill Quincy and his family for sure."

Dreko's eyes began to water off of the love he has for Q.

"Maybe he'll be alright." Tony said as the Intercom came on.

"Tony Blanco, you have a visit." The correctional officer announced.

Tony went upstairs to his cell to brush his teeth and comb his hair. Then he walks out the block to the visitation room. He sees his wife and his attorney.

"We have good news, take a seat." Tony's attorney, Mr. Holt, said.

"Your security cameras recorded the shooting. We can tell by the video that the agents never identified themselves. You need to thank Mrs. Smith for keeping those tapes and giving them to your wife. I've already given one copy to the Federal Prosecutors' office."

"So, Mr. Holt, do you think they will dismiss the charges?" Tony asked.

"I hope so with this evidence. It will be hard to convict you from looking at these tapes. Just sit tight, we should hear something maybe sometime next week. They only gave us 15 minutes, so we're gonna get up outta here."

"Okay, thanks Mr. Holt, and thank you too, baby."

"Tony, I love you." Jessica said as she got up and hugged her husband. "We'll beat this together, baby." Jessica smiled, kissed her man, and walked out of the visitation room, lawyer in tow.

Tony Blanco got up and returned to his cell block. Happy that he would soon be free.

Sunday Morning

Church is letting out. Mad Max walks to his car, and unlocks the doors. A woman walks up, but really it's Angel dressed like one.

"Excuse me, can I get a ride home?" The disguised Angel asked.

"I'm in a hurry. Here's $10, catch a bus. Now get outta my face. I got shit to do." Mad Max said, not paying attention to the face of the woman; thinking she was just a crackhead or a hooker. Angel takes a step back, takes his shades off, pulls a Mac-10 from out of the pocketbook he was carrying.

"Yo, Max!" Angel hollered.

When Max looked up, it looked like he saw a ghost. Angel let him have it. "Blatt, blatt, blatt." Emptying the 32 round clip, leaving Mad Max looking like patty meat. Blood all over the inside of the car. Angel pulled off his wig and took off, jumping in a silver Cadillac. Angel could see the whole church running outside through the rearview mirror to see what was left of the infamous Mad Max. As the Cadillac bent the corner, Angel pulls out his phone and calls Q.

"Ring, ring."

"Hello." Q answered.

"Yo, bruh, the war is over."

"What?"

"Yeah, it's taken care of." Angel replied then hung up.

Q figured Angel had killed Max, but he wasn't sure. Later that same day, Angel told him play by play how it went down.

Witness' say it was a woman that killed Max, but T. Loc wasn't buying it.

When everybody got together, Q told his brother, Tech, to lay low for a while because shit was hot. Tech loving money so much, he went to sell three keys to Champ over on the Southside. T. Loc had made Champ call Tech at gun point.

It was cold outside, so Tech decided to grab his jacket from the closet. While he was looking, he notices a bullet proof vest laying on the floor that Quincy had bought as a birthday gift last year. Tech snatched it up and put it on then left. When Tech got there he saw Champ at the door, so he grabbed his gun because Champ usually comes outside. Now all of a sudden, today he waving for him to come in. Tech gets inside. The door closes behind him. Instantly he knows that he is being robbed. But what he doesn't know, is that it's for his life.

"He forced me to call you, bruh." Champ said.

"Yo, you can live if you call Quincy." T. Loc said.

"Fuck you." Tech said as he pulled out his nine. T. Loc put three in his chest. The impact from the bullets caused Tech to fall through the glass table, blood flies everywhere from the cuts he received; Tech was bleeding so badly. T. Loc knew for a fact he was dead, so he grabbed his drugs and rolled out. Champ left, scared to death. Tech waits a few minutes, then gets up, bleeding like a pig, and goes out the back door into the woods and calls Quincy.

"Ring, ring, ring."

"Yeah." Q answered.

"Yo, bruh, come get me."

"What's going on?"

"T. Loc made Champ call me at gun point. The vest you got me for my birthday saved my life, bruh."

"Say no more. I'm on the way."

Quincy rushes to pick his only brother up. When he grabbed him, Tech looks like he's ready to kill something. "Bruh, I have to handle this."

"Already, bruh."

Q drove straight to T. Loc's crib. Before Tech got out of the car, he told his brother that he loved him and had to take care of himself, just in case he didn't make it back. They hug, then Tech gets out of the car. Q pulls off. Tech goes around checking T. Loc's windows. Lucky for him, the bathroom window was open.

Tech prayed T. Loc's girl didn't come home first, then he would have to do them both. Tech climbed through the window. Once inside, he searched the house. When he is satisfied, he took a seat in the living room, still bleeding, gun in hand. He waited for T. Loc to arrive. Growing restless, Tech got up and started looking for something to start a fire with. He went to the kitchen and looked under the sink.

Bingo! Lighter fluid. A smile slid across Tech's face as he grabbed the bottle of lighter fluid and returned back to the living room and continued to wait. He knew that he would catch T. Loc off guard, because T. Loc thought nobody knew where he stayed. What he didn't know, was Quincy had a girl at the DMV run T. Loc girls' name a while back, and he had gotten all the information that Money Mafia needed to pull the plug on T. Loc of needed.

A couple hours go by, headlights flash through the crib; it's T. Loc's car. Then the house phone rings. The answering machine came on; it's his girl.

"I've called your phone several times. When you get home, call me." T. Loc's girl said, then there was a beep and the machine went dead.

Tech cracked the blinds so he could watch T. Loc's movements. Before coming in, he stopped and talked to his neighbor for probably 20 minutes. Afterwards, he's on his way in, then another car pulls up. It was T. Loc's girl. Tech continued to watch as he walked to his girls' car and leaned in the window. They shared a brief conversation then she pulled off. "It's game time." Tech thought to himself as he watched T. Loc walk to the front door. The knob turns, he hits the lights, and sees a ghost.

"Yeah, what's up Loc?" Tech screamed as he pistol whipped him. T. Loc falls to the floor. Tech stands over him, pulls his shirt up and pointed at his vest.

"Yeah, saved my life." Then he reached down and snatched him off the ground and pushed him back on the couch. "Have a seat, and don't reach. I know your gun is on your left side." Tech said and then asked. "Why did you come for me?"

"I wanted your brother, he had my homie hit." T. Loc replied.

"Y'all hit our homies first."

"Well, it is what it is then. Go ahead, pull the trigger. I'm Westend for life."

Tech raised his 9mm. "Bloc, bloc." Fired two shots, ending T. Loc's life. As T. Loc lay dead, stretched out on the couch, Tech set the house on fire and walks out.

CHAPTER 18

When T. Loc's girl returned, she couldn't believe her eyes. Police were everywhere, along with fire fighters shooting water into her home. When the fire is out, police and detectives go inside and find T. Loc's body.

"Louise Westbrook, reporting live. Tonight, Tony Love was just found dead. Burned in his home. Police are saying that he was murdered. Tony Love, better known as T. Loc, is also one of the Westend crew leaders. I'm Louise Westbrook, reporting live, channel 5 news."

The next morning, the FEDs are all over Raleigh looking for Angel. Q knows they don't have shit on him, until his phone rings. He looks at the caller ID and sees it's his FBI connect.

"Hello."

"What's up?"

"The FED's are looking for Angel for selling to your Dollar. He set Angel up. I hear Angel sold him over 20 kilos."

"Shit, what they say about me?"

"They know you're the boss, and Tech and Angel are your

lieutenants. They couldn't give a statement about you selling drugs. They need Angel to snitch on you to make their case. There's enough evidence to pick Tech up on marijuana charges, but it only carries up to three years. So they won't waste their time on that."

"Thanks, Melvin, I owe you big time."

"The wife wants a trip to Europe this summer."

"Consider it done."

"Thanks, Q."

"No problem." Q replied then hung up and called Tech.

"Hello." Tech answered.

"Yo, bruh, where you at?" Q asked.

"The stash spot. I just took care of T. Loc."

"I'm on my way." Q replied, then hung up. He gathered his things and shot out the back door headed for the woods. He hops on his four wheeler and hits the path, knowing the FED's are watching his house. He pulls up to an old, White lady's house, hops off his four wheeler and knocks on the backdoor. She opens it quickly, knowing it's Q.

"Hey Q, it's been months since I've seen you."

"Yes, ma'am, how are you?"

"Baby, I'm okay. So what brings you here?"

"Been going through a lot these last couple days."

"So this will be your last visit, huh?"

"Yes ma'am."

"I knew this day was coming. Every time you walked through them woods bringing money. I knew one day you would leave forever. Before you leave, grab the keys off the rack by the door. I bought you a nice van and tinted the windows. I thought you would need it one day. See, White people can be gangsters too." She laughs.

Q couldn't do anything but smile.

"I have seven million dollars here."

"Mrs. Summers, you can keep a mill."

Baby, my husband sold heroin for 20 years before he was murdered. I'm very rich. You take that money and you go far, and don't you come back here. You hear me son?"

"Yes, Mrs. Summers. I'll make sure I send you a post card from time to time. Birthdays, holidays, check the mail box. "

"Okay, I will baby. Follow me so I can take you to your money." Mrs. Summers replied as she walked upstairs with Q on her heels.

When they got upstairs, Mrs. Summers went to her daughters old room and opened the closet door.

"The money is in here." Mrs. Summers said, pointing at the small door inside the closet behind all the old clothes she had stored inside. Q walked inside the closet and opened the trap door, and removed two duffel bags. He threw one over his back and dragged the other one down the stairs. He went to the garage and loaded the van. He hugged Mrs. Summers, kissed her goodbye, and then got in the van and left. Headed to the stash house in Spring Lake to meet Tech. It took 45 minutes to get there.

Hour and a half later

Once Q arrived at the stash house, Tech gives Q the run down about T. Loc, then Q fills him in on what their FBI connect Melvin had said.

"We gotta kill Angel, he's the only one that can connect us."

"But that's the Bro, big bruh." Tech replied as he put his head down. Digging in his pocket to grab his lighter, so he could light his blunt. He heard Q's phone ring.

"Yeah." Q said answering his phone.

"Don't play me Q. I want my four million tomorrow or you're a dead man." The voice on the other end said. Then click the phone hung up.

"Mother fucker." Q said.

"Who was that, bruh?" Tech asked.

"That was Mike."

"What he want?"

"I owe him 4 million."

"Pay him that, bruh."

"It's over, we're outta here. Did you send your family off yet?" Q asked.

"Yeah, I gave her all my money and sent them to Portland. She's got the ID's too."

"How many keys are left?"

"Angel has forty that he has put up back at his brother's house."

"Okay, he can keep that. It's seven million right here, you take three."

"Are you sure?"

"Tech, take the money." Q said pulling stacks of money out of one of the duffel bags he got from Mrs. Summers.

When the money was finally split up, they loaded the van, and went back to Raleigh to see Money's son. Q parked the van around the corner from Money's house.

"Tech, stay in the van. I'll be right back." Q says as he takes $250,000 and stuffed it in a small book bag and hops out of the van. Headed to Money's house. He knocked on the door and Money's girl Amanda answered.

"Hey Quincy, how are you?"

"I'm fine."

"Come on in."

"How are you holding up?"

"It's a struggle. Money is low, but we're making it." Amanda replied.

"I brought y'all something." Q said as he took the book bag off and handed it to her. Amanda opened it up and her eyes lit up and she began to cry.

"Q, thank you so much. Money left money at his mom's house, but they took it all for themselves."

"Don't worry 'bout that, there's $250,000 in that bag. Take the money and move away, that's all I ask."

"Well, we'll do just that. Carter deserves a new start."

"I have to run, don't worry. I'll find y'all, okay?"

"Are you sure about this?"

"Yes Amanda, I'm sure." Q replied then little Carter comes running up and hugs his leg.

"Uncle Quincy, will I ever see you again?" Lil' carter asked.

"Of course you will. I love you man." Q answered, picking Carter up and shooting him in the air.

"I love you too, Uncle Quincy." Carter said when Q put him down.

"Well, I gotta go, bruh." Q said then Tech pulls off, headed for the highway. When they pass the Shell Station, they notice that the FED's have Angel's car surrounded. So they stop and pull across the street to see what's up.

Angel gets out of the car with his hands up. When he does look, he looks straight at Q and Tech. He smiles then tears roll down his face. "That's my man." Q thought to himself.

Q sees Angel's lips move. He could tell he was saying Money Mafia, but his eyes told Q that he was thinking the wrong thing. By this time one of the federal agents grabs his left arm and brings it behind his back. Angel's gun falls from his right coat sleeve that he had hidden from the agents. Q tries to scream "no" but it's too late. Angel turns around and shoots the agent in the neck. Instantly killing him. The agents unload on Angel until he drops to the ground dead. Looking on, Q and Tech are in disbelief, not believing what just took place. Tech cranks up the van and pulls off headed for the highway. On their way to Winston Salem to one of their many condos.

When they got there, they just sit and get their thoughts together. Tech turns the TV on.

Breaking News

Today the Federal Prosecutors Office have dropped all charges against Tony Blanco for the murders of two FBI agents. There will be no further charges filed.

"Tech, oh shit. You hear that? Tony beat that shit, man I can't believe it. I know he's happy." Q said.

"Good for him, bruh. You know, we better get going." Tech said as he packed up a few things and headed out the door. Q did the same.

"I'll see you on Christmas. I love you, bruh."

"Love you too." Tech replied as he hugged his brother. "Be safe Q."

"You too."

Tech leaves in an all black Yukon heading West. Q, he's headed to Orlando, Florida to be with his wife and kids. He made it home in ten hours. Once he got inside, he took a shower and laid down with his wife. Toya stirs as Q gets in the bed, she opens her eyes and smiles.

"Baby, I'm glad you're home."

"I'm glad to be here, baby."

CHAPTER 19

One year later

Quincy was enjoying his new life. Since leaving North Carolina and coming to Florida, he bought into one of the Hampton Inns by Disney World. It sells out every night. His familys' last name has been changed to McNairs. Him and Tech speak a lot and is doing good down in Portland. He owns three McDonalds. The brothers visit each other every six months and Q also makes sure that all his homies family's get $25,000 a piece every Christmas. It's been only one year but that was the plan that had been set in motion. Q put up a mill for Dreko for when he gets out. Even though he was up, he was determined not to forget about his bro's.

Atlanta, Georgia

Fab's brother, Power, was just released today. The supreme court overturned his case. Fresh out, with revenge on his mind for his brothers murders. He boarded the first Greyhound bus headed for North Carolina to hunt Killah down and bring his life to an end.

3 months later, back in North Carolina
"Breaking News. Good morning, I'm Tamara Lane, reporting live from Raleigh, North Carolina. I'm here at 112 Spruce Street. The residence of Sarah Capps, 86 years old. She was found dead by her grand-daughter Janell Capps. The details of the murder have not been released yet."

Janell was on the verge of breaking down so she called her brother.

"Ring, ring."

"Hello." Toya answered.

"Toya, is Quincy there?"

"Yes, what's wrong Nelly?

"Someone broke in and killed grandma today."

"Oh Lord, no. Let me go get him. Quincy, baby, come get the phone." Toya hollered.

"Who is it?" Q asked as he walked over.

"It's Nelly."

"Why you looking like that? Hello." Q said when Toya handed him the phone.

"Quincy, grandma is dead." Nelly said.

"What? How?"

"Someone broke in and killed her, Q." Janell replied pushing words through tears.

"Sis, I'm on my way home, okay?"

"Okay." Janell replied then hung up.

DEA Office, Raleigh, North Carolina
"Agent Hurns, did you hear what happened?" Agent Pennell said.

"No, I didn't."

"Quincy Capps' grandmother, Sarah Capps, was found murdered this morning. She was badly beaten and they cut her fingers off."

"That's bad, Pennell, sounds like something personal. I'm sure Quincy will come back home to deal with this himself."

"Yo, Power, let's ride to the Westend and let them know we mean business." Powers partner, Nino Cracks, replied as they drove to Killah's hood.

"A, yo, Nino, pull over there where them niggas standing."

Nino bared the Charger off to the side of the street. Power rolled down the window.

"What's up? I'm lost, how do I get to Westend housing?" Power asked.

"Who is you?" One of the guys asked.

"Who is you?" Power shot back.

"I'm Westend, that's who." The guy said as soon as he finished his sentence. Power leans out the window with his Desert Eagle. "Bloc, bloc, bloc, bloc." Squeezing off round after round. When Nino Cracks hits the gas, they sped off. Three lay dead, later they ditch the old Charger.

"I'm killing whoever until I find my brothers' murderer." Power said.

The next day, Quincy arrives at his sister Janell's house.

"What's up, sis? How you doing?"

"I'm making it Q. I just can't believe this happened to grandma. She was loved by everyone."

"Janell, it was probably some junkie. I'm sure the authorities will find whoever did it."

"I hope so."

Janell nor Quincy knows that their grandmother's fingers were cut off.

Q's phone rings.

"Hello." Q answered.

"Bruh, what's up?"

"I'm good. You coming to the funeral?"

"Yeah, I'll be there. How's Janell, bruh?"

"She's holding up okay."

"Do they have any suspects?"

"Bruh, you already know. I'll holler back, a'ight?"

"That's what's up." Tech replied then hung up.

Q hung up and went back into the living room and sat with the rest of his family and friends then there was a knock on the door. "Coming!" One of Quincy's cousins said as he went to open the door.

"We're here to see Mrs. Janell Caps."

"Yes, I'm Janell."

"Ma'am, may we speak to you in private?"

"Okay, we can speak in the den." Janell said leading the officers to the other room.

"Mrs. Capps. I'm Detective Richmond, and this here is Agent Hurns. We have decided that your grandmother's death was a homicide. She was beaten badly, but what we didn't say was that her fingers were cut off."

"Oh my God." Janell began to cry.

"Mrs. Capps, do you know anyone who may have disliked your grandmother or anyone that may have wanted her dead?"

"No, sir. I don't."

"Well Mrs. Capps, I'm sure that you are aware of your brothers' dealings?"

"No, I'm not aware. What are you speaking of?"

"We know your brothers are dealers. We know that they have beef with the Westend crew, and from our investigation your brother is in debt with the Columbian Drug Cartel for four million dollars."

"Detective, what does this have to do with my grandmother?" Janell asked.

"We think that maybe this could be some sort of retaliation. I would like for you to take my card. If you receive any information, please call me." Agent Hurns replied.

"Don't tell your bothers how your grandmother was killed,

because if you do, we know the streets will bleed and that's what we're trying to prevent." Detective Richmond said.

"I don't want that, so only for their sakes, I won't tell them for now."

"Thank you, Mrs. Capps. We'll be in touch." Agent Hurns said. As Janell led them out the door, "You have our numbers, give us a call."

"Yes, sir, I will."

"Take care and we're sorry about your loss."

When they left, Janell informs Quincy of what they said.

Walking back into the living room, with a bewildered look on her face. "Brother, the detective said the intruder tied grandmas' hands during this robbery, and she died of a heart attack. They think it was some local crackheads."

Chapel Hill, North Carolina, The Marriot

Mike meets with the Mask Men. "That was some good work. Didn't think you would cut her fingers off."

"You asked us to bring Quincy out."

"Yes, I did. Has anyone seen him in Raleigh yet?"

"We know he's at his grandmas, but we haven't seen him yet." One of the Mask Men replied.

"Well, if you haven't seen him, that means he's not here. We're going to keep killing people in his family until he comes back out of hiding. A week after the funeral, I want you to kill his sister Janell. Cut her fingers off also. He'll show his face at the funeral, but will disappear like a ghost after that. Hold up, let me answer this."

"Hello."

"Hey, babe."

"Hey, love. How the kids?"

"Missing their father. How's the trip?"

"Baby, it's nice here in Kentucky. Next time you and the kids have to accompany me."

"When will you be back?" Weslyn asked.

"In about a week."

"Hurry back. I miss you."

"Kiss the kids. I'll call you later."

"Okay, babe. Love you."

"Love you, too." Weslyn whispered as she hung up.

"My wife knows nothing about this life. Clean Quincy up so I can hurry up and get back."

Back in Raleigh, North Carolina on the Westend, Killah's lil' cousin, Overkill, is now the sole leader of their crew.

"Today, someone came to our hood and killed three of our lil' homies right in this very spot. We're going to hunt down whoever did this and kill them." Overkill raised his voice to stress his point, amp-ing his comrades up. He was about to continue, until he looked up and saw a black Honda Accord creeping down the street. He really didn't pay it no mind until he saw the barrel of a shotgun appear out of the back window.

"Everybody get down!" Overkill hollered as shots rang out and then the Honda sped off.

"Who the fuck was that? Let's find them mothafuckas now!" One of the Westend crew members hollered.

Power and Nino both knew that they had to get rid of the stolen Honda they were driving, so they stashed the car on Spruce Street, not knowing where they were. Then walked to a Pizza Hut that was nearby and sat down to eat.

Overkill and a few Westend niggas are looking all over for the Black Honda that just did a drive-by in their hood. Then he gets a call.

"Yo." Overkill answered.

"Bro, we found the car over here on Spruce Street, close to Mrs. Sarahs' house."

"Good, hold tight. I'm on the way." Overkill spat and then

hung up.

Within minutes, Overkill pulls up. They search the car. Quincy looking out the window of his late grandmother's house, noticed Overkill up the street. Q looks, wondering what's going on, then he sees the hoodies.

Once Overkill leaves, later that night, Quincy sneaks down the street to see who the old Honda belonged to. He writes down the VIN and has one of his friends at the DMV back home run the numbers. Within minutes, Q finds out that the Honda is stolen. Now he's wondering why Overkill was looking at this car.

Wake County Police Department

"Detective Richmond, do you think Quincy had those Westend guys killed?"

"It's a possibility that he may think that they killed his grandmother, but I don't see them killing her. I believe the rumor about Quincy owing the cartel. Whoever killed those Westend guys. I strongly believe it was personal."

"So where do we start?" Detective Chambers asked.

"We wait until Quincy shows his face, then we make our move."

Back at his grandmothers house, Quincy flipped on the TV and turned it to the news.

"Good morning, I'm Tamara Lane, reporting live. It's 11pm, Friday evening. Earlier today, three young men were shot dead in Westend. It was a drive-by shooting that has shocked West Raleigh. The Westend is one of the most notorious neighborhoods in Raleigh. There are no suspects at this time. I'm Tamara Lane, reporting live. Channel 5 news."

Quincy sits watching the news, now he realizes why Overkill was searching that car. "Shit." Q thought to himself, "by that car being so close to his grandmothers house, it was only a matter of time before everything pointed at him.

Four days later

The funeral for Mrs. Sarah Capps is being held today. Q and his brother, Tech, attend. Unknowingly to Quincy and Tech, Mike has sent a hitman to see if they showed up. When Q and Tech arrived, the hitman sent Mike a text that read "I like what I see." As the funeral service goes on, the hitman remains watching the brothers' every move. Q spots him and realized that he never seen him before. When the service lets out, Q sent Tech to see who this strange man was.

"Excuse me sir, I didn't get to meet you. I'm Tech."

"Nice to meet you." The man said as he shook Tech's hand. "Mrs. Sarah talked about you and Quincy all the time. I was her yard worker. My name is Jamar. Mrs. Sarah was like a mom to me. Sorry for your loss."

"Thank for your support, and you take care." Tech replied, moving on to other friends and family. When Tech circled back around and met Q.

"Yo, who was he?" Q asked.

"Grandmas yard worker." Tech replied.

"Not wearing a $6,000 suit. He's lying." Q replied.

"So who do you think he is?"

"The FEDs. They know we're here, so we have to come up with a plan and bounce without them knowing."

"Facts."

After Mrs. Sarah was buried, a lot of the family went back to Mama Sarah's. Unknowingly being followed by Mike's hitman. As soon as they got to the house, Q pulled up on his sister Janell.

"Sis, you know the FED's were at the funeral. I'm sure they are outside watching the house. Me and Tech have to leave without anyone knowing. I need Jeff and Dave to switch clothes with me and Tech. Then go get in the whip and drive around the block and come straight back."

"Okay, I'ma go tell them now." Janell said as she rushed off to get her cousins.

Once they exchanged clothes, Jeff and Dave went and got into Janell's car and left the house. Seeing movement, the hitman calls Mike.

"They're on the move."

"Whatever you do, don't lose them. Call me when they stop and we'll be right there." Mike replied.

The hitman hung up, and continued to follow them as they turned back onto the same street they had just left. Seeing this, the hitman calls Mike back.

"Yo."

"Mike, I called you back to let you know they circled the block. Now we're back at their grandmothers house. Hold up, they're getting out. It's not them, it's a decoy!" The hitman hollered and then hung up.

Tech and Quincy both shot out the back door as soon as their cousins pulled off.

"Tech, I'm staying. You go back home. I have to find out who killed grandma."

"Bruh, I'm not leaving without you."

"A'ight, if you stay, it's a chance you may never see your family again."

"Yeah, I understand that, but you're my brother. I can't leave you."

"Okay, we'll do this together then." Q replied.

Utah

Killah has moved out West with his wife and kids. He has also changed his life and joined the church. He became a Deacon. On Wednesday nights, he teaches bible study to the kids and has formed a Big Brother program.

"Bae, it feels good to be home." Killah said.

"Thank you for the trip, the kids really enjoyed themselves." His wife said.

"Yeah, they did have a good time."

"Yes, they did." His wife replied, as she checked the answering machine.

"You have 20 messages. Message one: Kevin this is mama. When you get home, please call me. Beep. Message two: This is mama again, as soon as you get in, give me a call. Its an emergency. Beep.

"Baby, what do you think she has to tell you?" Shonda asked.

"I have no idea, let me give her a call." Killah replied as he dialed his mother's number.

"Hello."

"Hey mama, how are you doing?"

"Baby, I'm okay, just glad you called."

"Mama, what's the emergency?"

"Kevin, last week Mrs. Sarah Capps was murdered in her home."

"Mama, are you talking about Quincy's grandma?" Killah asked.

"Yes, baby, and that same day three young boys were shot dead in the Westend Housing Projects by a drive-by shooting."

"Is Billy okay?"

"Yes, he wasn't out there. But baby, they are all in the park with guns."

"Mama, What's Aunt Sonya's number?"

"919 457 3862"

"Let me call auntie, so I can get ahold of Billy before he kills someone or gets himself killed."

"Call me back, okay?"

"I will, mama." Killah promised and then hung up.

"What's wrong , baby?" Shonda asked.

"Quincy's grandma was murdered." Killah replied.

"Oh my God, no!"

"Three guys got killed in Westend by a drive-by shooter."

"Lord, please help them."

"I'm going to call Aunt Sonya so I can talk to Billy."

"Baby, I don't think you should do that. You are out of that life now. Please, stay outta that. We're happy and we finally have a good life." Shonda said knowing her words were going in one ear and out the other.

"I have to call, he's my family."

"I thought you loved us, but I see you love your homies more." Shonda's upset and storms out of the room.

Paying his wife no mind, Killah calls his Aunt.

"Ring, ring."

"Hello."

"Aunt Sonya, how are you doing?"

"Who is this?"

"Kevin."

"Oh, hey Kevin. I haven't heard from you in so long. I thought you were dead."

"No, Auntie, I'm alive. Where's Billy?" Killah asked.

"Baby, he's at the park with them thugs about to do something stupid."

"I need his number so I can talk to him."

"I don't want my son dead. 919 290 2019."

"Auntie, I'll do my best to save him."

"Okay, I love you."

"Love you too, Auntie." Killah hung up and called his cousin Billy.

"Ring, ring."

"Who is this?" Billy asked.

"Killah. What up cuz?"

"Who you?"

"I didn't stutter." Killah replied.

"Where you at?"

"I'm around, what's up?" Billy answered.

"What happened in the hood?" Killah asked.

"Man, someone came through the hood and iced three of the bros. Then did a drive-by the same day."

"I heard about Quincy's grandmother getting murdered."

"Yeah that shit is crazy, too."

"Y'all have something to do with that?" Killah asked.

"Lord, no. That's on the hood, bruh. But we found the car that was used in the drive-by over on Spruce Street." Billy answered.

"That's where Quincy's grandma lived."

"Right."

"Is Q in town?"

"I hear he was at the funeral, then he left the city."

"Listen Billy, don't do anything stupid."

"Bruh, I'm grown, plus this is my hood now."

"Alright then, accept what comes along with it, bruh. Take care, Billy." Killah spat then hung up.

When Killah got off the phone, he said a silent prayer.

"Dear God, I come to you in the name of Jesus Christ. I ask that you touch Billy and his friends. That they don't hurt anyone or get hurt themselves. Lord, if it's your will, protect them, by the Holy Ghost, Lord Jesus. I ask that my mother remain safe. I ask that you bring this war to an end. God if it's fair, take my life, so the younger guys can enjoy theirs. God, I ask that you watch over my family, keep me guided in your love, God. I thank you for loving me. Amen."

Killah opened his eyes and cleared his thoughts.

"How did it turn out with Billy?" Shonda asked her husband.

"He'll have to learn the hard way. I prayed for him. He's in God's hands now. It's nothing more I can do." Killah replied, shaking his head, knowing that Billy will probably get himself killed.

"Come on babe, lets go to bed."

Raleigh, North Carolina, DEA's Office

"I strongly believe Quincy and Trevon are in town." Agent Pennell said.

"How you figure that? And you didn't go to the funeral?"

Agent Hurns replied.

"Airport surveillance picked up Trevon one day after the funeral. If he's in town, Quincy's here too." Pennell said.

"How come no one seen them at the funeral?" Agent Hurns asked.

"Well for one, nobody was told to do surveillance on the family."

"You mean to tell me, two of the biggest drug dealers in North Carolina's history may be in town and no surveillance was set up?"

"Have patience, Mr. Hurns. Quincy will come to us."

"You said the same thing about Tony Blanco, when he got out, but we haven't seen him since."

"Oh but we will. And this time we'll take him down."

Day's Inn

"Tech, do you think them Westend niggas had something to do with grandmas murder?" Q asked.

"Bruh, I don't know, but you said they were looking at the car and searching it. I can't say who killed grandma, but we'll find out." Tech replied.

CHAPTER 20

Power and Nino Cracks decided to come out of hiding and hit club Red Velvet. It's the new spot in the city. When they pulled up, they notice one of the guys walking, had on the same hoodie as the last three niggas they buried.

"That's one of them niggas going in." Power noticed.

"Yo, Power, y'all go ahead in. I'ma park by the exit. I'ma ice this nigga for Fab's fam." Nino Cracks replied.

"Bet." Power said as he handed a fine Arab woman $200 to strap his gun to her inner thigh and follow her inside the club.

Once in the club, Power got his strap. The club is poppin'. It's women everywhere. But Power is focused; dedicated on putting this Westend niggas lights out. So he walks around the club and spots him at the bar. "Damn, it's like ten of them." Power thinks to himself. Modifies his stride, he slowed his momentum and eased up to the bar, in a slight drunken stagger. He called the waitress and ordered a Grey Goose.

"Yo, homie, you from around here?"

"Nah, bruh. I'm new in town." Power replied.

"What city you repping?"

"Cali, where you from?" Power asked.

"I'm from Westend. What they call you, fam?" Power looked him in the eye. "My name is Fab."

"Fab, huh? Last one around here wit that name got smoked."

"I heard, by Westend." Power answered as he eased his gun out from under his coat.

"Yeah, that right."

"So, what they call you?"

"They call me Too Bad."

"Well, Too Bad, Fab was my man. And this is for him." Power replied, bringing his Pistol in clear view. He shoots Too Bad in the face, knocking his lifeless body to the floor. Power began to unload on the rest of Too Bad's Westend crew. Billy fires back, "Bloc, bloc." The club is in pandemonium as Power goes to war with the Westend crew single handedly. Fire power being slung in every direction. Power runs out the back door entrance. Chasing behind him, a Westend member named Shonuff is met with Nino Cracks' barrel as he ran out behind Power. Nino Cracks doesn't hesitate, he pulls the trigger; ending Shonuff's life.

"For Fab." Nino whispered, then he ran back to the car and pulled off.

Within minutes, the police are all over the scene trying to learn information about what happened. No one was talking. Then Too Bads' girls broke rule number one; no snitching. She screams out loud, "He killed my baby!"

"Who, ma'am?" Detective Richmond asked.

"Some guy I never seen before. He walked to the bar. Him and Too Bad talked for probably five minutes. I heard him say that Fab was his man, then everything went crazy."

"Ma'am, do you remember how he looks?"

"About six foot, 215 pounds. Brown skinned. He had a black, New York snap back." Then she begins to cry.

Detective Richmond turned to his partner. "Put an APB out

on the description that she just gave us."

"Ma'am, I need for you to come by the station tomorrow morning so I can take a formal statement. I know now is a difficult time." The detective informed her.

As officers wrapped up the scene, Detective Richmond leaves to go see Billy in the hospital. 45 minutes later, Detective Richmond walks inside Duke Medical Center. Billy is in room 262.

"Billy, Billy."

"What the fuck you want?" Billy spat.

"I want to know who did this. Five people shot, and two dead. I come for answers, Billy."

"Well, I don't have nothing to tell you."

"The way it looks, is like someone or some group is trying to wipe you guys out. If you don't help us, more are going to die."

"Well you make sure you are around to pick the bodies up. Now get the fuck out my face." Billy spat.

"Okay, if that's how you want to play it." Detective Richmond replied.

"Yeah, exactly."

"Stay safe then, Billy." Detective Richmond said, and then walked out of the hospital room. Only to find Agent Hurns standing in the hallway.

"Detective, what are you doing here?" Agent Hurns asked.

"Following up on leads. You think maybe Quincy thinks Billy had something to do with his grandmother's murder?"

"Richmond, we don't have any leads pointing in that direction."

"Yes we do. The Westend crew now thinks that Quincy is behind this. This shootout started because the shooter was a friend of Fab's. What my hunch is telling me, is that the Cartel, Money Mafia, and Westend are all going to war. We have to stop them before the streets run with blood."

"When we catch Quincy in the act, we'll take them all down. Let me call Agent Pennell and fill him in." Agent Hurns replied.

Phone ringing.

"Hello, Agent Pennell speaking."

"Pennell, hate to bother you this late, but there was another shooting. Billy 'Overkill' Austin, new leader of the Westend crew, was shot today along with some of his friends. Two were murdered, one body at the bar and another at the back entrance. Detective Richmond thinks Quincy Capps is behind this. That maybe he hired a hitman."

"So he believes Quincy has resurfaced in Raleigh?" Agent Pennell asked.

"Yes."

"If Quincy's here, that means the Cartel is here. If the Cartel is here, Tony Blanco will show up soon."

"Keep me posted, Agent Hurns."

"I got you, I'll keep in touch." Hurns replied.

Back at the Holiday Inn, Quincy and Tech lay low, while trying to figure out who killed their grandmother. Blowing on that gas, Q flipped to Channel five news station.

"Breaking news. I'm Tamara Lane reporting live at club Red Velvet. Where five people were shot and two are reported dead. One of the witnesses said the gunman said the name 'Fab' before the shooting began. Fab was a member of Money Mafia who was murdered over a year ago. I'm Tamara Lane, reporting live."

"Yo, Q, did you hear what she just said about Fab?" Tech asked.

"Yeah, but it doesn't make any sense."

"Q, someone is hitting them that knows Fab."

"Yeah, but who is the question, right now I'm about to get some sleep though."

Next Day, Orlando, Florida

"Welcome to the Hampton Inn Resort."

"Sir, I would like a presidential suite."

"Name please?"

"Justin Harris."

"One second sir. How many days will you be staying."

"Seven."

"The total is $3,248. Will that be cash or credit?

"Cash."

"Here's your room key, room 262. Have a nice day, sir."

Once Justin got his key, he turned his head and began to head to his room. Where he noticed a familiar picture on the wall.

"Excuse me sir, who is this picture of?" Justin asked.

"Oh, that's the owner, Mr. McNair. He's out of town on a business trip right now."

"So he's the owner of this hotel?" Justin asked.

"Yes, sir. He has a few of these."

"Well, I'm looking to invest myself. Does Mr. McNair live here in Florida?"

"Yes, sir. Right here in Orlando."

"I'll check back in a couple weeks to see if he's back."

"Okay, enjoy your stay, sir."

"I will, thank you." Justin replied as he headed to his room. Once he got off the elevator, he went straight to his room and unpacked. Pulled out his cell phone and called Mike.

"Ring, ring."

"Hello, what's up, Jus?" Mike said as he answered.

"I'm good, like four million good."

"What you saying"" Mike asked.

"Your boy Quincy changed his last name to McNair and he owns a hotel right here in Orlando. He's out of town right now, so I'm guessing he's right there in Raleigh.

"Okay, thanks for the call, Jus."

"No problem, bruh." Jus said and then hung up.

"Yo fellas, Q has relocated to Orlando. I just received a call from one of my peoples. He's here in Raleigh right now. If we can't find him, we'll find his wife and kids and his sister Janell. I want his whole family dead, and I want it to look like the Westend crew that he's beefing wit did it." Mike said.

"Say no more Boss, we'll handle it." One of the masked men replied as he loaded his Desert Eagle.

2 Days Later

Billy is released from the hospital. Power and his partner, Nino Cracks, are laying low trying to stay off the police radar. Quincy and Tech have been asking around about their grandma but they still haven't received any answers. Back at Westend housing.

"Billy, what's good bro? Glad you made it out." Kai said.

"Yeah, me too, bro. Check this though. I seen that niggas face in the club, bruh. He ain't from Raleigh. I think this is Quincy's doing."

"Then you know it's time to turn the heat up."

"I feel you bro, but on who, though. I'm not certain it's Q."

"I got a perfect plan, bruh."

7:30pm Saturday

Kai and three Westend soldiers loaded up in an old, stolen Tahoe and headed to Spruce Street to Quincy's grandmother's house. Boosie, Q's cousin, was sitting on the porch with a hoodie on. When the old Tahoe turned on Spruce Street. Boosie, who was a certified gunslinger/hustler, noticed the truck and the four people inside. On instinct, Boosie pulled out his twin Berettas, but he didn't make a move. He waited until the old Tahoe got closer to be sure of their intentions. As the truck came closer, he sees a barrel of what looked like a shotgun. Boosie shot off the porch like Usain Bolt, blazing his Berettas, not caring about his own well being. The first three shots went through the windshield. The driver of the Tahoe slammed on the brakes. A shotgun rang out. Sounding like the God of Thunder. Boosie rolled, ducking for cover behind an old, oak tree and returned fire.

"Bloc, bloc, bloc."

"Boom, boom, boom." Buckshots hit the old oak causing

Boosie to duck for cover again.

Police sirens could be heard right before the Tahoe sped off. Relief overcame Boosie as he watched the Tahoe's tail lights disappear. Boosie jogged back to grandma Sarah's house where he called Q and informed him of what just happened.

"Ring, ring."

"Hello." Q answered.

"Q." Boosie said.

"What up, cuz?"

"This is Boosie. Them Westend Niggas just came through. I let 'em have it, though. I think they were coming for you."

"Calm down, bro. Go lay low, I'ma handle it."

"Say no more." Boosie replied then hung up.

DEA Office

"I did some background checks and Fab's brother, Maurice Reeves, aka Power, was just released from prison; the courts overturned his case." Agent Hurns said.

"Do you think that's who's committing these murders? Agent Pennel asked.

"That's a possibility because he got out the same day those three guys were murdered in Westend. The task force upstate said if someone killed his brother, he would avenge his death. We got us a mess on our hands. We need every officer on the street.

"There was a shootout on Spruce Street today."

"What? That's Q's grandmother's street."

"Yeah, there are no witnesses, and no one was killed."

"This time, you mean."

"We gotta get these guys off the street. It's too many dying."

"Yo, Power. We need to make another move on them fools." Nino Cracks said.

"I'm feeling you dog. Shit, we've been laying low almost a week now." Power replied.

"I know you've put a plan together."

"Yeah, you should've seen that pussy's eyes when I pulled that shooter out."

" I already know, big bruh. Them Westend niggas soft man."

"Yeah how 'bout we kidnap one of them niggas tonight. Y'all drop me off around 12:30am. They should be at the club, the first one I see. I'ma ice his ass."

"Let's do this. I'm wit it." Nino Cracks replied.

12:15 Sunday morning

"Yo, Tech, park right here. We'll walk. Hopefully, we can sneak up on one of them niggas. Lets go lay behind the bushes in the park." Q said.

"A'ight, come on, let's go." Tech replied.

Nino Cracks dropped Power off close to Westend. Power had planned to kidnap one of them at gun point. "Let me walk up to the park where they hang at with this hoodie. I might be able to get close to them that way." Power thought to himself as he took off up the street.

"Yo, bro, somebody is walking up. When I raise my hand, pull out on 'em." Q said.

"I gotcha." Tech whispered.

Power is walking up, wondering where everybody is at. He didn't see anybody, so he decided to take a quick piss.

"He's pissing now." Q said as he dropped his hand. Tech went into action.

"Don't move, nigga. You move your feet I'ma blow your ass up." Tech said as Quincy walked up.

"Take that hoodie off, matter fact, I'll do it. Keep your hands up." Q said as he snatched Powers' hoodie off.

"Yo, let me pull my pants up." Power replied.

"First, let me see your face. Who are you?" Q asked.

"I'm not Westend, so fuck you, nigga. Shoot if you're going to shoot." Power replied, not fearing death for even a second.

Out of the blue, Powers' partner, Nino Cracks, eased up

behind Quincy with his gun raised, ready to end Q's life.

"Do we have a problem here?" Nino asked. Q didn't say a word, he just kept his gun on Power.

"Yo, I ain't afraid to die. You bitches killed my brother. Be smart, you better finish me now, because if you don't, I'm killing all you niggas." Power said.

"Who killed your brother?" Q asked.

"You, punk ass, Westend Niggas."

"What's your name, bruh?" Tech asked.

"Power, and you better remember it."

"Power. Murder Cartel Power?" Tech asked.

"Who's your brother?" Q asked.

"Fab."

Upon hearing their homies' name, Q and Tech lower their weapons. Nino Cracks still has his 45 pointed at the back of Quincy's head.

"Power, I'm Quincy. Fab was my fam."

"Money Mafia." Power whispered.

"The one and only." Q replied.

"Nino, lower your gun. These are my brothers' people." Power said. Nino Cracks did has he was told. Then Power and Quincy dapped each other up.

"That's my man, Nino Cracks." Power said.

"Nice to meet you. Heard big things about you Q." Nino Cracks said as he dapped Q up.

"This is my brother, Tech." Q replied, introducing his brother.

"Yo, we might need to get up outta here." Tech replied.

"You're right, before somebody see's us."

They all left Pulin Park and went to a bar in Chapel Hill called Applebee's, so they could talk in a more secure environment. When they got there, they threw back a couple shots of Henny. Tipsy, Q asks, "So, Power, what's your plans?" Q asked.

"I'm looking for whoever killed my brother, so I can send 'em to hell." Power replied.

"Most of them are already dead, except Killah. He was their leader at the time when Fab was murdered. Where does he rest his head at?" Power asked.

"I don't know, bruh. My partner Angel, rest in peace, was about to punch his clock but his kids saved him." Q replied.

"How that happen?" Power asked, frustrated.

"Couldn't kill him in front of his kids. We haven't seen him in the hood since."

"Do you know who could tell us where he is?"

"The only one I can think of is his mother."

"I have to pay her a visit when we get back to Raleigh. By the way, who killed your grandmother?" Power asked.

"I don't know, I'm still trying to find out." Q replied.

Q, Tech, Power, and Nino Cracks chilled having a good time. The clock hit 3AM, Applebee's was about to close, then Q see's a familiar face.

"Yo, Tech, that big nigga over there, I've seen him before, bruh. I think he's been following me. I'm 'bout to approach this nigga."

"Let's go." Tech replied.

Power leaned over and flashed his Desert Eagle. "We got you homie." Power said.

Then Q got up and walked towards the big guy with Tech, power, and Nino Cracks right behind him.

"A, yo, big dog. Have we met before?" Q said.

"Nah, I don't think so."

"I've seen you in Raleigh a while back at the ice cream spot." Q spat.

"Nah, bruh, I've never been to Raleigh."

"Nigga, what you think I'm slow?"

"Look I don't know you man and I don't want no problems."

"Yo dog, you've been following me?" Q asked.

"Bruh, you tripping."

"Fuck that." Q says then punches the guy in the face. Then

Nino Cracks pistol whips him. Customers start running outside.

"Yo dog, you done fucked up big time." The big dude hollered,

Power kicks him in the face while the dude was on the floor; knocking the guys teeth out. The owner, seeing what was taking place in his restaurant, instantly rushed to the phone to call the police. Quincy saw the guy on the phone. "Dude's calling the police." Quincy hollered then they all rushed outside leaving the guy bleeding on the floor.

The big guy finally wobbled to his truck and called Mike.

"Ring, ring, ring."

"Hello." Mike answered.

"Quincy and three other guys just jumped me and kicked out my damn tooth. I'm on the way to kill his sister now."

"Dog, what the fuck happened?" Mike hollered.

"I stopped to get something to eat. I guess he remembered me from the ice cream parlor and Disney World."

"I'll have the other two mask there waiting. Don't forget, po-po is camping out next door."

"We'll take care of that also."

"Call me when you finish." Mike replied then hung up.

CHAPTER 21

Quincy and Tech are being followed back to Raleigh by Power and Nino Cracks.

"Bruh, was that the same nigga you were telling me about." Tech asks his brother.

"Yeah, bruh, I know that's him." Q replied.

"Man, we should've killed him. Niggas like that be the ones that send ya to hell."

Club Rosa. Lil' Kenny is having a ball with his Westend homies, while Billy is at home chillin' with his girl. When the club lets out at 3:50AM, they decided to stop by the Waffle House and grab something to eat.

"Yo, we gotta hit them Money Mafia niggas."

"Yeah, but the beef these days isn't wit Money Mafia. After Quincy tore the hood apartments down and built a Pizza Hut and a small shopping center, he left all that when he left the city. So far, since he left, Westend been controlling the city."

"Facts, facts. Right, you right." Lil' Kenny responded.

Quincy and them made it back to Raleigh.

"Q, I didn't get to eat so I'm 'bout to pull over at this Waffle House." Tech said.

"Alright, park on the backside." Q replied.

"Do you want something to eat?"

"Nah, lil' bruh. I'm good." Q replied just as Power pulls up beside them.

"What's good?" Power asks.

"Tech 'bout to run in here and grab something to eat real quick." Q answered. "We'll go get a couple rooms when we leave here." Q said.

"I'm 'bout to go grab me a plate, y'all good?" Tech asked.

"Shit, I'm coming with you. I'm hungry too." Power replied.

They both go in and sit at the counter and place their orders.

Lil' Kenny gets his homies attention. "Yo, that's the nigga sitting at the bar that we had the shoot out with at the club."

"You sure?" Ice replied.

"Homie, I'm more than sure." Lil' Kenny said.

"We can do him right now."

Ice got up and pulled his gun out and started walking towards Tech and Power. But Power spotted Ice's sudden movements and leaned over and told Tech.

"I think that's one of them Westend nigga's coming this way. When he bends the corner, we're going to plug his ass up." Power said.

"Let's do this then." Tech replied as he pulled out his 9mm.

Ice bent the corner.

"Westend nigga." But before Ice got his words out, shots rang out.

"Bloc, bloc." Tech's 9mm rounds spun Ice's body around, dropping him face flat on the floor. He never stood a chance. All of a sudden, shots rang out; men, women, and children jumped under the table in fear. Power and Tech are blazing back while making their way to the nearest exit. Lil' Kenny and his Westend crew were bringing so much heat. It was hard to make it out. But

Tech finds a way by shooting out the glass window while Power is still banging out.

"Yo, let's move!" Tech hollered as he jumped out the window. Power, not far behind him, taking a bullet in his left arm. Power falls to the ground. Tech rushes back, ducking bullets as they flew past him. He grabbed Power just as Quincy and Nino Cracks pull up. Nino jumped out of his car and laid cover fire as Tech helped Power to the car. Then Tech jumps in the car with Quincy and they sped off.

Within minutes, the police have Waffle House surrounded. Lil' Kenny, lil' Bro, Rex were all killed during the shootout, and an 80 year old White man was killed also.

At the time of the shootout, Mike's Mask Men are about to hit Quincy's sister, Janells' house. The guy Quincy and them jumped is about to kick in her front door and two other Masks are sitting outside the house. Where the police are staked out.

Boom. The Mask Man kicks Janell's front door open and rushes inside. The officers on duty are regular patrol officers. When they hear Janell's alarm go off, they rush out the door only to be met by AK47 Hellfire.

"Thratt, thratt, thratt." The two Masked Men body the police on sight, sling their AK's over their shoulders, and drag the officers dead bodies back inside the house.

Inside Janell's House
"Bitch, where the fuck is your brother?" The Mask Man asked.
"I don't know! I don't know!" Janell screamed; afraid.

The masked man shoots her in the head killing her, then Janell's five year old, hearing the gun shot, runs out the back room to his mothers' aid not realizing his mother is already gone. He grabbed her lifeless body.

"Don't hurt my mommy!" The five year old screamed.

The man smiled behind his mask and then shot the little boy and then turned and walked out of the house like it was a regular day in the neighborhood.

Nino Cracks and Power ride in silence as they follow Quincy and Tech to a nearby carwash. Power is pissed as he ties a shirt around his left arm to stop the bleeding. Lucky for him, the bullet went in and out. After they pulled up at the carwash, they all got up.

"Yo, thanks Tech, that was some hell of shooting you did back there. You saved my ass. I owe you big time." Power said.

"No problem. We're playing on the same team, bruh." Tech replied.

"Man, I'm killing their whole fucking hood. First, I'ma pay Killah's mother a visit, then I'm sweeping through their whole hood." Power said.

"Let's do it tomorrow night." Tech said.

"Nah, it's too hot right now." Q spoke up, taking charge. Let's get back to the room so I can get somebody to sew you up."

Westend Housing
Lil' Kenny calls Billy.

"Hello." Billy answered.

"Yo, bro, that fool we had a run in wit at the club, we seen him at the Waffle House and we got him."

"He dead?" Billy asked.

"No, we put the pressure on him but he got away. He killed Ice."

"He don't know Ice, so how that happen?" Billy asked.

"Ice was going to murk the nigga, but before he could get close, Tech and that other nigga popped off. So we got it in right there at the Waffle House."

"Remy, we gotta find that nigga and put him in a box asap. I'ma holler at you tomorrow though."

"Say less." Kenny replied and then hung up.

Agent Pennell House, 4:30AM

"Ring, ring, ring."

"Hello."

"Mrs. Pennell, I hate to wake you, but I need to speak with your husband." Agent Hurns said.

"Hold on."

"Wake up, Randy. The phone."

"Who is it?" Pennell asked.

"Your partner, get the phone."

Agent Pennell grabbed the phone. "Yeah."

"Pennell, it's bad. Janell Capps and her five year old son were murdered, along with the two patrol officers that we had posted next door." Agent Hurns informed his partner.

"I'm getting out of bed now. I'm on my way."

Quincy and them are back at their rooms. Power has gotten his arm sewn up. They are watching what took place on the news and they are saying witnesses are describing what happened. The lady on TV says we have another homicide that has taken place. We are going there live.

"Good morning, I'm Louise Westbrook. Last night, in this small neighborhood, four people lay dead. Two officers that were on duty doing surveillance work were shot dead right next door to Janell Capps' house. Where she and her five year old son were found shot to death."

Q and Tech couldn't believe what they were seeing. Without thinking, they both rush out of the room to the car and ran every stoplight on the way to his sisters house. They get there in 10 minutes tops. When they get there, they try to run inside but they're stopped by Detective Richmond.

"You can't go inside right now." Detective Richmond says.

Quincy and Tech breakdown crying as they see their sister and their nephew being carried out in two body bags.

Louise Westbrook is still talking, then she walks up to Tech.

"Sir, do you have a relationship with the victims?" The

reporter asked.

"Yeah, she's my fucking sister. Whoever did this, you're dead." Tech says and then walks off.

"That's the young brother, Trevon. The once drug lord who was never indicted. My prayers go out to the victims' family. Reporting live, Louise Westbrook, Channel 5 News."

"Quincy, I'm Agent Randy Pennell. I'm sorry about your sister and her son. But there's somebody out there that wants you dead. We put surveillance on the house because of the way your grandmother was killed. We feared someone would come for Janell next, trying to get to you."

"What do you mean how my grandmother was killed?" Q asked.

"Your grandmother was killed Mob style; they cut her fingers off."

"What!"

"I know this is news to your ears, but we asked Janell not to tell you."

"So why are you telling me now?" Q asked.

"I heard you beat the Cartel for a lot of money. Westend didn't do this, the Cartel did."

"I have nothing more to say to you, Agent Pennell. Do your job and clean the bodies up when they fall." Q replied and then walked off.

"Even if it's yours." Agent Pennell said to Quincy's back.

"Detective Richmond, Agent Hurns, ride with me. We're following Quincy.

Mike and his Mask Men sit in their room, watching the news.

"Y'all did a good job on Quincy's sister, but we have to kill Quincy later. It's getting too hot with the death of those two cops." Mike said.

"It doesn't matter about the heat boss. Me and my brothers can get around that. The head Mask replied.

"I know Odin, and I am very confident in you and your

brothers' skills. But as you know, I don't take chances. Were going back to Hawaii. We will finish him later."

"You're the boss." Odin replied.

Power and Nino Cracks left their rooms and headed to Westend housing.

Lil' Kenny gets a call from Billy. Billy tells him what happened to Quincy's sister and her son.

"It's the cartel that's hitting Quincy." Billy said.

Before Kenny could answer he heard gunshots.

"Bloc, bloc."

"Hold on, bruh. Let me go out here and see what's going on." Kenny replied. When he steps out on the porch, he sees people outside yelling. So he runs down the street to see what's going on. It's Lil' Man. He's shot in the stomach. Kenny rushed to his homies aid.

"Who was it, bruh? Who did this?" Kenny asked.

"I don't know, they said to tell Killah that they're coming for him for killing Fab. They shot me and pulled off." Lil' Man whispered.

"Get him to the hospital." Kenny yelled to one of his bros, then he runs back to the phone.

"Hello."

"Yeah, I'm here. What happened?" Billy asked.

"Someone shot Lil' Man in the stomach and told him to tell Killah that they were coming for him." Kenny replied.

"Did he see their faces?" Billy asked.

"Don't know, I didn't ask. But I think it's the same guy."

"Shit we gotta end this. I'll hit you back."

"A'ight." Lil' Kenny replied then hung up.

What Lil' Kenny and Billy didn't know is that Lil' Man told Power and Nino Cracks where Killah is laying his head at and where he's moved to. So now Power knows where to find Killah.

Lil' Man will go to his grave before he tells anyone in his Westend crew that he gave Killah up because they would kill him on the spot.

Sunday 1:00pm, Wake County Police Department

While in the break room, one of the officers was watching the News and saw what took place in Chapel Hill. Someone had video footage of a man getting beat by three other dudes at a Applebee's restaurant. The officer recognized Nino Cracks face and called Detective Richmond.

"Hello, Richmond speaking."

"Detective Richmond, I just saw on the news what happened in Chapel Hill at Applebee's. The same people were involved in the Waffle House shooting. There's got to be a connection." The officer said.

"Officer, good work. Call Applebee's and the Chapel Hill police department and get me a copy sent up to me as soon as possible." Detective Richmond said and then hung up.

CHAPTER 22

Two weeks have gone by. Janell Capps and her son had a double funeral. After the funeral, Detective Richmond picked Quincy up for the fight that took place at Applebee's. He was released on bond. Tech is wanted for the pistol that he possessed at Applebee's. No charges for the assault has been filed. Power and Nino Cracks are making plans to go out West to find Killah. Mike and his Mask Men are back in Hawaii and have more plans for Quincy. Killah finally called Billy and found out that he had been shot and that someone is looking for him for Fab's murder.

Today, Lil' Kenny took his girls to the mall to go shopping and have a good time. When they stopped at the food court, his girl let him know what was on her mind.

"Baby, I think we should move."

"I'm good here." Kenny replied.

"Well, I don't think so, baby. I don't think it's smart to stay here. Too much violence and I don't want to lose you."

"I'm through eating. Let's go." Kenny demanded.

"Don't get mad at the truth. I only want the best for us, baby."

"And I don't, huh?" Kenny asked.

Just as they were exiting the mall and heading to their car, Q's cousin Boosie was pulling up; he instantly spotted Lil' Kenny. Slammed his car in park and pulled his Berettas and got out and headed straight for Kenny. Kenny see's Boosie and pulled his 45.

"Get down, baby!" Kenny screamed to his girl as he let off the first shot missing Boosie's head by inches.

"Bloc, bloc." Boosie fired back. Kenny is hit in the head and the shoulder before he fell to the ground. Kenny let off four rounds.

"Bloc, bloc, bloc, bloc." Out of the four shots Kenny let off, he landed two. Hitting Boosie in the stomach and the chest. Kenny's girl rushes to his aid and calls 911.

It takes about three minutes before the police arrive. They're both taken to Wake Med where they underwent emergency surgery. Boosie never made it out; he died in surgery. Kenny lived but is under arrest for murder and weapons charges.

Back in Orlando, Florida

Quincy flew back home because he knew that Mike was gunning for him.

"Toya, baby. Before we left Raleigh, I owed someone four million for drugs. I believe that's why grandma and Janell were murdered. You still have the fake ID's?" Q said.

"Yes babe, I have them put up." Toya replied.

"Good we can go to the Virgin Islands. I have a offshore account already set up in those fake ID's names for you and the kids. I want you to leave today. I'll be there in a couple weeks."

"Quincy, I'm afraid." Toya whispered.

"Toya, I'm going to take care of this. I promise."

"Please don't go out there and get yourself killed. We need you Q."

"Baby, I'm going to be careful. Do you trust me?" Q asked.

"Yes baby, you know I do." Toya replied as she leaned over and kissed her husband.

"I have to go over to the hotel. I'll be back later."

"Be careful." Toya begged, fearing the worst for her husband.

"I will, babe. Kiss the girls for me." Q replied as he headed out to his hotel.

"Good morning, Mr. McNair. How was your vacation?"

"Not too good." Quincy replied.

"Sir, this guy checked in a couple weeks ago and was asking about joining in a partnership with you. Here's his card."

Q took the card. "Okay, thank you. I'm going back out of town for a couple weeks. I'll see you when I get back." Q said.

Q prepared himself to go to Hawaii. He knew the only way to keep his wife and kids safe, he had to kill Mike or be killed himself. To play the game you had to know the rules, and no one knew them better then Q.

Back in Raleigh North, Carolina

Billy is back on his feet, and tired of all the bullshit and has nothing but murder on his mind. Power and Nino Cracks have been laying low at the motel, but someone has informed Billy that Power looks like the guy that drove the car the night that Ice was killed at Waffle House. Billy and his team head up to the motel room that Power and Nino Cracks are staying in.

"No one in that room makes it out alive. We end this now, am I clear?" Billy spat at his crew.

"Already, bro."

Billy and his Westend crew stormed the hotel. One Westend member holding the hotel clerk at gunpoint so he couldn't call the police. The rest of the crew took the stairs. When they got to Power and Nino Cracks' room, Power peep what happening and him and Nino Cracks slid into the joint room next door. Right before Billy and his Westend goons unloaded a hundred rounds inside their room.

After hearing no movement, "Stop!" Billy yelled. "Go, go." He sent three goons inside.

"It's empty." One of the three goons yelled.

Billy walks in and notices the door that goes to the next room. But it's too late. The two dudes outside didn't see Power and Nino Cracks slide out of the room.

"Bloc, bloc, bloc, bloc".

Power and Nino Cracks take both of them out, then run downstairs.

"Bloc, bloc."

Nino Cracks kills the guy holding the motel clerk at gun point. Power hops in the car, having left his keys in the hotel room, he popped the panel under the steering wheel and began to hot-wire the car. "Bloc, bloc, bloc." Nino Cracks returned fire trying to hold his partner down. Giving Power time to work his magic.

"Hurry up, bruh. I can't hold 'em." Then the car came to life. He throws the car in drive. Instead of fleeing, Power hit the gas, hanging his Desert Eagle out the window.

"Murder Cartel nigga." Power hollered as he squeezed the trigger. "Bloc, bloc, bloc." Dropping two more Westend goons as they ran out of the hotel causing Billy to duck for cover.

"This is for my brother, nigga." Power hollered and then sped off.

Billy hopped in the car with one of his soldiers and gave chase.

Both cars are now in a high speed shoot out going up the highway.

Billy hanging his AK out the window. "Thratt, thratt, thratt." Shattering the back glass of Powers' black Blazer.

Nino Cracks returned fire. "Bloc, bloc, bloc." Causing Billy's Q45 to swerve. "I'm out of ammo, bruh." Nino said.

"Here, take this." Power said handing him his Desert Eagle. "Extra clips are in the glove compartment. Get these motherfuckers off my ass, bruh." Power hollered.

"What the fuck you think I'm trying to do." Nino Hollered as he leaned out the window.

"Bloc, bloc, bloc, bloc."

"Thratt, thratt, thratt, thratt." Billy squeezed, causing Nino Cracks to duck for cover.

"Shit, bruh. They're laying on the pressure." Nino said as he reloaded Powers' Desert Eagle.

Just so happens Agent Pennell and Agent Brown were riding by and saw the action taking place.

Pennell did a U-turn in the middle of the highway.

"All cars, we're in high pursuit of a black Chevy Blazer and a red Q45 headed Northbound on Newbern Avenue. Shoot on sight. Suspects are armed and dangerous." Agent Pennell radioed for back up.

"Yo, Billy. We have troubles."

"What? Take the next left!" Billy demanded.

"Shit, they're still following us." Billy's goon replied. Billy then turns around and shoots out the back glass of his Q45. "Thratt, thratt." He then hops in the back seat and starts spraying at the police.

"Thratt, thratt, thratt."

"This is Agent Brown. We're under fire. We need immediate back-up. Do you copy?" Agent Brown hollered in his radio.

"Copy. Back up is on the way, sir."

"Run the fucking light." Billy commanded. "Boom." The driver side of Billy's Q45 was hit by a Ford F-250 pick up truck, killing Billy's driver. Billy is shaken up, but he hops out of the car with his AK and pops in a fresh 100 round clip. "Thratt, thratt, thratt." He engages in a full blown shootout with the two federal agents. Billy hits Agent Brown four times in the chest area then takes off. Agent Pennell hits Billy as he runs. Billy falls but is quickly back on his feet.

"Agent down! I'm in foot pursuit of the suspect." Agent hollered in his radio.

"Thratt, thratt, thratt." Billy is spraying rounds as he ducks behind cars running through Walmarts' parking lot. Billy takes a woman hostage and tries to go inside Walmart. But the doors are locked, so he runs in a nearby clothing store. The FBI and the local police surround the place.

"Hi, I'm Brian Chambers , reporting live from the Walmart plaza here on Newbern Ave in Raleigh, North Carolina. Report has it there was a gun battle between gang members from Westend and two out of state convicted felons. Reports from Red Roof hotel, two men were killed and others injured. The gun battle continued on the highway. One car got away, but the other was in a two car wreck where one of the suspects died. From what witnesses say, the shooting continued. One man was shot but is still alive. During the incident, Agent Brown was shot and killed by Billy Austin. Who is held up in this clothing store and has taken eight hostages. We will keep you updated. I'm Brian Chambers, reporting live. Channel 5 News."

"Everybody get the fuck up and move over here. You speak or move and you're dead." Billy hollered.

"Man you need…"

"Thratt." Billy shoots him in the head.

"Who's next? That's what the fuck I thought. Now move." Billy demanded.

Everybody moved away from the windows to the corner of the store.

"You, shut the fucking blinds and give me your phone." Billy snatched the phone and called his mother.

"Ring, ring, ring."

"Hello."

"Ma, it's me."

"Oh, Billy, baby. What have you done?" His mother asked.

"Ma, I called to let you know I love you." Billy said and then hung up.

The store phone then rings.

"Yo, you. Get the fuck up and answer the phone."

The store clerk rushed and answered the phone.

"Hello."

"This is Agent Pennell. Is everybody safe?"

"For now." The store clerk answered, "But one person is dead."

"Okay, stay calm. We're going to get you to safety. Put Billy on the phone." Agent Pennell replied.

"It's for you." The store clerk said to Billy as he handed him the phone.

Billy grabbed the phone. "Yeah."

"Billy, this is Agent Pennell. The building is surrounded. You killed a federal agent. The only way you leave this situation alive is if you release the hostages and come out with your hands up."

"That's not going to happen. I already killed one hostage. If I don't get a bulletproof vest and a car in 30 minutes, I'm going to shoot another." Billy replied and then hung up.

"Get the chief on the phone. We have us a major stand off here. Agent Pennell said to his fellow officers.

"Yeah, this is Chief Roberts."

"Agent Pennell speaking. I hate to bother you sir, but I'm sure you're aware of the situation."

"Yes, I'm aware." Chief Roberts replied.

"The suspects name is Billy Austin. He's already killed one federal agent and a hostage. He's demanding a bullet proof vest and a car in 30 minutes or he'll kill another hostage."

"Agent, do your boys have eyes on the suspect?"

"No, not yet sir."

"As soon as you do, take him out."

"You got it, sir."

Back inside the clothing store

"You, lil' man, come over here."

"Yes, sir." The seven year old boy cried as he came over and stood next to Billy.

"Do you love your daddy?"

"Yes, sir."

"Where is your mother?"

"Over there." The little boy pointed.

"Come over here, miss."

The woman came over and grabbed her son. Billy stuck his hand in his pocket and pulled out a quarter.

"Do you see this coin?" Billy asked.

"Yes."

"If it lands on tails in 30 minutes, you're dead. If it lands on heads, then your husband is dead."

The little boy cries; afraid.

Billy looked at his watch. "Times up." Billy said then he flips the coin. It lands on heads.

Billy raises his AK47 and shoots the man in the chest. "Thratt."

The store phone rings. Billy walked over and answered it.

"Yeah, Billy speaking."

"Billy, we heard shots fired. What's going on?" Agent Pennell asked.

"I killed somebody else and I'ma keep dropping bodies until I get what I asked for."

"Okay Billy, don't hurt anyone else, your car is on the way. Just give me a few minutes."

"You have 20 more minutes to be exact. Then someone else dies." Billy replied then he hung up.

15 minutes later

The store phone is ringing again.

"Yeah."

"Your car and bullet proof vest are here." Agent Pennell replied.

"Park it in front of the store, and get back 500 feet. I'm taking two hostages and releasing four. I'll let them go when I'm out of the parking lot." Billy said.

"Just don't hurt anyone else, Billy."

"I won't as long as you do as I ask."

"We are, Billy." Click.

The swat team pulled the car to the front door. Billy looked outside to make sure everything was clear. Then he rushed to the car with two hostages in tow. When Billy turned the ignition, the steering wheel exploded. The hostages jumped out and ran. Billy jumped out also but he couldn't see. He tried to run back inside, but the door was locked. Swat team closes in. Billy squeezed the trigger on his AK47. "Thratt, thratt." Spraying wildly. Then he takes a bullet to his left shoulder. But regroups and continues shooting. "Thratt, thratt." He takes a shot to the stomach then in his side. He falls and drops his gun. Swat is closing in. Billy reached inside the car and grabs the bulletproof vest and straps it on.

Gathering his strength for one last stand. He took three deep breaths then stands. "Thratt, thratt."

The police didn't expect this because they thought he was dead. Three officers were hit. Then Billy collapses, blood coming from his mouth. He knows he's dying, so he closes his eyes and he gives in to eternity.

CHAPTER 23

I'm Jennifer Simms , reporting live. Four people have died here in the Walmart plaza. The suspect, Billy Austin, was shot three times by local authorities and federal agents. The deadly shootout took place right in front of this clothing store before the suspect was killed. Billy Austin was a leader of the Westend Gang. Will the streets be safe now? Only time will tell. I'm Jennifer Simms, reporting live. Channel 5 news."

Nino Cracks and Powers' pictures are being flashed all over the news for the murders they committed at the Red Roof Hotel.

Power and Nino stashed the car that they were driving and broke into an old abandoned house to lay low. By the time night had fallen. They both emerged from the old abandoned house. They needed a new ride, so they went car shopping. They came to an old apartment complex and found a black Mustang 5.0. Power sneaks up to the car an pops the lock in and begins to hotwire the Mustang. What Power didn't know was the Mustang had a built in GPS."

"Got it." The car crunk up. "Get in, let's go." Power spat.

When the car pulls off, the owner is watching. So he picked up the phone and called 911. Power pull out and takes Old Wake Forest Road. The car owner let the police know where the car was located. When Power pulls up to the stoplight, a patrol car pulled right in front of the old Mustang, blocking it's path.

Nino Cracks hangs his 40cal out the window,

"Bloc, bloc, bloc, bloc." Windows shattered on the patrol car.

Detective Richmond arrives on the scene and runs into the back of the Mustang. Nino Cracks hops out of the car and makes a run for it. But the patrol officer shoots him in the back.

Nino falls to the ground. Power takes off running. Detective Richmond is on his heels.

Power, knowing he couldn't outrun the detective, ran behind a bunch of apartments and waited for Detective Richmond to bend the corner. When he does, Power pops out and squeezed his Desert Eagle.

"Bloc, bloc, bloc, bloc, bloc." Detective Richmond falls to the ground dropping his weapon. His bullet proof vest saved his life, so far, but he's shot bad." Power smiles as he stepped over the detective and vanishes in the night. When officers arrive on the scene, they find Detective Richmond laying face down trying to hold onto his life. When the ambulance finally arrives, Detective Richmond take his last breath.

The department is shocked and they charge Nino Cracks with his murder. Even though they know that he didn't kill the detective. A state wide man hunt is out on Power.

Orlando, Florida

Quincy flew back home to send his wife and kids off. While doing so, he sees Power on the news and also see's that Billy was killed. As of now he couldn't help Power. He was focused and dedicated to dealing with Mike. After he seen his wife and kids off, he finally had a chance to lie down. Knowing that his family was safe, Quincy takes a seat at his mini bar and poured himself a shot of Henny. The last few weeks have been overbearing. Quincy knew the deaths of grandma and his sister were his fault, and his fault alone. "I should've never took that money." Quincy thought to himself as he downed the shot of Henny and poured himself another glass. After doing the second shot, he pulled out his phone and called his brother.

"Ring, ring."

"Bruh, what's good?" Tech said.

"I'm here, baby bro."

"You straight?" Tech asked.

"Yeah I'm good. Just thinking about grandma and Janell. The reason I called is to let you know I'm going after Mike. That's the only way to bring this to an end. I need to do this alone, though. I can't lose anymore family."

"What you saying, bruh?" Tech asked.

"I want you to sit this one out."

"Q, my family is gone, too. You ain't the only one in this. I'm going with you."

"Tech, this my business."

"I'll see you in Hawaii. Tech replied then click.

Quincy put his phone back in his pocket. "This nigga stupid. Lord, please keep my brother safe." Q thought to himself.

Four days later

Airport security called Agent Pennell and informed him that the pictures he dropped off of Quincy, they spotted him on one of their security tapes. Also he had received information that Quincy and Tony Blanco were cellmates in the county jail. A local snitch came forward and claimed that he was listening through his vent and overheard Tony Blanco telling Quincy about some weed and Stone was the suppliers name.

"Agent Pennell, I did a background check on Power a few minutes ago. He's Fabs' brother. He recently got out of the joint.

They say he's a killer and a member of the infamous Murder Cartel. He's here to avenge his brothers' death." Agent Hurns replied. "But most of the guys are dead or are in prison." Agent Hurns said.

"Killah is still alive." Agent Pennell replied.

"Yeah, but he hasn't been seen." Hurns said.

"He was the ringleader when Fab was killed."

"So, you think that he's looking for Killah?" Hurns asked then the phone rings.

"Ring, ring, ring."

"Hello, Agent Hurns."

"This is airport security. The person in the photos name is Quincy McNair from Orlando Florida."

"Are you sure?" Agents Hurns asked.

"Positive, sir."

"Thank you for your help." Agent Hurns said and then hung up. "Pennell, the reason we can't find Quincy Capps is because he's now going by Quincy McNair from Orlando Florida." Hurns informed his partner.

"Let's go catch us a plane."

This was the first time Q has used McNair outside of Florida. He was in such a hurry to get to his family, when he pulled his wallet out, he grabbed the wrong ID. So he went ahead and flew in the McNair name. This would be his first and biggest mistake.

Agent Hurns and Agent Pennell board a plane headed to Orlando, Florida.

"Pennell, we don't have anything on Quincy right now but a fight."

"Maybe this is our chance." Pennell replied.

Hours later, the agents land at Orlando International Airport.

"Mr. Bless, I'm Agent Hurns and this is my partner, Agent Pennell. We spoke on the phone about Quincy McNair."

"Nice to meet you, sir." Mr. Bless answered as he shook the two agents hands.

"I was wondering, do you have an address on Mr. McNair?" Hurns asked.

"One second, let me see here." The security officer said as he typed in Quincy's name. "Huh, yeah. He's coming up in the screen as an active flyer."

"What does that mean?" Agent Pennell asked.

"Active flyer tells us who is on one of our flights. It tracks his passport. From the looks of it, Quincy McNair caught a flight tonight headed to Hawaii."

"Mr. Bless, when is your next flight to Hawaii? Agent Hurns asked.

"Tomorrow night, sir."

"Book us on that flight."

"Alright, doing that now." Mr. Bless said as he continued to type "Done."

The next morning, 7:30AM, Hawaii

After Quincy's plane landed, he walked around to the car rental place so he could grab himself a rider. "While I'm waiting, I'ma text bruh and see where he's at." Q thought to himself as he pulled out his phone and began to text his brother.

Quincy: I'm here. Where you at?

Tech: The Trump Plaza

Quincy: Grabbing a rental. Be there in 30 min.

Tech: Room 330

"Damn, this nigga beat me here." Q thought to himself as he finished the rental process.

"Here's your keys, sir." The clerk said.

"Thank you, and have a nice day." Q replied then walked out the door and jumped in a grey 4runner.

30 minutes later, he was pulling into Trump Plaza. He parked, walked in, and took the elevator.

"Knock, knock."

"Who is it?" Tech hollered.

"Q."

Hearing is brothers' voice, Tech got up and answered the door.

"What up, bruh." Tech said as he let his brother in.

"Shit, I'm tired as hell. I think I got jet lag. I'll rest later, though. We need to get busy." Q replied as he walked inside.

They both chilled in the hotel for 45 minutes catching up. Then they both decide to go to Mike's hotel.

"We're going to follow Mike. Hopefully he'll lead us to his stash spot. That's where we'll roll his ass at." Quincy said.

"Sounds like a plan." Tech replied.

Quincy and Tech stake out outside Mike's hotel all morning, but they haven't seen Mike or his wife, Weslyn, yet. More hours go by. It's now 4:30pm.

"Yo, Q, wake up. Who's Lambo is this?" Tech asked as he woke his brother up.

"That's Mikes' shit." Q replied.

Q and Tech watched as Mike got out of his Lambo and walked inside his hotel. He didn't return for five more hours. Its now 9:30pm.

"Tech, it's on." Q said as he crunk up the 4runner. Mike switched cars, he's in a white Maxima. Q followed him up the highway until he stopped at a local fish market. He stayed inside for an hour.

"Bruh, what you think he's doing in there so long?" Tech asked.

"It can only be one reason. Hold up, here he comes now." Q replied as he crunk the SUV up.

When Mike leaves, he hops back on the highway, and drives for another 30 miles and stops at another fish market. Q is on his ass. Mike stays inside the same amount of time as he did at the last fish market. When he comes out, Mike heads back towards the city. Then he stops at a rest home. "Damn, it's late as hell. Why would he be going to a rest home this late?" Q thought to himself as he pulled the 4runner over.

"What you think he's doing?" Tech asked.

"I don't know. I'm 'bout to see." Q replied as he got out of the truck and snuck up to the window. Q watched Mike as he walked down the hallway and began to talk to an old man. Then they disappeared. "Who is this old man?" Q wondered to himself as he jogged back to his truck.

"Yo, what's going on?" Tech asked.

"Not sure. He was talking to some old man." Q replied.

"Old man?"

"Yeah."

"Look, there he goes." Tech said as they watched as Mike came outside carrying two duffle bags on his shoulders. "What you think's in the bag?"

"Gotta be money." Q replied.

"Yo, I should roll his ass now."

"Not here. Too many people."

Q and Tech watched as Mike threw the duffle bags in the car, hopped in the car, and pulled off. Q follows him for a few more miles. Mike pulls into this big mansion. Not being able to get through the gate, Q pulls over and waits.

"Whoever lives here, I'm willing to gamble, is someone involved in the Cartel." Q said.

"Probably so." Tech replied.

They post up for a few more hours, then they pull off. On the way back to the Trump Plaza the gas light came on, so they stopped for gas.

"Tech, get the gas, I gotta call Toya."

"A'ight, I gotcha." Tech replied as he got out and walked in the store.

While Q is on the phone, he notices a S550 Benz pull up. But when he sees who gets out, "Damn, that's Stone." Q thought to himself while he's talking to his wife.

"What's wrong, baby." Toya asked.

"Nothing, really. You remember when we were in Hawaii and

the agents pulled me over?”

"Yeah, I remember."

"Well, they said Stone was snitching on me, but I'm looking at Stone right now. Something isn't right, baby. I'll call you back." Q hung up, but not before telling his wife he loved her.

"Here, bruh. I bought you a soda." Tech said as he got back in the car.

"Thanks."

"What's wrong?"

"I'm 'bout to follow that white Benz over there."

"For what?" Tech asked.

"Stone's driving it."

"Bruh, I thought you said you got pulled and Stone was locked up."

"They did, but that's him right there."

Q follows Stone all the way back up the highway and across the overpass. Stone leads them back to some mansion.

"Yo, Q, we just left this place."

"I know, but I wonder who the owner is?"

"Let's wait and see."

Hours have gone by.

"Q wake up. We have action. It's like ten of them out there."

"Who's the guy in the black suit doing all the talking?" Q asked.

"Don't know. I can't get a good look at his face."

"He's moving like he's the boss."

"Do you think he's the one that had grandma killed?" Tech asked.

"Probably so." Q replied.

CHAPTER 24

Hawaiian Airport

Agent Hurns and Agent Pennell plane has finally landed. The hunt for Quincy is about to begin.

Meanwhile, Q and Tech are still staked out outside the mansion where they followed Stone to. They watched as Stone and his fellow comrades got in their cars.

"They're leaving now. Who are we following?" Tech asked.

"Stone. We hit him first then work our way up." Q replied, threw the truck in drive, and slowly pulled out behind Stone's S550 Benz. They followed him all the way to his mini mansion, then pulled to the side and watched as Stone got out of the car and walked inside. Popping the clip out of his 45, Q checked his ammo and Tech did the same. They waited another 30 minutes giving Stone time to get comfortable.

"Let's do this, bruh." Q said as he exited the truck.

"Say less." Tech replied as he hopped out behind his brother. They both snuck up and walked around Stone's house looking for an easy way in. Tech peeked through one of the windows and saw Stone with just a towel wrapped around his naked body and also some Hawaiian woman is walking around naked.

"I got eyes on, bruh. They're in the shower." Tech said.

"A'ight, I'ma check the front door." Q replied.

"You know this place has an alarm on it, right?" Tech said as him and his brother pulled their ski-masks over their faces.

Quincy turned the knob and to his surprise, the door was unlocked.

"It's open, bruh, come on." Q said as he walked inside, 45 leading the way. Tech followed right behind him. They walk down the hallway to the bathroom, they could hear the shower running and could see Stone hitting the Hawaiian woman from the back; they heard her moans. Q put his fingers to his lips then pointed at the shower. Tech took off into action, ripping the shower door off its hinges and grabbing Stone by the neck, dragging him out of the shower.

"Shut up, bitch. You scream and you're dead." Q said as he grabbed the woman and pulled her out throwing her to the floor.

"What's this about?" Stone hollered.

"Shut the fuck up." Tech said as he pistol whipped Stone in the face, causing several of his teeth to fall to the floor.

"Tape this niggas hands up." Q commanded the Hawaiian chick, throwing her a roll of tape.

She did as she was told.

"Tape his eyes up, too." Q spat.

Once she was finished, Q taped her hands, then him and Tech dragged them both to the next room, tied them both to the chairs and threw a pillow case over her head.

"Stone, who had my grandma and sister killed?" Q asked.

"I don't know." Stone replied as he spat blood.

"Who do you work for?"

Stone remained silent.

"I won't ask you again. Who do you work for?" Q spat.

Stone remained silent.

Tech then pulls out a K-bar, Rambo knife.

"Since you like to cut fingers off." Tech spat as he cut four of Stones' fingers off, then poured salt into his wounds.

"Aaaaah!" Stone tried to scream but the tape around his face muffled his sounds.

"Where is the stash house?" Q spat.

"Fuck you." Stone mumbled.

Q let off a round from his 45. "Bloc." Shooting the same hand that Tech cut his fingers off of.

"Aaaaah!"

"We can do this all day Stone. Now who the fuck do work for?" Q asked.

"Mike." Stone answered.

"Who does he work for?"

"His brother Justin and Tony."

"Where's the stash house?"

"Mike's hotel basement."

"Who lives in that mansion y'all were meeting at?"

"Tony lives there."

"Okay, now who had my grandmother and my sister killed?" Q asked.

"Q, is that you? I promise Mike had it done. I had nothing to do with that, bruh. I swear." Stone answered as he began to cry, knowing death was approaching fast.

"It's too late for that now." Q replied as he raised his 45. "Bloc, bloc." He shot Stone twice in the head; killing him instantly.

"What about the girl?" Tech asked.

"Kill her."

"Bloc." Tech ended her life as the gun bucked in his hand. Then they left out as silently as they came. Headed back to their hotel, but not before setting the place on fire.

7:25AM the next morning, Agent Hurns and Agent Pennell woke up to the loud sounds of their alarm clock. Once up and moving around, Agent Pennell cuts the TV on, the news flashes on. Last night, Willis Trump and an unidentified female was shot multiple times and was set on fire here in this mini mansion. Willis Trump was linked to the drug cartel. He is also the cousin to Michael Blanco, who owns several hotels here in Hawaii.

"Hurns are you hearing what I'm hearing?"

"Yes, Michael Blanco, do you think he's related to Tony Blanco?" Pennell said.

"Maybe, time will tell."

"Do you believe this is Quincy's work?"

"Who else do you think would kill someone like Willis Trump. Let's make some calls and see who this Michael Blanco is."

Mike, on the phone with his brothers, Tony Blanco and Justin Blanco.

"Did you send someone to pick up the shipments from the fish market?" Tony asked.

"What are you talking about, bruh?" Mike replied.

"Two guys went to the fish market and said you wanted the shipment for an emergency run."

"When did this happen?" Mike asked.

"Right after Stone was murdered." Justin replied.

"The only people that knows about the fucking stash houses are us and Stone. So y'all tell me what the fuck is going on?" Tony Blanco said.

"Do y'all think Stone gave the spots up?" Justin asked.

"Highly likely." Mike replied. "I'ma go check the hotel."

Q and Tech had already hit the fish market stash spot. Now they were searching Mike's hotel basement.

"Yo, Tech, it's like 500 keys in here."

"How are we going to get all this back to the Carolinas?" Tech replied.

"We rent a plane and pray we make it back safe. Shout out to Stone."

"Facts." Tech replied as they packed everything up.

9:30PM Michael Blanco arrives at the hotel and takes the elevator to the basement. When he gets to the door, he sees a note nailed to the door. He snatched it down and read it. It said, "You're too late." Mike opens the door and his heart drops to the floor. The money and the keys are gone. Mike calls Tony Blanco.

"Ring, ring."

"Yo." Tony Blanco answered.

"Big bruh, I'm at the hotel. The money and the work is gone. Stone gave everything up." Mike replied.

"Get Odin and the Mask to find out who did this." Tony Blanco ordered.

"I'm on it." Mike said then hung up and took the elevator back upstairs. When he leaves the hotel, Quincy and Agent Hurns are both following him. Only if they knew they were following the same person. While Mike is driving, he makes a few stops, then he notices that he is being followed by a black SUV. Mike pulls into a gas station and called one of his workers.

"Ring, ring."

"Yo."

"Ratchet, I think I'm being followed by a black SUV. I'm on my way back to the hotel. Take some pictures so I can see who's following me."

"I'm on it, Boss." Ratchet replied then hung up.

Mike pulls off from the gas station, slowly making sure that the SUV is close behind him. After a ten minute drive, he pulled into his hotel and then walks inside as his worker is snapping shots of Quincy and Tech. After he gets a few shots, he goes inside and shows Michael Blanco the pictures.

"Here's the pictures, boss." Ratchet said as he handed Mike his cellphone.

"Muthafucka, I'm going to kill this nigga. Find out where he's staying." Mike replied.

"I gotcha, boss." Ratchet replied.

Mike took the elevator down to the basement and took the

underground tunnel that lead to his hotel next door. Then he got in his red Bentley and headed to Tony Blanco's mansion.

Seeing Mike go inside the hotel, Tech got out of the SUV and walked across the street and inside the hotel. Agent Pennell saw him.

"Hurns, that's Tech."

"What's he up to?" Hurns said.

"Let's wait and see." Pennell said.

Once inside the hotel, Tech approaches the counter.

"Excuse me, sir. I'm here to see Michael Blanco, is he in?" Tech asked the hotel clerk.

"No sir. He has left for today."

"Could you let him know Robert Skywalker stopped by?"

"Yes, I will sir."

"Damn, how this nigga get away." Tech thought to himself as he turned and headed outside.

"Bruh, he's gone." Tech told Q as he got back in the truck.

"How that happen?"

"I don't know."

Q pulls off.

"Where we going, bruh." Tech asked.

"To the mansion they were at last night. I'm sure he'll show up there."

"Hurns, they're on the move, don't get too close." Pennell said as they followed Quincy and Tech. Quincy turns into the community and pulls on the side of the road.

"Pennell, where should we park?" Agent Hurns asked.

"Turn in this driveway so we can stay behind them. I wonder what they are doing parked here."

"Not sure, but it looks like Quincy pointing at that mansion over there." Agent Hurns replied.

"Yo, Tech, there's Mike on the side of the balcony. Who is he talking to?" Q asked.

"I see his face. Here, look through these binoculars, see if you know him." Tech said.

Q grabbed the binoculars and looked through them.

"He's facing the other way now. Okay, he's turning around now." Q said, then dropped the binoculars.

"Q, what's up? Who is it?"

"Tech, that's Tony Blanco."

"Do you think he's involved in the business?" Tech asked.

"I heard that's what the FED's were investigating him for." Q replied.

"What if Mike and Stone work for him? Then that would mean Tony would be responsible for grandma and Janell's murder." Tech said.

"Tony would never have our family killed."

"Well, maybe you don't know him as good as you think."

"Pennell, let me hold those binoculars in the glove compartment?" Hurns asked.

"Here you go." Pennell said handing Hurns the binoculars.

"I see the guy, Mike, and some more guys. One guy has his back turned. Come on, turn around."

"I'll be damned, Pennell. It's Tony Blanco. Here take a look." Hurns said as he passed the binoculars to Pennell.

Pennell took a look. "Yeah, that's him. Oh shit, Tony just shot one of the guys. We have to move." Pennell replied.

"No, we wait. By the time we get warrants, the body will be gone. We'll follow them when we leave."

At the Mansion

"Justin, who you think hit us?" Tony Blanco asked his brother.

"The Mexican Mafia or Demon Reigns. Who else? Justin Blanco replied.

"But the workers at the fish market said they were Black." Tony said.

"Here, Tony, take a look at these pictures." Michael Blanco replied passing his brother the photos.

Tony stared at them for a few minutes. "So it's Quincy. I never would have thought he would figure out that we had his family killed. Mike how did you get these pictures." Tony asked.

"I spotted a black Toyota 4runner following me, so I called the hotel and had Ratchet take pictures." Mike replied.

"If they followed you to the store, I'm sure they followed you last night and I'm willing to bet that's how they knew about the fish markets. Then they followed Stone and tortured him. That's how they found out about the money and the work in the basement. This is what we're going to do. Make a copy of these pictures, then send them to all the hotels on the strip. Have some pretty Hawaiian girls handle that. Once one of the hotels get in touch with you, you send Odin and the Masks to handle that asap!" Tony Blanco replied.

"Sounds like a plan. I'll put it in motion." Mike said.

"I'll help him with that." Justin replied.

"Tony killed that guy and he's acting like it didn't just happen. See bruh, Tony is behind this whole thing." Tech said.

"You're right, Tech. Let's go back to the room. " Q replied, heartbroken that his mentor was behind his family being murdered.

"Hurns, they're leaving, What are we supposed to do?" Pennell asked.

"We follow Quincy. He'll bring Tony Blanco out of hiding, trust me." Agent Hurns replied as he pulled off, following behind Quincy. Once at the hotel, they park and wait on Q's next move.

CHAPTER 25

Michael Blanco and his associates have moved the body that his brother, Tony, dropped. Then he went straight into putting Tony's plan into motion. The first thing he did after disposing of the body was get in touch with his home girl, Xena. He found her sun tanning on the beach.

"Yo, sis, I need a favor."

"Anything for you, Mike. You know that." Xena replied.

"I need you to get your best girls and hit every hotel on the strip and pass these pictures out." Mike said handing her a stack of pictures of Quincy and Tech.

"Who is this?" Xena asked.

"Someone that crossed the wrong people." Mike answered.

"What's in it for me?" Xena asked.

"$30,000." Mike replied.

"You know how much I love that paper. I'll get on this right away."

"Thanks, Xena." Mike replied then walked off. Throughout the whole day, Xena and her girls were up and down the strip passing pics out.

Back at Quincy and Techs' room

"Yo, Q, I'm hungry as hell. I'm 'bout to step out and grab something to eat." Tech said.

"Be careful, bruh." Q replied.

"I'm good, bruh. I keep that tone." Tech said flashing his Desert Eagle. "You hungry?"

"Yeah, bring me a burger and some fries."

"A'ight, I'll be right back."

Tech leaves the hotel, headed up Ocean Boulevard. While driving he sees a big line of limo's in front of the 40-40 club with a big sign that read Happy Birthday Weslyn. Tech stops at Wendy's and then shoots back to the room. On the way back, he see's Mike and Tony and the others standing in front of the 40-40 club, so he calls Quincy.

"Ring, ring, ring."

"Hello." Q answered.

""Bruh, I just seen Tony, Mike, and their crew out front of the 40-40 club. Some woman named, Weslyn is having a birthday party."

"Weslyn, that's Mike's wife. Come get me, we're going to that party."

"I think that's a bad idea, bruh."

"I have a plan."

"Okay, I'll be there in a few." Tech replied then hung up.

Back at the hotel, both brothers ate and then dressed up and left, headed to the party.

The federal agents following close behind.

"Hurns, they're coming out, dressed up." Pennell said.

"Where are they going?" Hurns replied.

"Looks like a funeral."

"Be for real."

"Stay close."

At the party, Mike got a text from his clerk. He pulled out his phone and checks the message. "They're staying at the Trump Plaza." Seeing this, a devilish grin appeared on his face as he walked over and spoke to his brother Tony.

"They're at the Trump Plaza, but let's enjoy my wife's party. We'll surprise them a little later." Mike said.

"We'll catch them when they're good and comfortable." Tony replied.

Quincy and Tech pull up to the party. When they get to the door. They don't have an invitation so Quincy pays the bouncer $1000 to get in. Once they walk inside, Quincy sees Mike and Weslyn with Tony Blanco and some lady that had to be his wife. So him and Tech walk over to their table.

"What's up, Mike?"

"Hello Quincy." Weslyn responds back. Where's Toya?" Weslyn asks.

"She couldn't make it, the kids were coming down with a cold, so she stayed home. But happy birthday to you." Q replied.

"Thanks, Quincy."

"What's up, Tony?"

"No, that's Justin." Weslyn tells him.

"Oh, my bad. How's life Justin?" Q asks.

"Very good."

"Weslyn, since it's your birthday, how 'bout a dance."

"Sure, Q. Why not." Weslyn replies as she gets up and follows him to the dance floor.

Mike sits at the table acting like he's glad to see Q. But all the while, wants to kill him. Tech smiles while keeping his hand on his Desert Eagle.

"Hurns, what do you think they are doing in there?" Pennell asked.

"I don't know but we need to find out." Hurns replied then his phone began to ring.

"Hello."

"Agent Hurns, this is Agent Ellis at DEA Headquarters. We

did a background check on Michael Blanco, come to find out his mothers name is Cindy Williams, but his father is the late Latif Blanco Sr. And guess what? They have another brother name Justin Blanco." Agent Ellis informed.

"Thank you, Agent Ellis." Agent Hurns replied then hung up.

"Pennell. Tony, Mike, and Justin are brothers; they have the same father." Hurns said.

"Now it's coming together." Pennell replied.

"Inside the party, Quincy and Weslyn share a dance while Tech waits at the bar. Two men approach Tech with guns drawn."

"Excuse me, sir. Will you please come with us?"

Tech sets his drink on the table slowly thinking about his next move. He goes to grab one of the guys gun. "Bloc." Tech is shot in the leg. People in the party run screaming. Q grabs Weslyn and drags her off the dance floor. Tech and the gunman wrestle. Tech pulled his Desert Eagle. "Bloc, bloc, bloc." Hitting one of Mike's bodyguards in the face and the other in the chest. "Bloc, bloc." Mike shoots Tech in the back. Quincy sees his brother get shot. "Bloc, bloc, bloc." Q slings rounds at Mike and Tony. The agents outside hear the gun shots and rush inside with guns drawn. Q and Mike are still engaged in a heavy shootout. Tony runs upstairs to grab his Dreko. Agent Hurns and Agent Pennell come in shooting. Quincy finally making his way to his brothers aid and pulled him behind the bar. Pennell and Tony Blanco are engaged in a shootout. Tony reaching his Dreko. "Thratt, thratt, thratt."

"You want some of Tony, come get it!" Tony hollared. "Thratt, thratt. Squeezing his Dreko, causing the agent to duck for cover. "I'ma Blanco." "Thratt." "I'ma Blanco, muthafuckas. I'ma send all y'all to hell." Tony hollered like a mad man. "Thratt, thratt."

Odin and The Mask rush upstairs to Tony's aid. "Bloc, bloc." Agent Hurns drops two of The Mask. Odin Supreme, not missing a step, "Bloc" knocked Agent Hurns head off with a single shot.

Agent Pennell shoots Mike in the mid-section as he runs

to his partner. Quincy grabbed his brothers' Desert Eagle and chased after Tony. Before he gets upstairs, Odin send shots in his direction. Q didn't even attempt to duck, he continued running, not caring about his life. One of Odin's bullets grazed his face as he raised Tech's Desert Eagle. "Bloc, bloc, bloc." All three shots hitting his intended target. Instantly killing Odin. Quincy stepped over his dead body as he continued his hunt for Tony. Once upstairs, Q locks eyes with Tony. Tony raised his Dreko and squeezed. "Click, click." Tony's out of bullets. Q raised his Desert Eagle and pulled the trigger. "Click." Q is also out of rounds. Q smiled at Tony as he threw his gun to the ground. Tony smiled back throwing his Dreko on the ground.

Q rushed Tony, squaring up, then throwing a series of combos. Tony, being a third-degree black belt, dodged Quincy's combos with ease. Tony counter-attacked with a round-house kick to Q's mid-section, dropping him to the ground. Q popped back up on his feet. Tony smiled. "Come to me." Tony said.

Q rushed Tony, causing his back to hit the wall. Q sent two hard blows to Tony's mid-section and after dropping his guard, Q delivered a clean uppercut to Tony's chin knocking him to the floor. Tony on the floor spitting blood. Q pulled a K-bar Rambo knife that he had hidden in boot and began to walk towards Tony.

"Bitch, you killed my family, turn your ass over and look at me." Q said.

Tony turns over on his back and spits at Quincy.

"They say your grandmother screamed like a whore when they raped her." Tony replied, coughing up blood.

This was something Quincy never knew. Quincy raised the Rambo knife and stabbed Tony 16 times, then he walked back downstairs to his brother.

"Tech, will you make it?"

"Yeah, I'm good." Tech replied as he tried to stand up. Once he's on his feet, he's hit two more times in the chest. Q dives to the ground. "Hold on, Bruh." Q hollered, grabbing a gun off the floor and shoots Agent Pennell in the face.

Tech is hit bad. The rounds went through his bullet-proof vest. Q runs to him and pulls him to his feet and carries him out to the SUV. Q could tell by the sounds of sirens that the police are getting close.

"Bruh, hold on. I'ma get you to the hospital." Q said.

"Q, I'm cold, bruh." Tech whispered.

"Trevon, hold on, bruh. Don't die on me." Q replied.

"Tell my wife and kids I love them."

"Just hold on, you'll tell them yourself. We're almost there." Q said.

"Did you get Tony and Mike?" Tech asked.

"Yeah, I got 'em, bruh. We did it together."

"I love you, Q." Tech said as he closed his eyes and drifted off to eternity.

"Nooooo! Trevon! Wake up man. God, take my not me brother man!" Q screamed then he pulled over and cried to himself.

Police arrive at the club and find Mike and Tony and the two federal agents dead. Police are everywhere. Quincy drove to the private airport where he has a plane waiting with the money and drugs loaded onboard that he took from Tony and Mike. Quincy carried Tech's lifeless body onto the plane. Then calls the owner and lets him know he's ready to leave. The news about what took place at the 40-40 club is all over the states.

"Hello, I'm Vickie Jennings reporting live here in Hawaii. Last night, Michael Blanco and two agents along with Michael Blanco's brother and associates were found dead in what appeared to be a brutal shootout. Why this happens, no one knows. But six people have died. If anyone has any information, please call the number at the bottom of the screen. Vickie Jennings, live from Hawaii."

One week later, Utah.
Power has found him a girl who's involved in the church, but he still hasn't been able to locate Killah. Power promised his girl

that he would go to church with her tonight. Power told her when they met that his name was Andrew Johnson, from Seattle, Washington. Since meeting her he's been thinking about living a different life. He vowed to avenge his brother Fab. So he knows when he sees Killah, he has to end his life.

Another week has gone by. Tonight, there's another service at the church, and Killah is the guest speaker.

7:00pm at the church. Killah is preaching, standing in front of a huge congregation.

"I'm giving my praise to God. If you're doing the same, let me hear you say, Amen."

"Amen."

"I know the Lord is the reason I'm able to stand here today. Coming from the streets, where there's shootings, drugs, you name it. But God touched me one day, and said 'Son, it's time.' God saved my life. He had his angels protecting me. And a few years later, I'm able to help kids with their lives. Trust God, he can help you though anything. Amen."

Power sat enjoying Killah's speech and didn't even know that that was Killah up there preaching.

When church was over, Power and his girl were on their way out, just as Killah and his wife. When they accidentally bumped into each other.

"Excuse me, brother." Killah says.

"No, sir, excuse me." Power replied.

"My name is Jeremy Sanders, and your name is?"

"I'm Andrew Johnson."

"So, Andrew Johnson, where are you from?"

"I'm from Seattle, Washington. And yourself?"

"I'm from South Carolina."

Killah and Power talk all the way out the door. Power and his girl walk Killah and his wife to their car. They stand outside talking for another ten minutes then exchange information.

"Well, you have a good night. Call me sometime." Killah said as he got in his car.

"I'll do that." Power replied and then him and his girl walked to their car.

Same night, Orlando, Florida

Quincy stashed the drugs and money and had a small service for his brother. Quincy gave Tech's wife 2.5 million for her and the kids. Since Tech's funeral service, Q hasn't left the house. If he would have just paid his debt, his family would still be alive. I've lost a lot of friends and I will tell anyone that reads this book, money is a beautiful thing, but there's a price to pay when you live in a drug dealers dream. Yeah, I'm very rich, but I live a private life in a fake name and I still look over my shoulder at times. I remember, every night growing up, we would hit the old field and play pick up get busted, and before we left, we would all dap each other up. That was the good ol' days. I never thought I would see the day that all of my friends would be dead. I wonder where Dollar and Remy are hiding at. One thing I did learn is everybody can't handle the pressure. So, when your boy turns on you, just remember I told you. By the grace of God, I didn't go to prison. But if you're in the game, it's a good chance that you will if you don't get killed first.

One year later

I just got back from the NBA All-star game out in Utah, me and my wife, Toya, was riding up the highway. I couldn't believe my eyes. Killah was on a billboard? I couldn't do nothing but smile. He's a preacher now and Power was standing in a row right behind him. If only he knew.

When we returned home, my wife took the kids shopping, while I did some paperwork. I went to the kitchen to grab a drink. I happened to look up and seen a row of black SUV's pulling into my driveway. I didn't wait to see who it was. I already knew it was the FED's. I ran downstairs in to the basement and hit the button for the underground tunnel to open up. I ran through and came to the door that leads to the storage house in the back yard where I kept my '68 Corvette. When I opened the door, the first thing I see were guns pointed at me, then I see a ghost; Tony Blanco.

"Oh shit, I thought you were dead." Q said.

"Quincy, Quincy. Mr. Fuckup, himself. You see Zeus here, he's my personal hit man. He's the one that killed Wicked at the club and sparked your war with Westend."

"What's going on here, Tony?"

"Quincy, I trusted you, so I gave you your dream, a connect. I had everyone you seen follow you and became part of your team to help you build your empire." Tony replied.

"So, the whole time it was you. Why didn't you just give me the connect?" Q asked.

"I had to make sure you could handle it."

"So, the FBI scene in Hawaii was staged?"

"Now you're catching on. I gave you credit. You're one hustling, muthafucka."

"Stone was a test?" Q asked.

"You're getting better my friend."

"So, you come to kill me?"

"Quincy, you played my family by four million. Then you took five more and 500 keys. I warned you in the county jail that if you fucked these people, they would kill you and your family. To answer your question, I'm here to kill you, Q."

"Tony, I watched you die. I killed you myself."

Tony laughs. "Quincy, you killed my twin brother, his name was Justin Blanco, and Michael Blanco was my brother, he was the youngest. My pops was the drug Cartel boss, but he died years ago."

"So, you're the boss now?" Q asked.

"Bingo." Tony said.

"How did you find me, Tony?"

"I had a friend of mine sell your wife this house. My sister used to live here. Q you made me over a billion dollars in two years, that's major. I never knew about the plans to kill your family. You were like a son to me, but your disloyalty is why your family is dead. It's your fault. The time for talking is up now. Where is my fucking money?"

"I don't know what you're talking 'bout."

"I wont ask you nomore, Q."

"Tony, I don't know." Q replied.

Tony takes a gas can full of acid, opens it, and pours it on Quincy's face.

"Aaaaah!" Q screams as he sees the left side of his face fall in his hands.

"Where's my shit?" Tony hollered.

Q doesn't say a word.

"Zeus, kill him." Tony commanded. "Bloc, bloc." Zeus let off two rounds. The first one ripped through Quincy's chest. The second one was a headshot.

"Zeus, throw his body in the pool." Zeus did as he was told. But Quincy's next doors neighbor heard the noise, so he looked out the window and seen Quincy's body floating in the pool. He waits until he sees Tony's car leave. Then he runs outside and dove in the pool and pulls Quincy out.

"Quincy, hold on man."

He then picks Quincy up and carries him to his car and rushes him to the hospital. Once they arrive, doctors rush Quincy into surgery.

"We're losing him, doctors. We're losing him. Flatline."

"Beeeeeeeeep." For the next 45 seconds, it's quiet. Quincy Capps has died.

Then the respirator came to life. "Beep, beep, beep."

"We have a pulse." The doctor hollered.

Keep reading for an
exciting sneak peak of
Cartel City

CHAPTER 1

Justice Santiago and his partner Amir Jackson pulled up to the Citco gas station bumping that new Kevin Gates. Justice parked and pulled out his phone to call one of his street Lieutenants to let him know he was at the spot.

After he hung up he reached into the ash-tray and pulled out a half a blunt and lit it up. 20 minutes went by before his Lieutenant Crazy K pulled up in his all black four runner. Crazy K parked beside Justice, and got out and hopped in the backseat of Justice's Caddy.

"Yo what's up Bro?"

"Not too much, you got that for me."

"Of course big bruh don't I always come thru?" Crazy K replied tossing a brown paper bag in Justice's lap.

Justice caught the bag and opened it to check the contents inside. After he was satisfied he reached over and hit the button to pop the trunk.

"Grab the book bag everything is inside. I'll meet you here sometime next week."

"I got cha Big Bro." Crazy K answered as he got out the backseat and grabbed the book bag out of the trunk slapping the trunk as he shut it back. Justice and Amir pulled off, with Crazy K heading in the opposite direction. Right before Justice got on the interstate he sped past a sitting state trooper.

"Shit," Justice cussed under his breath as he checked his rear-view mirror seeing the trooper pull out hitting his blue lights. Justice hit the gas pushing his Cadillac CTS to the max. He shot past the intersection making a left turn, then a right turn trying his best to lose the committed Trooper as he headed down Old Country Road. Thinking fast he handed his nine to Amir.

"Yo when I bust this next right toss all the guns out the window." Justice spat his adrenaline shooting through the roof.

"Aite Bruh hit the gas on this bitch." Amir hollered while looking back and forth watching for the perfect time to toss the hammers. Justice busted a right then another right. Seeing the opportunity Amir tossed their hammers out the window being sure to watch where they landed so he could come back and pick them up. Justice still didn't slow down. He kept pushing his 2018 Cadillac to the max until he seen the road began to intersect. He made a quick left turn, just as the trooper rammed the side of his car causing his vehicle to flip through an old field knocking him unconscious. When he woke up he was in the hospital handcuffed to the bed with two officers sitting beside him.

"Yo what happened, what am I doing here?" Justice asked the pretty nurse as she walked over to him.

"You were in a car accident. You suffered a concussion, and a dislocated shoulder. You were very lucky, you've been out of it for two days." The nurse replied.

"What about the guy that was with me?"

"Amir Jackson he's fine he walked away without a scratch. The police have him in custody." The nurse informed nodding her head toward the two officers sitting beside him.

"Well this is all for now Mr. Santiago. I have other patients to attend to. He's all yours officers." The nurse said cutting her eye back at Justice before she walked out the door.

One of the officers stood up and read Justice his rights, then they let him know what he was being charged with. Justice smiled to himself knowing that they didn't find the hammers that Amir had thrown out the window. All of his charges were traffic charges. <u>He would be out in no time</u>, he thought to himself. Later that same day Justice was released from the hospital, and taken to the county jail where he was given a $250,000 bond.

Justice Santiago was a known street General, and everybody respected his gun game and his ability to control situations, and the fact that his late mother was a Queen pin. From birth his mother had taught him the game, everything came easy for him. He was a natural born hustler. He possessed the same skill as his mother, a professional at getting money and making things happen, also making people disappear if need be. When he walked in his cellblock with his arm in a sling everybody knew who he was. Shit the city belonged to him. The real question was who didn't know him. It was clear that the Alpha had just stepped in the Block.

"Stunna Boy," someone hollered from the top tier as they watched Justice come in.

"You better know it," Justice hollered back as he sat his mat and bedroll on the floor.

"Yo Gee clean that cell up and move your shit out so the Bro can get that cell," Tone hollered.

"I ain't trying to give my cell up." Gee replied in frustration.

"You can move out or we coming down there and we're throwing you out. It's your choice makes no matter to me. I need some Rec anyway," Tone spat.

"Come on Tone, I don't want no problems," Gee begged.

"Then move your shit before it's gets ugly for you partner," Tone spat.

30 minutes later Gee's cell was cleaned and all his property

was thrown on the dayroom floor while Justice was having a conversation with someone he knew. Tone had sent someone downstairs to get Justice's stuff and put it in his cell for him.

"Yo where the fuck is my shit?" Justice hollered when he got off the phone.

"Cell 32 Big Bruh," Tone hollered.

Justice looked up and could have sworn he'd seen a ghost.

"Tone, damn fool. I haven't seen you in forever. Come down here and holler at me." Justice said walking into his cell, Tone walked in behind him, they shared a brief embrace.

"What you in for?" Tone asked.

"Traffic charges, reckless driving, speeding to elude, driving without a license, failure to stop at a red light. Shit crazy, but I'm good tho Amir threw the hammers out the window. I'm about to get on the phone, and call my girl Lisa, and tell her to come post my bond so I can get out of here."

"What you here for?" Justice asked.

"Shit bro I caught a body. Came home from work and found my girl in bed with another man. I snapped and deaded his ass."

"Damn, I'm sorry to hear that."

"I'm good with it. I should've killed my girl to, but I loved her too much. Fuck it. I don't regret it."

"Damn I don't know what to say, but thanks for the cell, you didn't have to do that."

"You good you are a Chapel Hill Stunna Boy like me, ain't noway you sleeping in the dayroom. Gee's a bitch ass nigga anyway he in here on a rape charge."

"Oh! That what it do Bro. Look let me hop on this phone real quick so I can call my girl."

"No problem bruh do your thing. I'll be upstairs if you need me." Tone replied then dapped Justice up, then he walked back upstairs. Justice walked over to the phone and dialed his girl's number.

'Ring', 'Ring'.

"Hello," Lisa answered.

"You have a collect call from 'Justice' from the Orange County Jail to accept this call please press five."

Lisa pressed five after hearing her boyfriend's name to accept the call.

"Hey baby." Justice said putting on his sexy voice.

"Hey Love, what happened?"

"I got caught up. I need you to come get me and Amir."

"Amir's locked up to?"

"Yeah I don't know what he's charged with. It couldn't be much since we didn't caught with anything."

"How much is your bond?"

"$250,000 thou."

"Damn boy, what did you do?"

"Caught a bunch of traffic charges, you coming or what?"

"You know I'm coming. Let me put some clothes on and call the Bondsman, then I'm on my way."

"Okay, I'll see you when you get here, love you."

"Love you too Baby."

When Justice got off the phone he went back to his cell and took a nap before he went and got himself in some more trouble that he didn't need right now. When he woke up he grabbed his towel, wash cloth, and soap and headed to the shower. When he finished he dried off and headed back to his cell to his surprise, he noticed Big Bruno standing by the doorway of his cell. Justice knew what it was but he didn't pay it any mind. Crazy K had already told him what happened.

"Bruno Cortez why am I not surprised?"

"Justice, you know we gotta shoot it. Ya boy Crazy K jumped my brother down in the Bottoms." Bruno spat. "I don't care about your shoulder, so don't even think of ducking no rec."

"Ducking rec you got me fucked up. Let me get dressed." Justice spat clearly frustrated with Bruno's bullshit.

"Yeah you do that. I'll be upstairs waiting." Bruno replied

then he walked off.

Justice went in his cell and put his shoes on then took off upstairs. On the way up he ran into Tone.

"Yo Bruh what's up? Why you moving so fast." Tone asked.

"That clown Bruno pulled up on me and said he wanted to go a couple rounds. I'm bout to go up here and feed his ass real quick."

"You talking about Bruno from the Bottoms?"

"Yeah that's him."

"What! Ain't noway, come on Bruh." Tone said as they both took off headed towards Bruno's cell.

"Yo you got a problem with my people?" Tone spat.

"Yeah he already know what it is, you don't have anything to do with this." Bruno said.

"Hell if I don't! He a Stunna Boy." Tone spat as he ran in Bruno's cell punching him in the face, hitting him with a mean combination. Justice without a second thought instantly fell in line, hitting Big Bruno over the head with the lock he had stashed in his pants before he left his cell. Hearing the loud commotion a couple of Tone's friends ran in Bruno's cell and began to beat Bruno senseless. Unconscious they drug Bruno out of his cell and threw him downstairs where more Stunna Boys continued to kick and stomp on his head until the Jailer came rushing in spraying mace and shooting inmates with stun guns. Through all the chaos Justice kept beating Bruno until he was hit with a taser, knocking all the fight out of him as he fell to the ground shaking foaming from the mouth as the Jailer turned up the heat.

After order was restored Justice, Tone, and a few of his homeboys were dragged out the block and thrown in the hole. Bruno was taken to the infirmary in critical condition. The very next day the Jailer that had stunned Justice appeared at his cell door banging on his cell window.

"Get your bitch ass up." The Jailer shouted.

Still badly bruised from the beating he had taken at the hands of the jailers Justice got up from his bed and slowly walked to his door.

"Oh you think you're tough. Coming in my jail thinking you running shit, this ain't the streets."

"Fuck you Pig." Justice spat through swollen lips as he stared the jailer in the eye, then he spit on the glass.

"We'll see how much shit you talk in a few minutes." The Jailer replied. Then two more jailers walked upstairs and joined him.

"Pop cell 3." One of the jailers said thru his radio

The door popped open. All three jailers rushed in on Justice and began beating him with their nightsticks. Justice tried everything in his power to fight back, but his efforts were fruitless. While being beaten his eyes landed on one of the Jailers name tag, he thought he recognized the man then darkness struck him as he drifted off to unconsciousness. They left him badly beaten on the floor.

Two days went by Justice was still in the hole no medical attention nor phone calls was giving as he sat battered in his cell he remembered the jailers name "Grant". He swore to himself to pay Grant back in the most violent way possible. Pacing back and forth he sat on his bunk and remembered where he recognized the jailer from. Grant was from the Bottoms. He remember seeing the crackhead jackpot mowing the yard of one of the houses that he had seen him come out of. "Yeah I got your ass now," he said out loud talking to himself. Then he became frustrated that he was still in jail and wondered why Lisa hadn't come to bond him out yet. Two more days went by. After his bruises were healed they finally let him back into population. As soon as he walked in the Block he went straight to the phone and called his girl.

'Ring', 'Ring'.

"Hello." Lisa answered on the second ring.

"Baby, why haven't you gotten me out yet?"

"I've been trying, they kept telling me you were at another jail. I didn't find out what was up until I bonded Amir out."

"So what's up?"

"I'm outside now with the Bondsmen, and your lawyer. The Bondsman is doing the paperwork now. You'll be out in a minute."

"Okay baby, love you."

"Love you too. Just be patient we're here."

"Okay." Justice replied and then hung the phone up and sat in front of the T.V. and watched as the Cowboys played the Eagles. While sitting down taking in his surroundings he noticed that he knew a couple of the guys in the Block. Justice dapped them up and kicked it with them until his name was called.

"Justice Santiago, pack it up you've made bail." The jailer bellowed. Glancing around the cell he had called home for almost a week. He packed up <u>Bout time someone follow instructions</u> Justice thought to himself as he grabbed his mat and headed to the door.

"A yo Styles Im'a put a hundred on your books. I'll call your girl later and see what's up with bail. Tell Dez I got him too." Justice informed while heading out.

"Good luck Bruh. I'll tell Dez what you said, when he wakes up." Styles replied.

"Stunna Boys we in here." A couple guys on the top tier hollered as loud as they could as the slider door came open and Justice walked out. Finally reaching the booking desk he spotted Grant and gave him a frightening smile.

"Fuck you nigga, you ain't shit pig." Justice taunted.

"Punk ass street thug. You'll be back, and I'll be waiting on your ass." Grant spat.

"We'll see won't we?"

"God damn it Santiago sign these fucking papers and get the hell outta my jail. You little piece of shit." Sgt. Cook growled.

"You know what Sgt. Fuck you too."

"I hope for your sake your ass don't come back here boy. I don't want you to end up like your mamma. You know you can't win we're the biggest gang in the World." Sgt. Cook shot back.

"Keep my mother's name out your mouth." Justice said as he signed his release papers. Handing the pen over Justice grabbed his property, his wallet, watch, chain and a few rings, then headed out the double doors. <u>This nigga Grant's whole family's dead he doesn't know who he's fucking wit</u>, Justice thought to himself. When he finally walked out to the parking lot. The first face he saw was his sexy girlfriend Lisa. He smiled to himself knowing he had the sexiest snow bunny in the city, and she had that paper. It was nothing more sexier than a bad chick with money.

"Hey baby! I was so worried about you. Are you okay?"

"Yeah I'm good, my Caddy is totaled, but I'm ok."

"Don't worry about the car. We'll get you another one. I'm just so happy to see you. Mama gonna take good care of you when we get home."

Justice smiled as Lisa hugged him tightly.

"I'm glad this is ok." Lisa whispered reaching down and gently rubbing the bulge poking from his Levi Jeans.

"Yeah we good ma, let's get out of here." Justice replied, then headed to the passenger side of Lisa 550 Benz.

"No baby, I want you to drive. I got something for you." Lisa said as she opened the passenger door and got inside.

Seeing this Justice got in the driver side, Lisa passed him her keys. Justice crunk the car up and pulled out of the jailhouse parking lot. When they got on the interstate Lisa reached her over and began to rub Justices crotch until she was sure that he was good and hard.

"Keep your eyes on the road baby." Lisa said as she began to unbutton Justice's jeans letting his eight inch dick free from its silk confinement. She gently stroked him before she leaned over putting her head in his lap sucking him slowly as he drove home.

Lisa was Justice's Queen, and she loved to please her man. It was nothing she wouldn't do for him. Putting her head game down it didn't take Lisa but ten minutes to drain Justice dry, swallowing his seed as she always did because she loved the taste of him. When she finished she wiped her mouth with the back of her hand, then grabbed a paper towel out of her glove compartment. She wiped her mouth again smiling to herself while watching Justice put his dick back in his pants. Twenty minutes later Justice was pulling into the driveway of their three bedroom home, they both got out, and held each other's hand as they walked inside.

Justice loved Lisa. They had been together for five years and had been through plenty of storms together. No matter what it was they always made it through because their love for each other was strong. The first storm came when they first got together. They had met each other at a college house party and hit it off quickly. After going on a couple dates things got serious. When it did Lisa's father didn't approve. He didn't like the fact that his baby girl was dating a black guy from the hood. He pulled Lisa to the side and had forbidden her from seeing Justice. Her father's words fell on deaf ears because Lisa snuck around to see Justice anyway. Until one day she became pregnant. She tried to hide her pregnancy for months but her father eventually found out and became angry that his baby girl was having a baby by a black man. Being a wealthy lawyer at a huge law firm. He felt his daughter would be an embarrassment. He was so angry, and humiliated that he gave her a hundred and fifty thousand dollars and told her that he never wanted to see her again. The money was transferred to her account, but she had nowhere to stay. Lisa went straight to Justice who was staying with his grandmother at the time. Saddened by her situation Vidah Santiago gave Justice her blessing, and he took her in with open arms, wiped the tears away from her eyes and told her everything would be okay.

Grateful that her man had her back she told Justice about the money that her father had given her. Justice was a street nigga, his mother had taught him the game before she died of cancer. He took fifty thousand, and hit the streets building himself a team along with his best friend Amir. In just a few months Justice and his Stunna Boys had taken the streets over. Money was coming in so fast from the guns he was selling that they bought a three bedroom house on the outskirts of Chapel Hill. The house sat on three acres of land. As time went by their good days became dark and cloudy. Lisa had given birth to a baby boy that they had named Pharell after Justice's mother Danielle. The baby was born premature, and had trouble breathing. Baby Pharell ended up passing away eight weeks after he was born. His death was a trying time for Justice and Lisa, but it brought them even closer. They formed an unbreakable bond. From that point it was them against the World. Even after the baby passed Lisa never went back to her father.

ABOUT THE AUTHOR

Durell Eubanks is a native of Burlington, North Carolina, who holds an Associate's Degree in Business Administration. His passion for writing and expressing himself stems from the many days and nights spent inside a prison cell, having to use his imagination to escape his confinement.

As a young child, his mother encouraged him to read and write poems to better express himself. Inspired by the many authors that he read, years later, he penned his own first debut novel, "I Am Tony Blanco."

For comments likes and shares
IG: Durell07Eubanks
Facebook: Durell Eubanks
Website: www.richworldpresents.com